bumped

SIBYLLA NASH

KAMARA PRESS

also by sibylla nash

Dreamcity

one

AFTER A FULL DAY of sightseeing in Paris with eight writers and then a sound check at the famed Olympia, I wanted nothing more than to close my eyes and sleep. Long and hard. I unlocked my hotel room, took two steps in, and flung myself face down on the bed, landing on top of the scratchy, green bedspread with my high heels and short trench coat still on. My room was the length of my arm span, which was fine on a day like today. Tiny, dark, enclosed spaces couldn't make me feel any worse.

I buried my face in the pillow and tried to stave off nausea. It felt like the beginning of the flu. It had followed me from Los Angeles to Paris and dug its heels in at the hotel along the Champs-Élysées. It didn't help that Paris hadn't gotten the memo that it was spring, or maybe I didn't read the memo that said to pack layers of clothes. Either way, it was damp and chilly outside. It was hard to look chic in goosebumps, no matter how cute my shoes were, and my Louboutins were hot, save for the beating they were taking from all the cobblestone walkways.

I checked the time on my cell phone. I had less than two hours before I had to wrangle everyone back on the bus for the purpose of the trip. They were here to write and report on one of the biggest hip-hop artists in the world, Cameron, performing at the Olympia. It was one of the oldest concert halls in Paris. He was signed to Savage Rhythms, the record label that employed me as a publicist and subsidized my stiletto habit.

My phone chimed, and a text message from my friend Justine came through. Growing up, we lived four doors down from one another in New Jersey and had been as inseparable as cake and ice cream at a birthday party. Now, living on opposite coasts, we were like caviar and a bottle of hundred-year-old scotch, good only on special occasions.

> Happy B-day Ellie! Hope you're enjoying your trip in the city of love! :> :>)

She included her usual assortment of happy faces and other crazy icons that always made me wonder if she dictated her text messages to her 12-year-old.

Bleh! Another birthday. I grabbed a pillow and put it over my face. Born four years apart, my sister Evie and I shared the same birthday. I'd much rather pretend the day didn't exist. I moved the pillow and rolled over on my stomach to send Justine a quick message.

> 35. Yaay. I'm working & how much fun can it really be w/my man on another continent?

Before she could reply, my phone rang.

"Happy birthday to you! Happy birthday to you!" Diego Rivera's baritone sang in my ear with only the slightest interference from across the Atlantic. I smiled, happy to avert a trip down memory lane. Even after two-and-a-half years of dating, his voice still made my stomach tingle with erratic butterflies... or it could have been the escargot from the other night. Two words. Never. Again.

"Thanks, honey! I miss you. How's New York?"

"It was great. Think I closed the deal. It's going to be big. We'll celebrate by taking a little trip to Majorca. Get you in a bikini."

"Hmph, bikini? I don't know about all that," I said as I sat up and unbuttoned my high-waisted pencil skirt. I would pass out if I didn't. An angry red indentation snaked around my almond-colored stomach like a belt. Not a good look. "Where are you going next? Frankfurt?"

"Yeah. I sent you flowers. Did you get them?"

Diego believed only flowers could capture the beauty and passion of a woman. He sent a different arrangement to my job almost every day. I told him to send me diamonds every day, and I would astound him with how passionate I could become.

"No, I didn't check the front desk, but I don't think I have any messages." I craned my neck to look at the phone on the nightstand. No lights were blinking. Not that it made a difference. The staff could leave a message saying, "Evacuate immediately. Assassins have over-taken the hotel," but it would be in French. I only knew essential phrases like "I'd like those shoes in a size seven" in four languages.

"Go check at the front desk and call me back."

I dragged myself to the elevator and studied my shimmering reflection in the gold-colored doors. My ready smile was on hiatus, and faint shadows lingered under dark brown eyes, a souvenir from being jet lagged. Those were the only nicks in the armor, though. Perfectly arched eyebrows, ready to be raised at the slightest amuse-ment or disdain. I had a flawless French manicure and pedicure. My peek-a-boo heels accentuated my long legs, my best feature, a throwback to my years of running track. Only a hint (and that's all I had, really) of cleavage peeked through in my pleated, keyhole halter top. Jet-black shoulder-length hair, with razor-cut bangs blazing a sharp path across my forehead, was straightened into a shiny curtain. My motto was *look good, feel good*, but it wasn't working for me today. The doors glided open, and thankfully, the ride was short. Downstairs, I was lucky enough to catch an English-speaking concierge.

"Hi, I'm Elle Nixon in room 24. Do you have a package for me?"

"No, but your car is waiting for you."

"What?"

She pointed toward a long, sleek sedan idling at the curb. It dwarfed the brightly colored, tiny Smart cars crammed together like forgotten toys up and down the narrow street.

Oh no they didn't. I specifically asked for a van to arrive at six. They were two hours early. I hoped they don't think I was paying for those two hours. I stalked outside and tapped on the driver's side window, wishing I knew how to say, "What the hell?" in French. It startled me when the back passenger side window rolled down, revealing a gorgeous bouquet of red and yellow roses. Behind the flowers was Diego, his wide grin bookmarked with only one dimple.

He opened the car door and stepped out as I wrapped my arms around him. He slipped his arm around my waist and pulled me closer. The tide of human traffic pushed around us. I forgot my headache as laughter spilled out of me. I nuzzled the crook between his neck and shoulder, drawing comfort from the familiar faint soapy scent still clinging to him.

"What are you doing here?"

"You know I wouldn't let you spend your birthday without me, even if you did go halfway around the world."

He was a man who knew my heart; he surprised me with a trip to the Givenchy emporium for a purse. It was a wildly extravagant gesture, but that was Diego—his spontaneity was the perfect foil for the life I had outlined and scripted for myself. Besides, when in Rome you do as the Romans, and when in Paris... you shop.

On the ride back to the hotel, we held hands in the backseat, his long fingers intertwined through mine. I rested my legs across his lap and gazed at his profile as he fired off text messages with his free hand, his thumb racing across the keys. He looked like Idris Elba's Stringer Bell from The *Wire.* He hated when I called him that. Bookish and intense, a strong jaw anchored his studious face. He wore the prerequisite glasses, and his head was always buried in a book, phone, iPad, or something. His tight goatee lent him the atti-tude he needed to deal with his clients. Tall and broad-shouldered, he wore his confidence like a tailored suit. As a financial advisor to A-list clientele, he had the ability to charm money out of many closed wallets. I lightly traced one finger across his lips, which sloped downward in a frown.

"What's wrong?"

He put his phone in his jacket pocket. "Nothing, now that I'm here with you." He turned his full attention to me, the top buttons undone on his tailored shirt, giving him a carefully composed casual air. When he wanted, he had a way of making you forget everything except the moment at hand.

Laden with bags, we arrived back at the hotel just in time. I left Diego in charge of herding the writers on the bus that would take them to the Olympia. I wanted to make sure Cameron and his band were ready to go. Cameron courted lateness like she was the only girl on the block.

Once we arrived at the Olympia, its famed red sign acting as a beacon, and everyone was settled, and the lights dimmed, I remembered this was why I loved my job. It was always about the music. Cameron walked out on the stage, cloaked in confidence, imbuing each step with a sexy swagger. His trademarked gravelly voice greeted the crowd, sending the women into a squealing frenzy with its sexy edginess. The stage went black as the sound of orchestral music filled the hall. When the heavy bass kicked in and the spotlight found Cameron, it was on. He radiated energy as he stalked from one side of the stage to the next, spitting out rhymes, singing verses, dancing, *and putting on a show* for 60 minutes.

We signed him a year ago because his mixtape had generated so much hype; it broke the record for downloads on iTunes. Blending his gritty lyrics with a sophisticated fusion of jazz and hip-hop and singing hooks that were catchy as hell had helped catapult him from the underground to multimedia superstardom. He had more YouTube views and Twitter followers than citizens in a small country. His first studio album went multi-platinum, and now he was an artist with something to prove. Did he have staying power, or was he a disposable cultural phenomenon? Hopefully, his performance at the Olympia would help seal his status as the newly anointed king of pop culture—for the moment. Unfortunately, the shelf life of pop icons lasted only as long as it took to refresh the page on TMZ.

Being in the same music hall where legends like Jimi Hendrix, Josephine Baker, Diana Ross and the Supremes performed was intoxicating. Cocooned in the dark, surrounded by pulsing bass, I breathed a sigh of contentment as Diego rested his hand territorially on my thigh. It had been a good trip. All the reporters interviewed Cameron and would file their stories with their respective outlets when they returned. The performance and the crowd's response would be a great centerpiece.

After the concert, we all piled into a restaurant along the Champs-Élysées and sat five tables deep. Savage Rhythms had a very generous expense account. Thanks to them, on this trip, every meal was an event unto itself and lasted for hours. Each course was a delectable orgasm for the tongue. Laughter and wine flowed easily all night. Diego was in his element as he regaled everyone with his stories. One of the female writers, Scarlett, seated to my left, said, "Lucky girl! Your boyfriend flew all the way here from LA just to spend your birthday with you?"

I glanced at Diego; his head was bent in deep conversation with Cameron. "I am pretty lucky, aren't I?"

"Or it must be gold-plated down there... you must know some tricks!" She laughed, tipsy from one cocktail. I saw the way she eyed Diego. As for the next junket, this is what I saw: ~~Scarlett Jackson~~.

Later, a rousing round of "Happy Birthday" was butchered over a dish of tiramisu with a candle in it as everyone in the restaurant serenaded me. It was close to 2 am by the time we stumbled back into my hotel room, giggling like teenagers. Somehow, I'd managed the trip from the restaurant with a bottle of champagne still clutched in my hands. I found two plastic cups and poured in the remaining drops.

"A toast to my sister Evie," I said solemnly, hiccupping only once.

"To Evie," Diego repeated.

The following day, the dull throbbing in my head from a combination of jet lag and hangover made it impossible to move, much less talk. Wrapped in the gauzy pre-dawn light, Diego gathered his things in the shadows; we fumbled a kiss before he left on the train to Frankfurt. I was to pick him up at LAX the next night, Monday.

If I had known that was to be our last moment of normalcy, I would have held onto it and him longer. Savored the barely there scent of his cologne and the strength in his arms wrapped around me. Instead, he disappeared into the morning as I tried to recapture sleep before getting on my flight back home.

two

ON MONDAY, when I returned to Los Angeles, I was feeling so run-down. I went to visit my doctor. No big surprise there with the schedule I kept. I had crisscrossed the country three times and made one overseas trip in the last three weeks. I wasn't quite at the level of George Clooney's Ryan Bingham from *Up in the Air*, but I was getting close.

New York for Letterman. Arizona for Wango Tango. Back to LA for Jimmy Kimmel. Off to Paris for my artist Cameron. As a music publicist, it was the same on both coasts and any continent: schmooze, smile, handhold, and get blamed for any bad press suffered by my artists. Take the red-eye, land in the morning, and go straight to the office. Sounded glamorous on paper, but after eight years, it was about as exciting as surfing the 'net on dial-up.

I had expected my convo with Dr. Madison to run something like:

"Elle, here's a prescription for Amoxicillin. Take one every eight hours for ten days and slow down, get some rest. This bug is really getting around."

Instead, as I sat perched on the examining table, shock had unhinged my jaw. It felt as loose and flimsy as the paper gown gaping open at my backside when she said, "Elle, you're about six weeks pregnant. Here's a prescription for prenatal vitamins. No alcohol, and ease up on the caffeine." No alcohol and caffeine? She might as well have said, "lay off on the breathing."

I always assumed if I were to have a kid, it wouldn't be easy. A turkey baster, test tubes, or surrogate mom would be involved or, at the very least, months of trying. At 35, my eggs were supposed to be a cycle away from being on life support from what all the magazine articles and websites touted. I had happily stood in line and bought tickets to the myth that motherhood and careers were divergent paths, and to choose one was to forsake the other.

After the doctor dropped her bombshell, I drove back to my office in Beverly Hills on autopilot. I ignored the tall palm trees lining the sidewalks, their fronds swaying in a lazy salute to the sky. One that was perfectly blue as long as you didn't look northward where the Hollywood Hills jutted toward a sullen, gray cloud of smog and exhaust. It was a typical April day, a balmy 70 degrees. Standard for LA. Or at least it was typical this morning when I left for the doctor's office. Now everything had changed. I had a passenger traveling with me. The sharp stench of tar stung my nose, and the staccato beat of a drill thrummed a budding headache as I tried to merge into one lane to get out of the way of the roadwork. Crater-sized potholes littered the streets, adding an obstacle course feel to the process. The stop-and-go traffic was second nature and allowed my mind to wander.

The subject of children had never really come up between us. We thought they were cute when they were someone else's accessories and did the obligatory "oohs" and "aahs" over the rug rats of acquaintances. We didn't exactly share a kid-friendly lifestyle. Unapologetically married to our careers, we were still young enough not to have any regrets. We wanted to have kids someday in that vague, hazy future sort of way, as in "someday I want to climb Mt. Kilimanjaro." But today was never that day.

I had the media elite on speed dial. Getting some of my B-list and unknown clients into A-List events? Not a problem. Getting an upgrade to first class without the required mileage points? Could do it in my sleep. Knowing the best bars in eight different cities in four countries when on a layover? Easy. I could also make a mean vanilla martini. I knew the best caterers in town. If you needed to buy a last-minute dress that would turn heads at the Grammy's, the address was already programmed into my GPS. These were all precious skills to have in my world. Breastfeeding and changing diapers? Not so much.

Hollywood made it look easy, but they had an army of personal trainers, chefs, nannies, therapists, pool boys, and plastic surgeons on hand to keep them looking and feeling young. Motherhood was nothing but a set prop for them but, for me, way above my pay grade. You might as well ask me to build a rocket ship that ran on flax seed oil. I shook my head to restart my thoughts. Babies were supposed to be a blessing... gift-wrapped in stretch marks. I was unnerved by the guilt that came rushing in for being so thrown by Dr. Madison's news. My maternal instinct was on hiatus; maybe it would kick in once the hormones started flowing.

I checked my dates just to make sure when I arrived at my office. I tossed an envelope of receipts on my desk as I flicked on the computer. It was not a corner office... yet. It had just enough room for a leather loveseat and coffee table, horizontal file cabinets, four platinum album plaques on the wall, and my desk. I kept the look minimal. No need to get too comfortable here.

Once the computer loaded, I clicked on my calendar. It filled the computer screen as I scrolled through the weeks. Last month had been busy (as usual) with juggling listening parties, album release parties, accompanying my acts to television studios, sitting in on interviews all the while attending mandatory staff meetings, pitching media outlets, creating publicity plans, and trying to do more while my budget was sliced and diced because of the economy. *Aha.* I found the date I had been looking for, the listening party for Sexual Chocolate, the new "it" girl group. That was the last visit from my monthly friend... March 8th. I *was* late. So used to it being on time, I didn't even notice it was mid-April, and a week had passed after its expected arrival. It was the last thing on my mind with everything that had been going on. I also vaguely remembered doubling up on the pill, thinking it would be fine that one time. Guess not.

Even though I was picking him up from the airport later this evening, I sent a text to Diego, *"OMG! Call me, important."* I sent him another text with *"911,"* just in case it wasn't clear. If I was freaking out, he needed to freak out with me or be the voice of reason. Hopefully, he will see my texts during a layover. I hadn't heard from him since he left yesterday morning.

The smoggy Hollywood Hills were visible from my window in the penthouse suite. I slipped on a Bluetooth headset for the office phone and stifled a yawn as I stared off into the distance. The row of Bobbleheads that lined my desk nodded and stared too. They were my "yes" men. I started running calls as I listened to my voicemail and checked my email. Benny, a product manager, had left me several messages, each one escalating in tone until I needed to be a dog to hear the high pitch shrill formerly known as his voice, which was a sharp departure from his native tongue of mumble. I hated talking to him, but just like a colonoscopy, sometimes it was necessary.

I called him as I checked my email. First up? The online proof for my parents' 40th wedding anniversary "surprise" party invitation. Gala was more like it. Everyone and their unborn knew about it except my father, further perpetuating the old wives' stereotype of the clueless man. Right below their email was one from my mother with 15 "small little changes" ranging from the menu to the music to the guest list, and she wanted to know when the invitations were going out. She was inviting friends and family from out of state and wanted to give them enough time to plan. She long ago made me rue the day I gave her my email address. I offered to let her handle the arrangements more than once, and she would always demur that I knew best. Right. It was four months away, but I felt more pressure from planning this than I had for any other event in my professional career. I'd worked the Grammy's, the AMA's, fielded questions at press conferences about nude pictures, affairs, drugs, you name it; I'd seen it all and had to write the press release about it. Even attending a soiree at the White House was less complicated than this.

I scanned the invite again before clicking "accept" for the proof. In a few days, I'd have the pleasure of printing out labels and mailing 100 invitations to friends and family. I wish I had the type of assistant who would do my personal tasks. Getting Veronica to do the bare minimum of work-related tasks was hard enough.

Another email came through—this time from Triad. Triad, an indie record label snapped up by a major, was the closest competitor to my current employer, Savage Rhythms. They were looking for a VP to head up their publicity department and were a cautious suitor. Finally, after two months of eyeing one another, we were just getting to first base. They wanted to meet with me more formally on Friday. I sat up. Their email made me remember the goal at hand... and I lived by lists and goals. The minute I swung my tassel to the other side and graduated from college, I knew I wanted to make it big in music... except I couldn't sing or play an instrument. *Hello, publicity.* I was supposed to have been vice president of publicity at a record label by 35. My 35th birthday was now behind me. I was behind schedule. Triad could put me back on track.

I didn't even want to think about how I would handle the whole maternity leave issue. No matter what the law said, I knew they would strike my name off the short list of contenders if I looked bloated or even gave off a whiff of morning sickness.

Before I sent them an email saying yes, I checked my calendar to make sure I was in town. I'd gone as far as I could go at Savage, and unless my boss suddenly sprouted a second head and hit the talk show circuit, she was going nowhere, which meant I was going nowhere. I had skyrocketed right to the glass ceiling unless they invented the title, "Most Seniorest Director."

I needed to get Benny off the phone. I had been half-listening to his ramblings. How he accomplished much as a manager was the Eighth Wonder of the World.

"Benny?"

"Yeah?"

"I don't think I'm hearing you correctly when you say she's 'suddenly sick' and can't make the press day I've been busting my behind to set up for the last month. I mean, please tell me you're kidding."

"Chantal's not feeling well and-"

"Look, you wanted to be THE MAN so badly, Mr. Run-Everything-Through-Me. Just get her to the Four Seasons by noon."

"I'll see what I can do."

"You were her product manager and wanted to make the jump into artist management. Make it happen. Chantal can't afford to blow off the *Weekly Reader,* much less *Rolling Stone.* You know the last time she had a hit record? FIVE YEARS AGO. News flash, she ain't on top anymore. Just get her to press day and make sure she's sober... and wearing underwear." Just to be safe.

I pulled off my Bluetooth and leaned back in my chair. My morning was spiraling into that out-of-control region. Most days, I lived for the thrill of extinguishing wildfires. I loved being the invisible puppeteer pulling the strings, creating the reality that the media would hand-deliver to the masses. If there was a problem (and with the potent mixture of Twitter and celebs—there was always a problem), all I had to do was put a spin on it and tip off TMZ, Radar Online, and any other hot gossip sites of the moment. Problem solved. Sure, most people would think it's only music, and I'm only a publicist. It's not like I was solving global warming or the food crisis in some Third World country, or our own country for that matter. But I lived in L.A., where entertainment was more powerful than religion unless you were Mel Gibson, and found a way to combine the two. My pops would say, "Might as well FedEx yourself to hell since you're going there anyway," for even saying that. But it was true.

After this morning, though, I seemed to have lost my enthusiasm for converting the masses. I was dragging, and the calls I was getting made me want to fast-forward to the end of the day when I could go home and curl up with Diego.

I put on some old-school Lenny Kravitz to keep me going as I slipped on my earpiece and again became the mouthpiece for Savage Rhythms. After fielding an hour's worth of panic-stricken and/or attitude-laden conversations with everyone from magazine editors to managers to our own promotions department, I was beyond stressed. I had long ago sucked dry my tall double latte from Starbucks and was considering licking the bottom of the cup to see if there was any spare caffeine. I would have to ease off the caffeine in steps; going cold turkey would kill me. The only thing that kept me going was the thought of seeing Diego in a few hours. I checked my cell but didn't see any text messages from him. Even though our schedules kept us on different coasts half the time, we always managed to text/IM/Skype/Facebook/Tweet, or call one another a few times a day. Social media made it so easy to stalk the ones we loved. Diego was on a serious social media blackout because he had updated nothing since yesterday morning when he left my hotel.

I couldn't dwell on him for too long. Decisions. Decisions. Was it better to have Chantal float into press day and let anything fly out of her mouth? Or cancel and do some serious ass-kissing to the twenty or so journalists already on their way to the scheduled "Meet and Greet"? Either way, she was screwed because the album sucked. Known for her powerhouse vocals, her newest album sounded like Auto-Tune 101 with tracks recorded from her cellphone. Even the little boy on YouTube singing a Lady Gaga song into his banana was better than her.

Chantal showed up thirty minutes late at the hotel, looking crazy. Wearing oversized sunglasses and a garish scarf to hide a blond weave that had seen better days in its former life as a house cat. Her husband, a fame whore extraordinaire, was glued to her side and had the nerve to include his demo in the press kit. The only spin I could put on it was groveling and bribery. I promised more exclusives than I had artists.

I was washing my hands in the hotel bathroom when Chantal stumbled in to freshen her lipstick.

"I think it went well, don't you?" she asked as she puckered her lips in the mirror.

I looked around and then scanned the stalls for any feet. No witnesses. "Seriously? I mean, were we just at the same event?"

"What do you mean? They loved me."

I grabbed paper towels from a cute wicker basket and dried my hands. "We've worked together at what, two, three labels now? I've known you long enough to not have to kiss your ass as much. Whatever you're smoking or drinking, you need to quit. You're destroying everything you worked so hard to get and those people out there? If you don't know this already, they're not your friends."

Chantal had that raw talent that could move you to tears or a "go on and sang girl" shout with just one note. I didn't want to see her fail. I walked out, knowing I'd hear from her manager or my boss, Melanie, about what I said. I didn't care. The entertainment industry was littered with fallen stars shot down by shooting up. My job was to enable them by spoon-feeding excuses to the public. As a hired hand, I was to *never, ever* upset the talent. I should have just canceled the press day.

Back at the office, I kept one eye on the clock as the light of day slowly faded. I needed to get to the airport to pick up Diego, but it didn't feel right. I should have heard from him by now, and his silence was troubling.

three

DIEGO and me had this thing. On a good day, he drove me crazy. Crazy like crazy for him, crazy in love. On a bad day, he drove me crazy. Crazy like master samurai Lorena Bobbit. Crazy like his ass makes me so mad because the spontaneity I loved about him made it difficult to plan things with him, and it drove me nuts. Some days I didn't want to speak to him, but I still needed to see/touch/breathe him. And on a day like today, I just needed him.

We had met at an industry event. It was a premiere party for an independent movie a friend of a friend of a colleague had worked on. As usual, that night at the party, I was the center of my universe. Drink in hand, The Ruby—ruby red grapefruit juice and vodka, I worked the room. The cocktail mix of attendees was chilled. Hoochie mamas spilling out of too tight dresses hoping for a second glance, broke wannabes passing out business cards, headshots, and in some cases, thumb drives of their work, and then they were the suits. We worked full-time in the entertainment industry, and we worked the room in our own quiet yet expensively clad, desperate way. No matter who you were in L.A., every party, every event was just another opportunity to get your hustle on. Everybody was looking for the next big thing to bandwagon.

There were just some people who had to attend every single party, no matter how big or small. I was one of them. I chatted up the press and reacquainted myself with those I hadn't seen since the last fling. Fortunately, I had a gift for faces. I never forgot one. It was an asset in an ego-driven town like Hollywood, where most deals were initiated outside of the office. I talked up the label's new acts, got a couple of bites of interest for a cover story on Nikki, the president, and a guest hosting gig for Chantal on MTV (pre-crackhead days). It wasn't a bad night. I could have left then, but like a good little party girl, I could never go until I was sure there was no one else to see me and nothing else to be seen.

1 a.m. was always the rush to get that last groove on, the last chance to meet and greet. Last call before the town shut down at 2 a.m. unless you're in the know and knew where to find the after-hour joints. I was waiting for my car when we met. He dominated the side of the valet stand. He staked out his patch of cement like he owned it. His tailored suit fit his six-foot-plus frame like he was born wearing it. He looked good, and he knew it. He was smooth. From his bald dome to the undercurrent of confidence like an electromagnetic field surrounding him, I knew acquisition was his specialty. I could feel his dark eyes studying my long bare legs like roadmaps guiding him to redemption.

He was on his cell and spoke in a low voice, not like some poseurs who spoke loud enough so everyone could hear their good fortune. He looked sharp in a dark blue Ermenegildo Zegna suit and crisp white shirt. When I stood next to him, he ended his call.

"I saw you hustling the room in there. I asked my boy about you, and he said you do publicity at Savage Rhythms."

I shrugged my shoulders. "Give your boy a gold star," I answered none too kindly.

I pulled out my phone and dialed my office to escape his intense gaze and give my hands something to do. Even though it was late, my boss was known to leave me messages at all hours. Surprisingly, there were none.

"I'm Diego," he continued, and offered his hand.

I slipped my phone back into my purse before I shook it. "I guess there's no need to introduce myself, seeing you already have a dossier on me."

"You're witty. I like that," he said.

I chuckled, "That's a first."

"What? You disagree?"

"No. Most people usually just say I'm a smart ass."

"Well, I'm not most people."

"You would say something like that."

He flashed a smile. "What's that supposed to mean?"

"Nothing. Forget it."

Just then, the attendant pulled up with my cherry-colored Audi T2. Diego followed me to my door and handed me a card. There was no flash of light, no explosion of stars to signal that he would forever change my life. I took the business card he offered and jammed it into my Prada bag filled with other cards procured that evening.

"Call me next week. I want to talk to you about some of your acts."

He disappeared into the silver Maserati Spyder that sailed up behind me with the personalized plates that read SMOOVE.

It was almost a month before we spoke. I was closing the loop on several items in preparation for the holiday. Mostly, I was trying to figure out my expense report and how much personal stuff I could write off. The label was shutting down for a week. When my phone rang that evening, it was him. I agreed to meet him for drinks at Lola's in Santa Monica on Christmas Eve. I had also done my homework on him. I learned he was a financial advisor, adding serious star wattage to his client list.

Diego was there and waiting for me at the bar when I arrived. On the drive over, I kept wondering why was I going to meet him? Especially since I had sworn off men. My previous two relationships had gone the way of nuclear fallout. No survivors. Edgar wanted me to choose between him and my job. Like that was going to happen. I sent the engagement ring back to him in a hurry. After him, I fell hard for someone off-limits, the-ex-who-shall-not-be-named. I was ready for more, but he wasn't. Love was more about timing than compatibility, and I had the timing of a blind and deaf cat burglar.

Diego seemed different. He made me curious. He had that way about him. He dropped morsels of information like a crumb trail. Just enough to lure you in. He let me know he was interested but didn't push. Over drinks, a French martini for me and Campari for him, we talked. Something clicked. Whereas when I walked into Lola's as an indifferent spectator, ready to blow him off after the buzz faded, I suddenly found myself wanting him to want me. It was that inexplicable shift in the balance of power, a power I would never regain. It was like discovering the potential in an outfit after seeing it on someone else.

"You like to play games, don't you?"

"Why do you say that?"

"Because you answer my questions with questions."

"What's the matter, not up for the challenge?" I teased.

"See, that's my point."

"What point? That wasn't a question. So that doesn't count," I took a sip of my drink. "What do you want to know?"

"When was the last time you fell in love?"

"The question should be, have I ever fallen in love?"

"Well?"

"Haven't you heard? Eating a piece of chocolate can give you the same high, and it's cheaper."

I grabbed his hand and pulled him out onto the tiny dance floor. It was 70s night at Lola's, and I wanted to get my disco groove on. I fell for him that night because he made me laugh. A deep, gasping-for-air-I-can't-believe-he's-so-silly type of laugh. We had gotten a Soul Train line started on the dance floor, and when he did a John Travolta *Saturday Night Fever* routine with a *split,* he had me.

At the end of the night, he suggested we meet for some coffee or "something" at some point. I played along. Gave him the home digits like it had never crossed my mind. Let him think the thought of "us" was only his idea. Didn't matter. We both wanted the same outcome.

* * *

Traffic was a little lighter as I traveled the surface streets to LAX. I took LaCienga straight down to Century Boulevard. The sun had officially left the sky when I passed the giant donut at Randy's Donuts. Even though I knew it would take him a while to go through customs and I could be a little late, I ran every yellow light. I parked my car in the Central parking complex; it wasn't that crowded for once, and I hurried over to Terminal 2. I waited at the base of the escalator and checked my watch every five minutes. I watched as tourists rubbernecked looking for stars, and Angelenos, too self-involved to care about anyone else, convened in front of the luggage carousel. Suitcases for Flight 1, Air New Zealand, tumbled out. Diego's flight. I double-checked the email with his itinerary on my phone. Right day. Right time. Right flight. No Diego.

I searched every face as the crowd swelled and then thinned out. I checked my cell again and tried to call him. It went straight to voicemail. Mild panic introduced an extra thud as I felt my heart rate speed up. Soon, the carousel was empty, and I was the only person standing there. The ticket window was no help. They wouldn't tell me whether he had gotten on the flight citing privacy rules. I tried calling him again, but his cell was off and went directly to voicemail. I sat in my car and willed my phone to ring. Fear gnawed at me, causing me to second-guess everything. Should I leave and wait for him at his house? Stay at the airport and wait? Did he miss his plane? Was he hurt? Why hadn't he called? Did he get my text? I was going to burst if we didn't hurry up and have a conversation about this baby. *Our baby.*

After waiting an hour, I drove over the hill to his home in Tarzana. The dark silence was crushing. I had been hoping somehow our wires had crossed, and his house would be lit up, and music would be playing when I arrived. Instead, the lights from the alarm control panel mocked me as I disarmed it after I let myself in. My heels echoed as I walked across the marble foyer and dropped my purse on the settee in the living room. I took a shower and tried to formulate a plan. If I hadn't heard from him before morning, I'd have to figure out who to file a police report with and how. As flakey as he could be about making plans, once he made them, Diego was anal about being on time. For him not to show up, something was wrong. I could feel it deep in the pit of my stomach.

Would I have to involve the German consulate? I climbed into bed and hugged the pillow as I tried to fall asleep. I still expected to hear his key in the lock; the slightest sound sent a burst of hope, only to deflate when I didn't hear his footsteps or him calling my name.

Visions of dirty diapers and stretch marks danced in my head all night while I simultaneously cursed Diego. Why hadn't he called me? And I worried about him. Was he hurt? Is that why he couldn't call? Early the next morning, a commotion downstairs pulled me out of a deep sleep. It sounded like banging. I thought Diego had forgotten his keys, so I grabbed my robe and practically sprinted downstairs. The cool marble floor felt like ice on my bare feet.

"Just a minute!"

Pulling my robe around me, I swung open the door and was met with a lawn full of men and women in suits and uniforms. Unmarked and marked police cars with lights flashing, casting an eerie bluish-red haze in the predawn light, lined the street. I blinked. Was this a dream within a dream? The chill of a morning breeze sent a flock of goosebumps racing across my chest and chased the sleep away, leaving no doubt that I was awake.

My legs went boneless, and I had to lean against the door for support. Something must have happened to Diego.

"Is he ok?" I coughed the words out, almost afraid to hear the answer. Instead, a man thrust a bunch of papers as thick as a novella in my face. He introduced himself. Agent Walsh, FBI. He had the pallor of a desk jockey with a shock of red hair capped off with piercing blue eyes. He looked like a hardened Conan O'Brien. I found it difficult to concentrate as he explained he had a search warrant for the house because I kept looking for the TV cameras. This had to be a joke.

My mind struggled to keep up. Why would they need to search his house?

"What happened? Is he in the hospital?"

Agent Walsh gave me a strange look. "Ms. Nixon, we don't know. To our knowledge, Mr. Rivera never boarded his flight."

"Wait, why are you here?"

"We have a search warrant," he said slowly.

Search warrant? I backed away from him. A sigh of relief escaped from my lips as some of the tension loosened up in my neck and shoulders. I switched from crisis mode to crisis management. This has to be a mistake. I started planning the publicity campaign around the lawsuit Diego could file. I could press some of my media contacts and see if they would do a story on it. Upstanding, prominent financial advisor harassed by law enforcement. I could practically hear the sound bite on the 5 o'clock news. Talk about pain and suffering, not to mention embarrassment. His swanky neighborhood was home to more than a few stars and business titans who valued their privacy. This little display wouldn't win him any friends.

Strangers milled in and out of Diego's house carrying boxes. Papers. Laptop. Computer. File folders. His grass was littered with lawn jockeys on cell phones. I had snuck upstairs to change and was wrapped in one of Diego's sweaters and a pair of my jeans. I felt like a little kid pretending to be a grownup as I watched the agents dismantle our life together. My thumb was numb from pressing redial on my cell. My calls went straight to Diego's voicemail. I could barely keep a grip on the phone because a thin sheen of sweat coated my hands like surgical gloves. *They knew my name.* They knew he had never boarded the plane from Frankfurt. It was getting harder to cling to the belief that this was a case of mistaken identity. *I was starting to wonder if I needed a lawyer.*

Downstairs, sitting in the great room across from Walsh, I folded my arms across my chest. My stomach rumbled, and I could feel a hollow pit of hunger expanding.

"What is this all about?"

"The government believes Mr. Rivera breached his fiduciary duty as an investment adviser and misused funds his clients entrusted to him."

I just stared at him. Waiting for the punch line. An uncomfortable silence sat between us until finally I said, "You can't be serious?"

"If you have any information that could be helpful-"

"That's crazy. You think Diego ripped off his clients? Is that what this is all about? He would never do that. You obviously don't know him." My head had started to throb.

"And you may not know him as well as you believe. Did you know he's married?"

I put my hand up as I stood up. "I know what you're trying to do, and it's not going to work. We're done. I don't have to listen to this. I'm going to recommend to Diego that he get a lawyer and sue you guys for everything you're wor-"

I took a few steps and stumbled. The ground rushed up to greet me. Everything went black.

Coolness stung my cheek. I was at the center of a black dress shoe convention when I opened my eyes and found myself on the cold marble floor with various police and federal personnel staring down at me.

Agent Walsh kneeled beside me and checked my pulse. "Everything's fine. Get back to work," he ordered.

I struggled to sit up, but hands gently forced me back down. "I'm fine, just..."

After a few moments, the gawkers dispersed, and I was allowed to sit up. A glass of water, one crystal goblet, and ice wrapped in paper towels magically appeared in front of me. I sipped the water slowly and held the ice pack to a pulsing knot that seemed to be growing on the side of my head.

"Are you sure you're ok? Low blood sugar?"

"All that FBI training, and you couldn't catch me? Really?"

"I'm sorry, you dropped so fast. Do you usually pass out like that?"

"Yes, it's a hobby of mine." I put the glass down and tried to stand up again.

This whole scene seemed like something out of a bad reality show. However, there were no camera crews around to capture the police and FBI tearing apart Diego's life. Our life. And Conan O'Brien was the ringleader.

"Listen, your boyfriend's in a lot of trouble, and depending on what you know, and when you knew it, you could be in trouble too."

"If he's in so much trouble, why do you only have a search warrant and not an arrest warrant?" Years of watching *Law & Order* were finally paying off.

"Mr. Rivera likes his women spunky; I'll give him that. Mrs. Rivera, his wife in Miami, she's a lot like you. Very sharp."

"Divide and conquer. The only thing that's missing is the bad cop. Doesn't work when you play both roles." I brushed him aside and headed up the stairs, ignoring the business card he tried to hand me. I needed to change. I had to go into the office, and there didn't seem to be anything else I could do at the house.

I closed the bedroom door behind me and reapplied the ice pack. *Wife.* That had to be a mistake. Some divide-and-conquer bullshit. *Wife.* I don't know why I protected him so much in front of the Feds. Yes, I do. I loved him. But a *wife*? How could I miss the signs that he had a wife, another life that existed outside the bubble of us? Was I that caught up? Or were they just *that* wrong? All you had to do was take a headcount on death row of those exonerated by DNA tests to know that snap judgments and prosecution sometimes went together like cookies and milk. By the time I made it to my car, I could hardly drive. Car horns blared at me so badly that I pulled over. A tremor had snaked its way up my leg, rendering it useless. I could barely press the accelerator.

Competing thoughts banged around in my head, shattering my focus. I couldn't process any more information. I pulled back onto the road when the traffic was lighter. During the entire drive, my phone buzzed, and I let every call go to voicemail after checking it first to make sure it wasn't Diego.

four

AT WORK, I valeted my car and headed to my office. On my way up, I bumped into my boss Melanie; she was VP of Publicity. We rode the elevator together. She was a dead ringer for Star Jones (pre-weight loss). She was carrying her little ankle nipper of a dog in a Louis Vuitton monogram pooch pouch. A tiny head, no bigger than a golf ball, with a white strand of hair swept up in a ribbon, poked out of the little zippered opening.

Melanie eyed me before she asked, "Everything okay?"

I shifted from one foot to the other, realizing how I must look wearing a pair of jeans, Coach sneakers, and a hot pink t-shirt. My hair was hastily thrown back in a low ponytail, and a mad dash of lipstick streaked across my lips. Top it all off with a big knot on my head... It was a far cry from my usual photo shoot-ready ensembles.

"I'm fine. I slipped in the shower," I said with a little too much pep in my voice, "and look at this little guy, you brought little ummm, Pippy to the office."

"It's Pepper. His nanny had an emergency and couldn't come in. Water main break or something... and mommy couldn't let her little babsy-wabsy stay home all by his wittle self."

I sighed and forced a smile.

"So, kiddo, let's go over your publicity plan for Cameron after lunch, 'kay? I have a meeting with Nikki at 3 p.m. and want to update her on everything," she said.

"Sure, 1:30 work for you?"

"That's fine. Thanks, kiddo." She started down the hallway and then came back. "If you want to talk about anything, let me know." She eyed my forehead again before taking off to her office.

Kiddo. She drove me crazy with that; we weren't more than five or six years apart in age, but to hear her talk, I was the incompetent baby sister tagging along to the office. I couldn't even sweat it today.

I took a shortcut through the maze of cubicles that made up the support staff in the center of the floor. Every cubicle was its own island of drama. Phones ringing, punctuated by voices yelling from inside an office looking for something that hadn't been done. A variety of music jumped out at me from the open doorways, reminding me of spinning the dial on the radio. Wu-Tang Clan. Usher. Patti LaBelle. It was the typical chaos of Savage Rhythms. Usually, it was a source of energy for me, but this morning it was plucking the one fragile nerve I had left. I couldn't wait to get to the quiet sanctuary of my office.

The first thing I saw when I opened the door was a pair of Raf Simons Crocodile Pocket sneakers resting on my coffee table. They belonged to the outstretched legs of Cameron. A tattooed bicep peeked out from his white short-sleeved shirt. He was relaxing on my leather couch like he owned it and talking on not one but two cell phones.

"Yeah, so why don't you text me those pics? I need to see what you look like; know what I'm saying?" he said into one phone, his mouth twisted up in a smirk. "S'up cutie?" he asked when he finally noticed me.

"Oh no, I don't care how much your sneakers cost, but you better get them off my furniture. You are not home," I told him while walking over to my desk and dropping my Gucci tote bag on the floor.

The first record label I worked at was dominated by hip hop, so I was used to claiming my respect from the jump. As a female in the business, it was eat or be eaten alive. You almost had to de-feminize yourself to dodge the bullet of being placed in the category of hoes and bitches that seemed to encompass the spectrum of all women except their mommas, in most cases anyway. That's why I admired Nikki so much. She made it in a man's world, playing by a woman's rules. Everybody who was anybody agreed that she was *bad*, in a scary, very threatening way.

"It's like that? You have no love for me? You know I pay the bills around here," he said. His smile faltered as he caught a glimpse of my face. "Damn girl! What happened to your head? Yo, I gotta go," he said into both phones.

"Nothing. I'm clumsy." *Why didn't I wear a hat? Or a turban? Would I have to answer questions like this all day?*

Cameron was long and lean. Even underneath the baggy jeans and a t-shirt, he had a sinewy, muscular look. His cocoa brown skin had a natural shine to it. He was good-looking, not in a pretty boy way. No, he definitely looked as though he could and would handle his business. His swagger exuded raw masculinity that had all the admins preening and primping whenever they heard he would be in the office. He carried the burden of growing up in middle-class suburbia and channeled his anger and indignation about *not* living in the hood into music. Because he didn't come from the street, he wore the scowl of defensiveness, constantly feeling as though he had to prove he was just as tough.

"Look, last time I checked, the label is still called Savage Rhythms. There are 14 other acts here, and they are all pulling their own weight, so deflate that big head of yours," I said as I checked my office voicemail, wishing he would go away.

"I don't see anyone else in this joint going triple platinum out the box. You got flava, kid. I like you," he said, smiling as though I were supposed to be honored about that.

"Just get your feet off my table." My head was pounding like someone was doing the Macarena on my temples. Usually, there was an easy camaraderie between us. He understood the art of selling yourself, your brand, better than most artists. Made my job easier. This morning, a tense current seemed to bounce between us.

"No, for real," he continued, "everyone else in this joint be tip-toeing around me and shit, kissing my ass when you know they probably dogging me out behind my back. You know how you do in LA. But you always keep it real, know what I'm saying?"

"Why are you here? And stop talking to me like Ebonics is your first language. There are no cameras rolling. You can drop the project bad boy image... a'ight Chauncey?"

Cameron Caine was his stage name. Yep, I went there.

He finally swung his long legs off my coffee table and looked at me. His face was unreadable. He flashed me a brief smile.

"Where's your boy?" He was up and off the couch, prowling around my small office with feline grace.

"My boy? Who are you talking about?"

"That cat Diego."

My throat went dry, and the air felt like sawdust.

"I been trying to reach him. I can't get that cat on the phone for nothing."

"And what does this have to do with me?" I said when I really wanted to shout, *"OMG! Me too!"*

"We were talking 'bout putting some things together, know what I mean? Now he's ghost."

"Well, that's between you and him."

"I can't reach him, so now it's between you and me."

I hung up the phone in the middle of listening to my messages.

"You better take five steps back and get out my face with that noise. Don't come at me with this bullshit, Cameron. Not this morning." I pushed back my chair and stood up. I was hungry. Suffering from caffeine deprivation. Diego might be married. And I was pregnant. The way I felt, I was *thisclose* to leaping over my desk and putting him in a half-nelson wrestling hold. I could take him down quicker than a big cat hunting buffalo. We stood facing one another. The door opened, and his manager Casey poked his head in and broke our tense standoff.

"Dawg, Nikki's in her office. I'm gonna play the remixes for her. Come on down." Casey stopped and looked from Cameron to me. "Everything alright in here?"

"Everything's everything, right Elle?"

I sat down in my chair and slid it closer to my desk. "We're cool."

Casey grabbed a duffel bag he must have left in my office, and they walked out. He looked like an intimidating big bear of a man, but if you poked him, he would giggle and jiggle like the Pillsbury Dough Boy. He was one of Cameron's friends from his pre-prep school days, and he was also Cameron's Achilles' heel. Mixing business and friendship was rarely a good combo. It was like playing Russian roulette backward, loading all the chambers but one. Riding along on the coattails of Cameron's success, Casey was less effective as a manager yet highly skilled as an ass-kisser. Cameron seemed to hold on to him, the idea of him, as his way of keeping it real. Whatever.

I gulped down a few deep breaths before stalking out to Veronica's cubicle.

"I don't care how cute he said you looked. Don't you ever let Cameron, or anyone else for that matter, in my office when I'm not here. Understood?"

Veronica was the department assistant but doubled as an undercover groupie. Pushing 25, she was severely testing the limits of gravity coupled with too many Krispy Kreme in her little halter-tops and miniskirts. Every day was casual Friday for her. The addendum to the dress code that recently came out - no piercings below the neck should be visible. That was for her.

"Fine. Sorry. I didn't think you'd mind."

"Well, now you know."

I stomped back into my office and closed the door. I looked down at the ring on my finger. Diego had given it to me a few months ago.

It was an 18k white gold ring with amethyst and tsavorite gemstones delicately shaped into a violet with a single leaf. We were on Rodeo Drive and had popped into the Chanel store when I saw the ring. A bloom full of colors, deep reds, yellows, and lots of purples, I fell in love with it as soon as I saw it. Diego bought it for me on the spot.

He had always been spontaneous. Generous. Someone like that couldn't be like the someone the Feds were painting him to be. Why hadn't he called me? My brain felt like soft butter. If I didn't pull it together, I would get nothing done but the backstroke in a pool of self-pity.

My hands were still shaking. I couldn't concentrate. I closed my blinds, and a feeling of paranoia threatened to immobilize me. I called Justine but got her voicemail. She was an actuary at an insurance firm with a dry, analytical demeanor that could immediately suck all the drama out of any situation.

A series of work-related flash fires sprouted up, leaving me no time to obsess about my personal life as I tried to extinguish them.

We had signed an act out of backwoods, Arkansas, and his manager called and screamed at me because she didn't like how his press package looked. I had to put her on hold to hunt down the A&R guy to find out about a missing music file that was supposed to have been sent to one of the daytime talk shows. An editor from *People* magazine received the release I did on Cameron and needed a high-resolution jpeg of him sent to her five minutes ago because she was on deadline. Besides dealing with the mags, every Tom, Dick, and Harry that had a blog with a whiff of traffic felt like they should be on my press list, and I had to deal with their requests. While juggling the phones, Melanie sent me an e-mail asking what happened to the *Sexual Chocolate* review in *LA Premiere*?

I took a deep breath and closed my eyes. He promised me. It was Tuesday. New music Tuesday was like the elimination round on *American Idol*. The pressure was always on to see how many units an artist could move, what the reception would be on that first day, and how many features and reviews would run in the dailies and weeklies.

I grabbed a copy of the weekly entertainment magazine from my overflowing inbox. I flipped through it. Twice. No review. Harlan promised he would run the review of the girls this week. Had me jumping through all sorts of hoops, rushing to get him the music so he could have enough time to do it.

This was not good. Melanie was as fickle as they came, and depending on which way the wind was blowing, she would disavow any knowledge of my actions quicker than the Secretary from *Mission: Impossible.* We had another marketing meeting to go to later on, and they were all going to be asking the same thing... what happened to the *LA Premiere* review? That was supposed to be the lynchpin of our progress report.

The hype gods were smiling on me because I was able to redeem myself a little by calling the right person at the right time. I called Liza at *The Ellen Show* about another one of our acts. She had a last-minute cancellation for Thursday, and I could slip Sexual Chocolate in there because the girls were local.

It was only Tuesday afternoon, my second day back, and already I felt overwhelmed and craving the weekend. Unable to sit still, I had to get out of the office. Like a homing pigeon, I was headed to the Coffee Bean down the block. Beverly Hills, like all of LA, was changing. Construction was relentlessly tearing down the old and making way for newer, bigger, better, shinier housing that very few could afford in this market. Sidewalk closures, the repetitive sounds of jackhammers, and traffic were all part of the ambiance. Everything was changing.

I checked my voicemail messages. Sandwiched between ten calls from television producers, managers, writers, and magazine editors was a message from Blake, my landlord/roommate.

"Elle, it's Blake. This is my fourth message to you. Whatsup? Call me back. It's important."

Between traveling and now the "Diego" situation, I had failed to return Blake's calls over the last two weeks. He traveled just as much as I did. He had my share of the rent. I had left it out before I went out of town, and he had cashed it. What else could he want?

I erased his message with good intentions to call him and called Diego instead. I tried his cell phone, the home phone, and his office. All voicemail. He had disappeared off the grid... on the day his house was raided. If the FBI knew he hadn't boarded his plane, could *he* have known they had a search warrant? Innocent people didn't just disappear, at least not on shows like *Snapped, 48 Hours Hard Evidence, The Devil You Know,* and all the other true crime shows I DVR'd. My mocha ice blended was almost gone by the time I got back to my office.

"There's someone waiting for you in the lobby," Veronica said with a heavy attitude as I squeaked past her in my sneakers. She could have had three heads, and I wouldn't have noticed, so entrenched in my own melodrama.

"I just walked through the lobby and didn't see anyone. Do they have a name?" I snapped.

She glared at me, "I don't know, the receptionist didn't say, just some red-haired guy in a suit and long coat."

I blinked. I went back to my office and closed the door. As I leaned against it, I felt like hellhounds were hot on my heels. What was he doing here? It was like having a nightmare follow you to work, and it wasn't even my nightmare.

Sucking down deep breaths, I walked out to the lobby. Agent Walsh was flipping through the pages of a *Billboard* magazine while Dru 'n Damon, another one of our bass-heavy hip hop acts, was piped in through the speakers. Debbie, the receptionist, didn't even try to hide her curiosity. She glanced at me with one eyebrow cocked as her fingers whizzed across her phone's keyboard. Probably texting and/or tweeting about my latest visitor to her spies in the inner office. Everyone knew a Fed when they saw one, thanks to the persistent rumors of Savage Rhythms being built on the backs of ill-gotten gains and laundered money. "What to do in case of a raid" was actually part of the first-day orientation spiel to the uninitiated. The question on her face was as plain as day... why was he here to see me?

"Mr. Walsh, come in," I said. I should have called him Dr. Walsh to confuse her, but the rumor mill would have me on death's door if I did that.

He unfolded his long legs and casually dropped the magazine on the tabletop before following me. We didn't say a word until I closed my office door.

"Nice office," he said.

"What are you doing here?"

"You rushed out this morning, and I still have a few questions." He pulled out a little notebook.

"You know where I work, and I didn't even tell you my name, but how hard would it have been to get my phone number? You should have called; I would have saved you a trip. I don't have any answers for you."

"I thought it might be more comfortable for you to do this on your turf, but if you like, you can come to my office, and we can do this in a more formal setting."

"Do what? What do you want from me?"

"I have a few questions to ask you about your boyfriend."

"Do I need a lawyer?"

"I don't know, do you?"

"I don't even know what you think I should know."

"Has Mr. Rivera contacted you?"

I could feel the ice blended mocha rising from the base of my throat.

As I sat down, my right leg started shaking. I tried to cross my legs at the ankles, but it wouldn't stop. I don't know which freaked me out more, him or my leg?

"I haven't spoken to Diego since I saw him two days ago in Paris. He left that morning to take the train to Frankfurt, and he was fine. I was supposed to pick him up from the airport last night, but *as you know*, he wasn't on the plane. I don't know what started this, but he's a great guy. He wouldn't; he just couldn't do something like this."

"We're investigating several complaints from his clients. We have a half dozen banks ready to sue Rivera Financial for fraudulent loans."

For a moment, it felt like a hand was around my throat, squeezing the air out. "You know, you should check out his partner Jeffrey Coogan. I always warned Diego about him. He just seemed shady." Not my best *Columbo* moment, but it was all I had. I sat back and folded my arms across my chest.

"We have Mr. Coogan in custody, and he's cooperating."

"Oh."

Didn't see that coming. A thousand questions convened on my tongue, but none were able to launch, or so I thought.

"Cooperating? What does he know? What was he saying? Sued by banks?" Belatedly, I realized I was speaking aloud.

"I know this is hard for you. I see it often in these cases. I'm looking for leads in tracking Mr. Rivera. Do you know of anywhere he would go? Could you write down a list of friends and their numbers you believe he would contact?"

"His parents are dead. He's an only child. You say he's married, and he stole from his clients. Enough to get the FBI involved. The Diego I know is brutally honest. I thought we would probably get married one day. I don't know how I can help you when it sounds like we're not even talking about the same person."

After a few more moments of getting nowhere, Walsh stood up to leave. "So, are you going to be ok?" He replied off my blank look, "This morning, your fainting spell?"

"Yes, I'm fine, thanks." That sounded much better than saying, "If left to Mother Nature, in nine months, I'd have cankles and wouldn't be able to see my feet."

"Look, I know this is tough, but it will only get worse. The banks have already petitioned the courts to place Rivera Financial into bankruptcy, and it's only a matter of time before they liquidate his assets. When you speak to him, tell him he should come in and talk to us."

Agent Jonas Walsh left his card on my desk before he left. He was an FBI Financial Analyst. I tried reaching Diego. Cell. Voicemail. Home phone. Voicemail. Text. Unanswered. If I knew how to do smoke signals, I would be lighting matches.

When good hormones go bad... that was my mood in a nutshell. I drove over to Diego's office. It's not like I was getting any work done in my office. What did Walsh mean when he said Coogan was cooperating? I'd met him a few times, and he had a different girl on his arm every time. He never introduced her, like she was just a disposable piece of décor. His arrogance was bar none. Life was turning into this riddle, and I felt like the answer was somewhere in his office. It had to be. Stuck in lunchtime traffic, I realized I could have hopped on a pogo stick to his office faster than traveling east on Wilshire. A small bright light shone on me when I found a meter, with time still left on it, in front of the former home of mega-talent agency ICM. Diego's office was only two blocks away. I walked up the driveway on the side of the brick building and stopped at the guard's desk outside in the parking garage.

Gil was hunched over his small portable television, watching one of the many carbon copy judge shows. The empty bank of elevators was behind him.

"Hey, Gil." I made sure to keep the swollen knot away from his point of view.

Gil glanced up. "Your friend's pretty popular these days." On the counter, he had a bowl of baby carrots swimming in a gallon of ranch dressing.

"I bet."

Gil slammed his fist down on the desk and exploded, "That's bull!"

"What?"

"Sorry. The judge just entered a verdict."

"Gil. Focus," I said, hearing the impatience creeping into my tone. "What's going on with Diego? You said he was popular."

"Right." He shrugged his massive shoulders before picking up a carrot. "Place was swarming with 5-0 this morning. They took a bunch of stuff out. I had to let 'em in cause no one was in the office. I coulda joined the force if I wanted. My knee-"

"-Gil. Why did you have to let them in? Where's Sharon? Did the police say what they were looking for or why?"

"When the 5-0 show up with warrants, it's not my job to ask questions." Munch. Munch. "Place been a ghost town all last week."

All last week? I was suffocating in my thoughts, struggling to make sense of it all.

"Could you let me up there, please?"

Gil tore his eyes away from the small set and looked at me. His face softened. "You could get me into a lot of trouble if anyone finds out..."

"I won't tell, I promise."

Gil nodded. I hurried over to the elevator and pressed the up button. On the fifth floor, the doors silently glided open into the lobby of Diego's firm. A loud ding announced my arrival to no one.

My heart slammed into my rib cage as I walked past the receptionist's desk. Usually, on any given day, the phones were ringing off the hook, and five staff people were on computers doing whatever it was they did. They always looked busy. Now it was empty. A few computers were missing, but the rest were still on. File cabinet drawers hung open, long abandoned by their contents. Most disturbing of all was the eerie quiet.

I went to the corner office, which was Diego's. It was empty. There had been several framed photos of us lining his desk. They were gone. There used to be degrees hung on the wall. Gone. His file cabinets were empty, and his computer was gone. I sat down in his chair and spun around slowly, taking in the bare shell of the room. I opened the drawers on the side of his desk, looking for *anything* that could tell me something. Empty. I closed my eyes and rested my hands on my stomach. The elevator ding startled me, and I realized I had fallen asleep.

"You okay up here?" Gil asked, lumbering into Diego's office.

Wiping the drool off the corner of my mouth, I yawned. I was exhausted. "I'm fine. I was just thinking."

I grabbed my purse and headed to the elevator. We rode down in silence until the door slid open.

"Thanks for the CDs the other day. My little sister loves them."

"You're welcome." Gil's sister had been in the hospital recovering from a bone marrow transplant; she had leukemia. I had given him a bunch of CDs of artists on Savage Rhythms, which he uploaded onto her iPod. I knew what those hospital stays could be like, a vast terrain of boredom only broken up by moments of utter discomfort and pain as doctors and nurses poked and prodded. Evie had sickle cell anemia, and we spent many days and nights in the artificial cheeriness of the children's ward.

Instead of returning to the office, I walked to a cafe on Robertson. As far as I was concerned, they had the best Caesar salad with tuna and capers. I couldn't think straight. I was so hungry even though I had just inhaled an ice blended 30 minutes ago. My stomach was an abyss, and no matter how hard I tried, the gnawing hunger wouldn't go away. Just the routine act of eating helped calm my nerves. I made my mind blank and just concentrated on the food. I ate at a table outside facing the street. The usual potent mix of smog and exhaust were my tablemates as I watched the tide of Hollywood dealmakers-in-training rush in for takeout. The unemployed writers were easy to spot. They were in no particular hurry as they gazed over their laptops into some fantasy life just beyond their reach. I tried to pretend as though this was any other day. I hid behind my sunglasses and tried to throw off an everything's-cool-vibe. Inside, I was treading water.

* * *

About a quarter to six, when I was making the move to pack up and go home, Melanie came rushing into my office with Pepper in tow.

"Will you do me a huge favor, kiddo? I have a 6 o'clock with Chantal and her manager, and of course, she's bringing in her two dogs, and they're just bullies. Some mean-tempered Pomeranians," she paused and gave Pepper a loving pat on the head. "I don't want Pepper exposed to them. Will you be a doll and watch him for me? The meeting shouldn't last more than 30 minutes."

"Aww, Mel... where's Veronica? Why can't she watch him?"

"Veronica? She had a doctor's appointment or something. I don't know. I just remember her asking if she could leave early today."

A year ago, that would have never happened. Before Melanie embraced the joys of puppyhood, she was a super Type A personality with ice-cold Red Bull running through her veins. She went through assistants like a drunk at an open bar. After Pepper came into her life, she no longer stayed late, as she had to rush home because the nanny left at six, and "Poor Pepper couldn't be by himself for too long."

"He's not going to chew up any of my stuff, is he? He's trained and all of that?"

"Of course, kiddo," she smiled and looked at me as though I were the office simpleton. She dumped a bunch of junk on my coffee table. "Here are some toys. His brush. He loves being brushed. His wee-wee pad and some tissues."

"Hold up. What's the tissue for?"

"Just give him a little wipe once he goes on the wee-wee pad. We don't want mommy's little boy to have wee-wee on his fur."

"Melanie, I love you and my job, but I have limits. Wiping Pepper's little ahhh-tushy is not going to happen."

"Oh. Well. I understand. I won't be too long." She put Pepper down and walked out of the office, hesitating at the door as she glanced back with large pools of doubt clouding her eyes. I waved her away.

"He'll be fine. What's the worst that could happen?"

Pepper was a mellow Maltese weighing all of five pounds. He wasn't hyper like most little dogs, running around in circles and barking at the air. Melanie placed him on the couch, and he didn't move from that spot. He had on a cute sweater emblazoned with rhinestones (Mama Melanie thought the air conditioning was too high in the building) and a diamond-studded collar with a dog tag that read: Mel's Boy Toy.

I looked at Pepper, and he looked at me before closing his eyes and falling asleep. If I didn't choose motherhood, is that what I was destined to become in another five or six years? A sugar momma to my pet? I shuddered.

While returning phone calls, I opened a can of peanut brittle I had bought from a little display in the kitchen. Co-workers were constantly hawking some school fundraising products for their kids. On any given day, it looked like a swap meet with raffle tickets, candy, Girl Scout cookies, nuts and fruit or catalogs for stationary, and candles assembled on one of the tables in the office kitchen.

Pepper perked up his little ears at the sound of the can opening. He hopped off the couch and trotted under the desk to sniff around my feet. He looked like a fluffy cotton ball with a black nose.

"I'm letting you know now, you mark your territory on my shoes, and I'm going to be using you to remove my make-up," I told him while crunching on peanut brittle. He sat up on his little hind legs and shook one of his paws at me.

"Aww, look at you! Now I know what Melanie does on Friday nights, teaching you cute tricks."

I dropped a little piece of peanut brittle to him. He caught it in mid-air and snapped it up.

"You are just the sweetest thing!"

I tossed him a few more pieces before my phone rang. I was in the middle of a call with an editor from *Nylon* when I heard this annoying wheezing sound. Was the air conditioner on the blink again? I spun around in my chair to gaze out the window while I talked. Already, darkness was starting to stain the sky. That annoying sputtering started again. I turned down my stereo to get a better idea of where the noise was coming from.

"Hehph, hehph" and then a long gasp and another round of coughs. I rolled the chair over to the air conditioner, but the sound wasn't coming from there.

"Hehph, hehph, hehph, aackkkk!" I turned around slowly and rolled the chair back to where the sound was coming from. I looked under my desk, and Pepper was hunched over and choking.

"What the he-? Let me call you back!" I hurriedly yanked off my earpiece and got on my hands and knees to see what Pepper was doing underneath the desk. Mouth wide open; it looked like he was trying to hack up a lung.

"Not on the Gucci, Pepper!" I shoved my tote bag out of the way and grabbed him. He felt like a sock full of feathers. I could feel every rib as he tried to suck in air. A rush of panic made me light-headed as I sent a hurried prayer, "Lord, please don't let this dog die on my watch!" His little heart was pounding as his chest heaved in and out. I snatched the phone off the hook and dialed 911. A message came on and put me on hold. I hung up. Pepper's wheezing was getting more frantic.

I held him in outstretched hands and gingerly tried to shake him. Melanie walked into my office as I held him upside down, saying, "Don't go to the light, Pepper, just spit it out!" Her scream startled me, and I dropped him. An arc of hot urine sprayed all over me on his way down as he coughed up the offensive peanut brittle at the same time.

"What are you doing to my baby?" Melanie screeched. She scooped Pepper up and inspected him.

"He was choking on a piece of peanut brittle, and I was trying to dislodge it."

"You gave him peanut brittle?"

"I don't know CPR or the Heimlich maneuver, so I thought shaking would help."

"My poor baby! He's allergic to nuts!"

"I didn't mean to hurt him."

"What were you thinking? You could have killed my baby! I have to get him to the vet."

I followed her down the hall, dripping with pee, still babbling. "Do you want me to come with you? I could explain what happened to the doctor."

"No. Thank. You. Elle. You've done enough already."

I leaned against the wall and sighed. I ignored the unspoken questions asked and answered in the eyes of the spectators still in the office.

"Show's over. Elvis has left the building," I told them as I made the walk of shame to the restroom to clean up. I couldn't even take care of a dog. How was I supposed to raise a kid?

five

I MEANT to return Blake's call; unfortunately, the intent was lost in the haphazardness of the day. I didn't think about Blake again until I arrived home and found him in our kitchen. Actually, I knew he was there as I trudged upstairs to my place. His fragrant fingerprint lingered in the air the way the day smelled after a fresh rainstorm. His unique scent, with a twist of Issey Miyake, was faint yet distinctive. It proclaimed his presence as I swung open my front door.

Tara Hill was a gated mini-suburb within the larger suburb of Culver City, housing over 400 condos. The exterior was nothing to brag about. Brown stucco with the required muddy "Tara Hill" brown for the doors and patio fences. The interior was something else altogether. I loved the cathedral ceiling in the living room, and my balcony reminded me of being ensconced in a tree house as spring sprang up around it with the neighboring shrubs and plants blossoming in a fit of green.

I kicked off my sneakers, my feet aching from not being in heels, and slammed the door behind me. Blake poked out his head, covered with nubby blond twists, from the kitchen doorway.

"You know I like a stocked fridge. Where's the food?" he said, as he gave me a frown.

"Had I known you'd be back in town..."

"You would have done what?"

"Left the takeout menus on the counter. What else? Give me a sec. I have to change."

I slipped out of my stained jeans and top. Pepper was like a furry thermos storing a gallon of warm pee. Disgusting. I couldn't get the smell out of my nose even after I took a shower.

Afterward, I walked back to the kitchen and forced a smile as I stood on my tippy-toes to tussle his twists, loving how the natural kinky curl of his hair tickled my fingertips. Touch-up queen that I am, I don't feel it too often.

"Hey, back up off me. I go to Arden's place smelling like perfume, she'll swear I was out screwing some chick."

"When did you get hair? You were sportin' a baldie last time I saw you."

"You know how Blake do, like to change it up some."

"You look good. Not that you need me to tell you that. I'm sure you say it to yourself daily."

"Haha, make jokes at Blake's expense. Blake can't help it if God gave him all this." He gestured from his head to his toes.

"Talking about ourselves in the third person again? You must have landed another gig. Who are you doubling for this time? Danny DeVito?"

"Don't hate on a brutha, Elle. Especially when you're looking at Will Smith's stunt double in his next $100 million action flick." He accentuated his point with a slicing karate chop move before bowing.

"That's great. Glad you're back cause the air conditioning went out," I said as I walked down the hallway. I didn't want to talk to Blake about what happened, still couldn't wrap my mind around it.

"Hey Elle, that's why I've been calling you. I sold the place." His words stopped me in my tracks. I walked backwards down the hall back to the kitchen.

"Excuse me? Did you say you 'sold the place'? What do you mean?"

"I'm saying, we're in a recession. I was getting ready to lose this spot and had to do a short sale... and I'm moving in with Arden."

"Why couldn't Ms. Money Bags give you enough dough to cover this place? When were you going to tell me all this?" My head felt like it was going to explode.

"I'm not going to ask Arden to bail me out. Look, I'm telling you now. This spot is sold."

"I have to move?"

"Well... yeah. I mean, the new owner wants to live here. It wouldn't be cool to have you lounging around in your Victoria's Secrets. His wife wouldn't like it."

I punched him in the arm. "That's not funny. Did you even think how this would affect me?"

"No, you never entered the equation. I'm drowning, and this was a way out."

"You didn't even tell me it was on the market. When did you show it?"

"It was on the market for one day, and this offer came in. I got a call. We swooped in here one morning, no biggie. Cash deal."

"I pay you rent every month. What do you mean you're losing this place? You could have at least offered it to me first!" I folded my arms across my chest. Blake started laughing. An infuriating, long, drawn-out, gut-busting laugh. I swatted him again.

"Ow!" He backed away from me, rubbing his shoulder while trying to control the last sputtering of his laughter.

"What's so funny?"

"This was a cash deal, and I know you don't have that kind of loot. I peeped your credit report when you filled out your rental application for this spot. Lucky you wore a short skirt that day."

"My credit's not that bad. Name me one reason I couldn't get a loan." My voice cracked a little, and beads of sweat popped out on my forehead like microwave popcorn.

"Your credit's not that great either. You over-extend yourself every month. Baby, you look good, but you're broke as hell," he softened his voice a little to take away the reproach when he saw how my face had fallen. "You wear your mortgage on your back, babe. You have no assets. You're late-"

I held my hand up. "I get it. You can stop. You made your little point."

"Well, you asked."

"Well, now, I'm asking you to shut up."

"What's the big deal? Why you trippin'?"

I walked over to the patio doors. The scratchiness of the lawn carpet tickled my bare feet as I shuffled to the balcony rail. A blanket of darkness had fallen. Hidden high in the trees, the sounds of the night littered the air like a bevy of shooting stars. The laugh track from a sitcom. A baby crying. Mr. Harrison giving his weekly piano lessons. Blake came over and stood beside me. I leaned against the railing as a tidal wave of exhaustion threatened to bring me to my knees.

"How long do I have to pack?"

"You being a tenant and all, have 60 days to vacate... but the buyer wants to move in sooner, so I told him I would talk to you." He turned his soft brown eyes on me and gave me his most charming smile.

"What the hell? Blake? You want me to find another place and have all my stuff packed up in less than 60 days?"

"Move in with your man. You spend most of your time over there."

The frenetic energy of the frightened moved me into the living room, where I paced the confines like a wild animal cornered before collapsing onto the couch.

"Of course." *If I could find him.*

"Take all the time you need. Just be up out of here at the end of the month."

"I thought you said I had 60 days?"

"How long have I been trying to call you?"

Exhaustion, fear, hunger, and the why-me look of the damned played out across my face. My drama meter was off the charts. Hormones raging. The tears took their opportunity to make a mad dash for it down my cheeks.

"What else can go wrong? This is the worst. Day. Ever. I'm not even going to go into the usual work crap, but I'm at Diego's house when the Feds raid it. Saying they have a warrant to search the place like he pulled a Madoff or something, and I haven't been able to get in touch with him all day, and then I pass out on the ground in front of all these cops." The words flew out of my mouth as though tossed by a tempest raging inside. I pressed my lips together; I couldn't believe I was blabbing stuff to *Blake,* of all people. But Justine hadn't called me back, and Diego was MIA. I had to tell someone. It was either Blake or a barista at Starbucks.

"Diego got raided by the Feds? Best believe he did something to get on their radar."

"And you know this how? From your vast experience playing a background FBI agent on a TV show?" I said as I pulled out a bunch of tissues from the container on the end table and blew my nose.

"What's up with the fainting? You okay?"

"I don't want to talk about it. Why don't you go back to Arden's and leave me in my misery?"

I got up and went to the bathroom to wash my face. I checked my phone and saw I had a million voicemail messages, texts, and calendar alerts. It was almost 7:30. Krave. Shit. Double shit with sprinkles on top. It was an in-store signing for a new group at one of the few remaining record stores in the city. It had been scheduled for weeks, and I totally forgot it was tonight. I needed to be there because I had the group's pictures and CDs in my car's trunk. How could I let this slip through? I was supposed to be the bridge between the group and the store, helping everything run smoothly and dealing with any media requests that might have come up... I closed my eyes. Just when I thought the day couldn't get any worse.

Blake ordered Chinese food and watched the game while I sequestered myself on the patio and tried to save my job. I spent the next 30 minutes on the phone with the group's manager and the record store. Fortunately, the manager had some pictures and CDs on him. I tried Melanie on her cell to see how she made out at the vet with Pepper. When her voicemail answered, I left a message. Hoping against hope, she hadn't heard about this mix-up. *This was big.* In what felt like a blink, I was losing pieces of myself. They were being swept away by a huge, unforeseen gust of wind, and I couldn't catch them fast enough. Diego. My job. I never forgot an event. Ever.

I came back into the living room, about 20 pounds lighter from being chewed out. Blake was on his feet, pacing and yelling at the television. I told him he would make a perfect Little League Coach. When his cell started blowing up, he looked guilty.

"Arden's probably wondering what the hell happened to me. I gotta go. Don't try to be superwoman up in here lifting something heavy cause I don't know if my homeowner's insurance will cover you if something happens."

"I'll be fine. Thanks for your concern."

Blake left with the promise of returning in a few days to pack some of his belongings.

Almost three years ago, Blake was looking for a roommate. I knew him through a friend of a friend of an acquaintance—LA thing. It was perfect; we were both never around. I had moved around and traveled so much that I never really had the inclination to accumulate anything other than clothes. Blake traveled even more as a stunt double, working on films in exotic locations and doubling as a personal trainer during his off time. Real estate was hot at the time; loans practically threw themselves at buyers. He and many others bought more houses than they knew what to do with, and now that the economy had tanked, he was cutting his losses.

His full-time and most demanding job was as the patsy/lover for Arden Blackwell. A true career climber, she went from Arden Who? To A-List Arden, thanks to a sex tape that "accidentally" leaked to the press. She turned her insecurities into a cottage industry with a reality show, book, clothing line, and whatever else her business managers managed to sell. She kept everyone on a short leash, including Blake.

Meanwhile, he trained her, kept her in shape, and gave her an ass that caused whiplash. He would freshen up at the condo whenever he was in town or needed a break from playing Blake Bigelow Male Gigolo. It was an arrangement that worked out well... until now.

Once the house was quiet, I slipped between my sheets, fully dressed, barely remembering to kick off my slippers. I still hadn't heard from Diego. Not knowing where he was and if he was safe kept sleep at bay. I knew he would be able to straighten everything out if he were here. I clicked off the light and grabbed my phone. I wanted to keep it close in case he called.

six

MY EYES FLICKERED OPEN. For a moment, with the gray haze of morning softening the shadows in my room, I didn't remember. The deep coma of sleep had wiped away the events of the day before... and then my cell phone rang. A flood of memories rushed through like high tide. I slid my finger across the touch screen to answer, pulled the covers over my head, and groaned when I realized it wasn't Diego.

"Hey girl, sorry I didn't get back to you yesterday. What's going on?" Justine said in her usual machine gun, rapid-fire way.

I slumped down in bed even more. "It's 6:30 in the morning," I said as I stifled a yawn.

"I would have called you last night, but Lena's driving me crazy with all this Sweet 16 nonsense, and I have these last-minute reports due, so work is nuts. Are you all right? You sounded stressed in your message."

I gave her the short and dirty version of events, too tired to put a spin on it.

"You should come back home until you figure things out. Especially since you're going to be a mama."

Justine was the typical, I'm-a-mom-come-over-to-the-dark-side-with-me type of mom. The kind that felt everyone should procreate. To not do so was selfish. I knew her, and she was probably already planning the baby shower.

"Go back to Mariner's Pike? Are you kidding me?"

"Geeze Ellie, you act like we're some hick town using mail carrier pigeons. You grew up here, remember?"

"How could I forget? Listen, I have to go. Breathe a word of this to anyone, especially Déjà, and I'll hunt you down and force you to learn how to Krump."

I really hoped things would be resolved today. The authorities would realize they were looking at the wrong guy, his clients would miraculously find their money, and the banks would discover it was just a mix-up. Everything would go back to normal. My visit to Dr. Madison never happened. My little fainting spell could be attributed to... hell, a change in air pressure sounded good.

If I didn't speak the words again, didn't give weight to their possibility, maybe the situation would evaporate. Wishful thinking, I knew, but if I had one late birthday wish, it would be that yesterday (and part of Monday) never happened. Any of it.

Somehow I made it out of the house. I don't remember showering or getting dressed, and I wasn't on the phone for once. Wrestling with my thoughts and fighting traffic was all I could multitask.

After yesterday's Krave debacle, I couldn't afford another screw-up. Especially if I wanted to jump over to Triad. Fuck-ups traveled faster than the speed of light in this town, and only men could recover and get promoted to bigger and better jobs. Mistakes, no matter how old, stuck to women like lead stilettos and put a drag on our careers.

* * *

Years ago, after a (now ex) fiancé gave me an impossible ultimatum, I developed the brittle skin of the jaded. After him was an ex-who-shall-not-be-named that dumped me. Those experiences made me believe that falling in love should be akin to setting up a business deal. I would interview the applicants, weed out the deadbeats and losers, put the potentials on probation, and cull a finalist. We would level-set our expectations, develop an action plan, and then conquer the world together. Unfortunately, qualified applicants had been at an all-time low—maybe it was geographical. Forget the Bridge to Nowhere; LA was the "land of dates that led to nowhere." Until I met Diego. Some days he made me forget how to think. Sent the pheromones racing through me. Made me forget everything but how to wear his name on my lips.

I fell so hard for him that I swear I was walking around with a concussion for the first few months. It helped that he was the perfect accessory that looked right at every event. When we went to parties, and he loved to party just as much as I did, I didn't have to worry about him being the territorial wallflower stressing me while I worked the room. We worked the room together. Big dreams. He wanted to build up his cadre of clients to include the Hollywood A-list. With my contacts and his business acumen as a hotshot financial advisor, we would run this town.

The problem with me and Diego? Sometimes I felt as though our merger was just another acquisition for him. Maybe he collected hearts like some people collected rare cars. Something to be stored but not actually used. Maybe a wife wasn't such a far-fetched idea after all. Maybe it was all just a big mistake, one that could be resolved if he just called. The problem with me? Maybe I loved being in love too much.

* * *

I kept my head down at work and managed not to kill any small animals, and got through the day with no drama. Now, I was late for an engagement party. One that I would have loved to ditch, but it was probably poor form since I was the maid of honor. I'd been set up on a blind date years ago with someone, totally not my type, think: Mr. Bookman from *Good Times*. He raved about a friend of his, also from New Jersey. He introduced me to Freddie, and we've been friends ever since. Not sure what happened to the guy.

Hopefully, Freddie wouldn't be too upset with me. I was always late, and I had promised her I would be on time for the engagement dinner at Swanks in Beverly Hills. I swung by the house to change. It took me forever to find something to wear. Everything felt a little snug (that's what I got for having everything tailored), and made me self-conscious. I finally decided on a pair of distressed low-riding jeans and a beige off-the-shoulder peasant blouse.

Would people know? Could they tell? A part of me wanted to crawl into bed with a pound of chocolate-covered strawberries. Make that two pounds. I would inhale the first pound and take my time savoring the second. Somehow, I would manage to consume all while safely cocooned between my sheets. My hand shook while I put on my mascara and freshened up my powder to hide the matching luggage sets underneath my eyes. Don't stop. Keep moving. It was the only remedy my family ever used in times of crisis, and we always seemed to be in some type of crisis mode.

I was blasting an Angela Bofill song on the way to Swanks. "I Try" seemed so appropriate. The minute I stepped into the restaurant, I heard Freddie's distinctive laugh slicing through the undercurrent of talk, the clattering of dishes, and the background music. It was a tight squeeze as the hostess led me to the back room. The main dining room was no bigger than my living room, and every seat was full. The walls were sponged a gorgeous shade of sky blue, and the flickering candlelight heightened the mingling scents floating about. Spicy seafood gumbo. Ox tails. Collard greens. By the time I reached the party, I felt like the Venus flytrap in the *Little Shop of Horrors*. FEED ME! All the usual suspects were seated and accounted for. My heart sank a little when I saw two empty and expectant chairs at the end of the table. I knew I would have to spend a good twenty minutes acting as Diego's GPS, explaining his absence.

Six couples were already seated, and various snippets of conversation floated about. Frederica and Nigel dominated the center of the long table. Freddie wore a skin-tight black dress with a blood-red feather boa draped around her neck, while Nigel was resplendent in an off-white silk shirt. Freddie was a large woman in size and voice. She used to do theater. She was pure drama, from her impeccably done face to a voice that could inject high drama into simple phrases like "please pass the salt." Whereas I don't remember ever hearing Nigel speak more than two sentences. He was small and slender with a nervous quality that took form in the shape of wide damp circles underneath his arms.

As usual, when the clique clicked, banter around the table centered on who was vacationing where, who purchased what stock, new cars, and all the delights to be had with an excess of disposable income. At least it used to be. Since the group was purely new money, the recession had sliced and diced their income. Lately, talk centered on how much they had saved by downgrading from a nanny, chef, and housekeeper to just making do with a nanny who took on the additional duties of a housekeeper or chef, and, in some cases, a gardener.

Freddie air kissed me from across the room before pouting, "You're late. I hope you're not this late on my wedding day."

"And ruin your day? Never," I blew a kiss back at her and made what I thought was the Girl Scout's sign of honor.

Freddie let out a gusty laugh that spilled over into the spirits of other guests.

"Like they would let you in," she sputtered.

"You were probably the only Girl Scout selling rum cookies," Tina chimed in.

"You mean she was the only Brownie spiking the brownies at the bake sale," said Maia. I never liked her. With blond locks, she always had a way of lobbing off barbed jokes with a smile that didn't reach her eyes.

"Yeah, she was her own best customer," added Freddie.

"Obviously, you all must have consumed a little too much haterade. You need to stop because it ain't cute. Let's focus on the business at hand, Freddie and Nigel. I'd like to propose a toast."

I grabbed a bottle of wine and filled my glass before pushing back my chair and standing up. Everyone raised their glasses in anticipation. "A toast. To Freddie and Nigel. Your love serves as an inspiration to us all. May all your days and nights be filled with happiness, love, and one another."

A chorus of "here, here's" swept around the room as glasses clinked against one another.

"And a toast to you, happy belated birthday," Freddie said, raising her glass to me.

Even though I dumped my purse and jacket on the chair next to me, it did nothing to hide Diego's absence. My glass of wine sat untouched as I traded gossip with Tina. She was going on about her divorce, so I didn't have to talk much.

A feeling overcame me; I knew it wasn't a test run. I hurriedly excused myself and made a dash for the bathroom. I rushed in and headed for the nearest stall. After getting up close and personal with the toilet bowl, I had to sit on the floor for a few minutes and hold my head between my knees to stop the nausea from rolling in. The variety of stale and putrid scents assaulted my nose. My stomach was still doing a series of flips, but finally, I could stagger out to the sink and splash cold water on my face. When I opened my eyes, I was shocked to see a man standing behind me. Were the police following me? Was I being set up?

"What are you doing in here?" I asked. My eyes locked on his in the mirror's reflection. Why did I stop carrying mace? It didn't look right on my Tiffany key ring. Damn. What was I supposed to do? Stop. Drop. And roll. Wait. That was from those safety lessons in 5th grade in case of a fire.

"What are *you* doing in here?" He walked over to the sink next to mine and washed his hands.

My eyes traveled around the bathroom in search of an escape.

Two lime green urinals stuck out like penises during a bikini wax. The door swung open, and another man walked in.

"Oops. Didn't know there was a private party going on," he said and ducked out.

I grabbed my purse from the sink and left. I stopped at the bar and got a cranberry and club soda. Back at the table, Tina asked, "Where were you? You were gone so long that I went to check on you, and I didn't see you."

"You know me, I needed a refill, and uh, I went outside to make a phone call. I wasn't getting good reception in here." I held up my glass to her and took a sip.

The party was interminable. A word I had never, ever uttered to describe a party. By now, I would have hijacked the party, and everyone would have been singing "Happy Birthday" to me. But in the new world order of things, I didn't want to bring attention to myself. I just wanted to go home. Every time I wanted to leave, someone would give a toast, or Freddie would launch into one of her long stories about how she met this or that person and how we were all so special; that's why she wanted to share her special day with us —the bridal party. Blah. Blah. Blah. For those of us who had known Freddie for a minute, we all just prayed the third time was a charm. I was tired of budgeting for her bridal shower and wedding every two years. You would think she would have stopped with the gift registry after wedding number one.

Finally, when my migraine kicked in to the tune of "Kung Fu Dancing," I left. Of course, that move garnered a chorus of "Are you alright?" "Elle's the first to leave, there must be something wrong." I mumbled something about work and left. Tongues would start wagging once I stepped out of hearing range.

By the time I got home, I was stripping before I took my keys out of the door. My trail of clothes led to the bathroom. I kept the lights off. Turned the shower on high and let the warm stream of water soothe my fractured nerves. I sat on the bathtub floor with my back to the faucet and let the water wash over me. The roar of water rushing past my ears was comforting. I stayed that way until the water turned cold. I barely remember crawling into bed. The chime of my cell phone jerked me out of an already fitful sleep. I shivered as a playful night breeze zipped across my naked body. I had crashed on top of the sheets.

It was a text message.

> We need to talk. Astro's at 8 am?

Even though I didn't recognize the phone number, I knew it was Diego.

seven

THE MINUTE the sun started to stain the morning sky, I rolled out of bed. Not like I was sleeping anyway. Men avoided that phrase, "We need to talk," like it was the main cause of permanent erectile dysfunction. So, hearing Diego volunteer it, I was on edge. *We need to talk.* In the shower, his voice tickled and teased my already frayed nerves. *We need to talk...* about my wife. Concentration was just as fleeting as sleep. I dropped a glass of water. Damn near took my eye out while applying mascara. Had to come back home because that gnawing feeling of leaving the iron on was actually correct.

When I left the condo the second time, a woman stepped in front of my car as I exited the side gate on Jefferson Boulevard. She walked over to my car and smiled. She looked like a college student with her hair pulled back in a ponytail and a warm-up suit. She tapped on my window. I rolled it down halfway.

"Are you Elle?"

"Do I know you?"

A sudden flash of light blinded me when some guy appeared out of nowhere and started snapping pictures.

"What are you doing?" Instinctively, I blocked my face with my arm as I tried to blink away the blindness caused by the flash.

"Your boyfriend swindled a lot of people out of money. How did you two spend it?" The woman asked as she shoved a digital recorder toward the open window.

Horns honked behind me. I looked in my rearview mirror and saw a few cars lining up behind me, waiting to get out. I peeled out of the driveway away from the reporter and headed east on Jefferson. The road was shimmying before my eyes as I started to shake. I was afraid to pull over, afraid someone else would start taking pictures.

My phone rang. It was Justine. Using Bluetooth, her voice filled the car.

"Are you sitting down?"

"I'm driving."

"Maybe you should pull over."

"I can't, so just spill it."

In a tone that could have been describing how to build a database to figure out HMO costs, she said, "Diego was on *GMA*. They called him a disgraced financial adviser because he stole more than $30 million from his clients."

Another chorus of angry horns blared simultaneously like they were in a marching band as my car swerved into the other lane. I jerked the wheel to get back in my lane.

"You're kidding me, right?" I sucked in my breath. This had to be a mistake.

Hyperventilating, panic attacks, hives, they used to be foreign to me. I thought I was going to pass out at the wheel from the shallow breaths that came fast and furious.

By the time I reached our little out-of-the-way spot in Silver Lake, I felt like I was going to jump out of my skin. I had fallen down some crazy rabbit hole and couldn't get back up. I sat there with my hands still gripping the steering wheel. My interview with Triad was Friday morning, tomorrow. It couldn't come fast enough. What were the chances my name could stay out of the news until after the interview? Fortunately, I wasn't mentioned on *GMA*, but who did that female reporter at my gate work for? Was that the angle she would use for her story? Could I become a target simply because I was accessible, or did she really believe it? I pinched myself. Hard. Just so I could feel something other than fear. A sharp rap on the window startled me. I almost peed on myself.

I scowled as I rolled down the window a crack; it wasn't Diego. It was a youngish guy; he could have been 25 or 35, hard to tell. Men aged in the reverse of dog years; they would age one year every seven years.

"Yes?"

"You ok? You don't look so well."

"I'm fine, thanks."

He shrugged and pulled up his hoodie before jogging out of the parking lot.

Astro's. The small diner was far from the confusion, yet the drama was still consuming me. Consuming us. Inside was checkered with customers. An eclectic mix of bohemian-lite artists—the kind that believed suffering for their art meant they would drive a Prius instead of a Benz. There were also seniors on board for the discounted specials and scenesters just crawling in from a wild night of partying before heading back to their oh-so-trendy homes in Silver Lake.

I quickly scanned the restaurant for Diego before heading to a booth in the back. The sticky fingers of nausea tickled my throat as I tried to avoid the potpourri of breakfast scents surrounding me. Cheese eggs. Strawberry jam. Bacon. Strong coffee. Beautiful by Calvin Klein. And I had to pee. My head pounded. No matter which way I turned, there was no escape. I made a fort out of the little plastic jelly containers. Checked my messages at home—just in case. Reapplied my lip-gloss. Realized no amount of concealer in the world would eradicate the shadows under my eyes. Wanted to hop behind the counter and help. As I waited, I needed to do something. I tapped my foot, trying not to think about how much my bladder felt like it was going to burst. I didn't want to go into the bathroom and miss him. *If* he was going to show. How did he get back into the country without being detained? *We need to talk...* about us.

Funny how he would choose this place to meet. How he remembered. We had stopped here only once, eons ago. Wondering now if it was because he's been here before with someone else or if our time here was indelibly etched in his mind. We came here after a party thrown by one of his clients in Glendale. Flirtatious laughter. Heavy necking in between double-entendres volleyed back and forth. It was the foreplay leading up to our first time together. It was, as I thought, the beginning of a long time for us. In hindsight, it was the climax.

The reporter's voice kept creeping into my thoughts. Swindled. Did he purposefully steal, or did he lose the money in a bad deal? If I had to choose, I'd rather have him be an incompetent investor than a competent thief.

The one car missing from my train derailment of thoughts was about the pregnancy. Denial seemed to be a great place to hang out. Better than accepting the fact that a faulty contraceptive, well, carelessness, and the cruel hand of fate, conspired against me. If ever there were a time NOT to be pregnant, this would be it. Unable to wait, I went to the bathroom. When I came out, I ordered.

My hand was still shaking as I downed a glass of orange juice and nibbled on a piece of toast, hoping it wouldn't open the floodgates of nausea. As each minute passed by ever so slowly, it felt like everyone was staring at me. I paid the waitress and then went outside to wait. I sat on the curb in front of the door and watched the morning traffic whiz by. My feet were tip-tapping on the cement, keeping time to some song I had never heard. In lieu of my traditional uniform of a pencil skirt and tailored shirt with heels, I was slumming it in a pair of black slacks and silver flats. Nothing felt right. My pants were a bit snug. How long before I started showing?

We need to talk... Hi honey, my name's not really Diego—I'm a polygamist, and I'm stealing money to buy a compound in Utah. A few more customers straggled in. I squinted at them as the hard sun beat down, making everything appear fantastically washed out. My hands gravitated to my necklace. My fingers brushed against it to make sure it was still there. That some things hadn't changed. I couldn't help but wonder if the necklace would appear on a list of items to be seized by the Feds at some point. Along with the ring, my purse, and the many other expensive trinkets Diego was fond of giving me.

The Feds swooped in, as they should have, and reclaimed all of Madoff's ill-gotten gains. How long would I be able to stay at his house? How long would it take to liquidate his assets? The morning chill had all but evaporated, and a dry heat was hot on its heels. It was unusually warm. The weather couldn't decide if it was spring or summer. Not that there was too much of a difference unless you lived in the valley. Things hadn't been the same since El Niño some years back.

I rummaged in my bag and grabbed my phone. No new messages. No texts. The tap dancers in my head kicked in full blast as I continued to swim in a sea of nausea. I struggled to stand up. I stumbled back into the diner and made a beeline for the bathroom. After a not so pleasant visit with the sink, I leaned against the wall. Could I really survive nine months of random nausea? Morning sickness, my ass. I glanced at my watch. If he wasn't here by now, I knew he wasn't going to show. His affinity for promptness was from being raised by a military father. No matter the occasion, he always arrived early. Always sat facing the doorway. I always believed those were just his quirks. Now I couldn't help but wonder if they were something more.

I closed my eyes and took a series of short, deep breaths. I knew Diego. He wouldn't do this. I would find a way to prove them wrong. If it scared me, I could only imagine what he was going through. We'd beat this. I had to get to the one other person who could help me answer some questions.

eight

NO SOONER DID I get onto Los Feliz Boulevard to start the slow-speed chase to the office than my phone started blowing up. It was a code red at the office, and unless Scottie was going to beam me up somewhere, I wouldn't be stepping foot into Savage Rhythms for another 45 minutes or longer. I was navigating three freeways, and all of them had their fair share of morning commuters. Sitting in traffic, with a giant garbage bag to my right covering up the mountainside, trying to contain a potential mudslide, I felt powerless.

Dodger's Stadium. Downtown. Tops down. Talk radio. Hip-hop. My brain struggled to shift into crisis mode as I tried not to let thoughts of Diego take over. I needed details. I had to have all the facts before I could put a spin on it, before I could process it emotionally and understand what I was supposed to be feeling. Indignation? Embarrassment? Anger? Sorrow? I had a steady grip on confusion, but that was it.

I pulled into the parking lot of my office, feeling discombobulated. Melanie had called and left very curt messages on my voicemail. Sexual Chocolate was getting funky about doing *The Ellen Show* today and was threatening to pull out. Between Melanie, Veronica, and Aaron, the group's manager, I wanted to throw my cell phone into the nearest garbage can.

When I walked into the office, the first person I saw was Helene, a product manager. Benny's ego was a peanut compared to Helene's super-sized one. Always talking about the latest diet fad on the one hand, yet she was the first person in line whenever there was a free lunch. I usually tried to avoid her on the good days. Built like a linebacker, arms folded, she blocked my path.

"Elle," she said, elongating my name like I was some reticent fourth grader. "What's going on with Sexual Chocolate?"

"You're the product manager, don't you know?" I asked as I tried to squeeze past her.

"My name is not Benny, and you can't bully me around like you do him."

"Bully? What are you talking about?"

My cell vibrated. I snatched it out of my purse and pressed talk. "Hello?"

"-ey–Elle?" It was Diego. My heart fluttered. His voice was breaking up.

"I need the updates now, Elle. I'm pitching them for an endorsement, and I-"

"Just a minute!" I turned my back to her and started walking to the front entrance so I could get better reception. "No, not you. Hello?"

"Elle? I'm talking to you." She was right behind me as I pushed open the doors and walked into the reception area.

"Hello? D, can you hear me?"

Silence greeted me on the other end of the line. The call dropped. Frantically I start going through the received calls log, trying to find the number Diego called me from. I turned around, and Helene was right in my face. For a second, I couldn't even see straight. Helene's moon-shaped face swam before my eyes.

"Elle!"

"WHY THE HELL ARE YOU ON MY BACK?"

Helene did a dramatic gasp and clutched at her neck. "You don't have to yell at me. I was just asking a question!"

Diego's number showed up as unavailable. "Dammit!"

A hysterical ball of frustration from the last few days erupted, and I threw my phone at the wall in front of me. It felt like PMS to the nth degree. I wanted to stomp my feet and howl out the madness and fear roiling in my stomach. Before the cell could even hit the ground, Helene opened her mouth like she was auditioning for a role in the *Scream* franchise.

The elevator doors glided open. Nikki Savage, founder and president, and Tonya McKenzie, the VP, looked shocked as Helene started shrieking, "You're crazy! This was uncalled for and unprovoked!"

"What are you talking about? Maybe you should back that big ass up and try to understand the term 'personal space.'"

"Ladies!" Nikki's voice fired a warning shot. She shut both of us up with that one word. "Let's take it inside."

"Did you hear that? She insulted me!" Helene said as she walked into the suite of offices.

"I don't have time for your little melodrama, Helene." I picked up my phone from the floor and had to hunt around for the battery before I marched into my office and slammed my door. I ransacked my desk looking for the card Walsh had left the other day. I found the card and called his number as I set up Google Alerts on my name and Diego's. Google would send me an email every time we were mentioned on the Internet. Walsh answered on the second ring. He sounded surprised to hear my voice.

"Look, a reporter showed up outside my door this morning. What's going on with this case? What information does the press have?"

I sank down into my chair as Walsh talked. $26 million. Diego allegedly stole $26 million from clients. Not $30 million. The story didn't mention the $15 million in fraudulent loans from various banks. Yippee. Almost everything he said after that faded into oblivion, although a few phrases leaped out like: fugitive, shell corporation, and prison. My chest tightened, squeezing all the air out. I couldn't breathe. With the type of high-profile clientele Diego had... the media would be all over this. They had issued a warrant for his arrest this morning.

"What about Coogan? You said he's cooperating."

"You should probably get a lawyer."

"I don't want a lawyer. I just want to know what's going on. Do you have evidence that proves Diego is guilty?"

"Yes."

My stomach dropped. I clenched the phone tighter to keep it from slipping out of my hand.

"What? What proof do you have? Because I don't believe he could do something like this, and if you're just taking Jeffery's word... he's trying to save his ass. He'll say anything."

"I can't discuss that with you. Best advice I can give you? Lawyer up and tell your boyfriend to turn himself in."

I hung up and just stared at the window. What was I supposed to do? Walsh's words reverberated in my head, and I felt my chest tighten. I knew Diego. The man I fell in love with could not do this. But how could I help him? Where was he? Why didn't he show up at Astro's? I sent a reply to the number he texted me from last night.

> I'm pregnant. Why weren't you there this morning?

I waited.

I was hoping he would text me back with an explanation that would make all of this go away. After letting, I don't know how many calls go to voicemail; when I finally answered, it was human resources. They had summoned me for a meeting.

* * *

"Dana, I don't care what you say. You can write me up or whatever, but I'm not apologizing to her," I announced as I sat down in Dana

Delgado's office, the head of human resources. She tittered around like one of those little birds always hopping about. Top heavy with stick legs, her voice was light, as substantial as a summer breeze, making it easy to forget she had ever spoken, except for today.

"I'm not asking you to apologize. Unfortunately, Elle, I'm going to have to let you go."

"Go where?" I paused. "You're joking, right?" She met my questioning laugh with an uncomfortable silence.

"Unfortunately, not. As of this moment, you are no longer an employee of Savage Rhythms. I'll need your badge and your key card," Dana said, pausing only to push up her glasses, which were constantly sliding down her bridgeless nose.

I gripped the chair's wooden arms as if that would make the churning feeling disappear.

"Excuse me?"

Dana refused to make direct eye contact with me as she shuffled a few papers in front of her.

"I'm sorry, Elle, but this behavior is just unacceptable, especially after you were warned before."

"Warned before? You're bringing up an off-hand comment I made two years ago?"

"It was an insensitive remark that could have contributed to creating a hostile work environment."

I called Terry from A&R a "ball-less bastard" for not coming to me directly with an issue, and *I'm* the one who got reprimanded.

I got up from my chair. I stumbled to the window, watching brightly colored cars zip along Wilshire. I took a deep breath. "So, you're firing me? For what exactly?"

"Well. Let's see. You physically assaulted another employee."

"What? I never touched her!"

"You verbally abused her, and you threatened her. If we keep you on, she could later sue us for allowing a hostile work environment to exist."

I turned around and stared at Dana in disbelief. I opened my mouth several times before any words could actually come out. For a moment, I just gazed at the shrine to her Stepford-looking family hanging on the wall behind her. Kids. Husband. Pets. All of them wearing color-coordinated outfits, even the dog and cat. They were moments in time captured and mounted in frames. Happier times that were incongruous to the hysterical thoughts belly-dancing in my head.

"Assault? That phone thing was an accident, but had I known I was going to be fired, I wish I did have something to hit her with."

"Elle."

"I've given three and a half years of my heart and soul to this company, and this is how I'm treated? You're just going to 'let me go' and not even ask to hear my side of the story?"

"I don't have to hear sides. I looked at the tape."

"Oh. So, then you're letting Helene go as well?"

Dana shifted in her chair. "Elle, don't make this harder than it already is."

"Harder for who? You still have a job."

"I just need your badge and your key card."

"The key card is in my office." I unclipped my badge from the waist of my pants and tossed it onto her desk.

"I'm sorry, Elle."

"Not now, but you will be."

Rob, one of the beefy security guards, cracked open Dana's door and asked if everything was okay. Dana nodded, but her eyes told him not to go too far. I didn't even care. I just talked louder.

Dana tried to talk over me by informing me about COBRA health insurance options, and if I wanted to keep my cell phone, they would put the bill in my name. Her words blended together and were like an energy drink for my rage.

"Helene's Barney-looking ass hounding me for some damn updates isn't considered harassment? Did you see that on the tape? Her chasing me into the main reception area?"

"Name calling will not help the situation."

"What situation? You just fired me. I can say whatever I want. You just fucking screwed me over for some political bullshit or that damn dog."

"What?"

"How was I supposed to know he couldn't eat peanut brittle? Am I a vet?"

"Elle, I have no idea what you're talking about."

"It doesn't matter. I worked hard to get here and even harder to stay." I laughed. "You fired the wrong one. Hostile environment? When I finish suing you for wrongful termination, working for the Taliban will seem like a trip to the spa compared to this."

"Really Elle, is this necessary?"

"Fuck you, Dana." My mouth had long ago stopped listening to my brain. I was glad the conversation was over because I didn't know what I might say next. How many times did my dad tell me, "You talk too damn much, don't know when to shut up." Without Melanie and Dana in my corner, I'd have about as much chance of getting my job back as Helene would have getting on a *Maxim* magazine cover.

I stalked out of her office and slammed the door behind me. Rob and Trevor escorted me to my exiled Eden and stood guard while I disassembled my life and compartmentalized it into a few boxes. Bobbleheads. Platinum plaques. A few framed pictures. My Grammy credentials from last year. A fern I had nursed back from the deeply dehydrated.

"These are my CDs. See?" I flipped open the cases to show Rob and Trevor before flinging them into an open box.

"Don't even sweat it, El. It's really fucked up what they're doing to you," said Trevor despite Rob's scowl.

"Thanks, Trev."

"You need help with those boxes?"

Trevor carried my three boxes as I made a pit stop at the ladies' room. It was like the Jolly Green Giant was sitting on my bladder, and the urge to go was overpowering. As I left the office for the last time, I was the invisible woman. I hid behind my Jackie O. sunglasses, blinking back unspent tears. A trail of averted eyes and hushed voices followed me out of the front entrance and into the elevators. I knew Pamela was probably popping the champagne bottle before my big toe even crossed the threshold. She was a director of publicity, and with me out of the way, she would probably be promoted to senior director. I probably saved Melanie the task of firing the publicity coordinator because of budget cuts.

I had Trevor throw the boxes in the passenger seat. I started the car and punched the accelerator. I screeched out of the parking garage and headed to the one place that could help me clear my mind and sort out the swirling jumble of thoughts bumping into one another.

nine

RETAIL THERAPY. *Look good, feel good.* That was my coda. No job. No insurance. How was I going to afford prenatal care for a kid whose father allegedly owed $26 million? It would be years before he could even afford a box of diapers. Normally, in high-stress situations, an impromptu and immediate vacation was always the remedy, in which case a new bikini or island wardrobe was the order of the day. My credit cards were maxed out. I didn't have enough cash to swing a weekend in Santa Monica, much less Aruba, but a new dress would certainly help things along. Maybe something with a floral print. I headed over to the Glendale Galleria. I wanted to shop anonymously, and the Beverly Center and The Grove were just extensions of my social scene. I was bound to bump into someone I didn't want to see and have to explain why I was out in the middle of the day trolling the sales racks.

I punched the button on the radio, and the speakers came to life. A familiar bass line filled the car. I couldn't place the song. It kept niggling at me. Where had I heard this before? It only served to take my mind away from my more immediate problems for a few minutes as I felt the stab of hunger pangs. No doubt precipitated by the newfound resident in my tummy. I gripped the steering wheel and tried to focus on the traffic.

Even though the behemoth Americana at Brand, Glendale's answer to the Grove, was right around the corner, I was a stalwart Galleria fan. It housed all my favorite stores for me to get lost in. I planned my map of attack as I circled the parking structure on the hunt for a spot.

I was a walking zombie navigating my way through the mall. Nothing felt right. My slacks were a little tight, and my back was hurting. Shopping at 11 in the morning on a weekday. No calls to return. No press packages to send out. My man was MIA. And the crème de la crème... in seven months or so, not only was my waistline going to balloon to the size of a small country, but I would soon be the moral compass for a little person.

My knees buckled slightly, and I felt a tentative hand on my elbow.

"Are you alright, ma'am?" The voice belonged to a kid working at a mobile phone kiosk.

"Did you just call me ma'am?" Maybe my first stop should be the beauty counter.

"Yes, ma'am."

"Don't do it again."

I gave him a look that sent him scampering back to his booth as I beat a hasty path to the crowded MAC store. After elbowing my way to a space at the counter, I had a chance to glance in the mirror. If pretty was a state of mind, I was about as far south as you could get. A rabid raccoon greeted me from the other side of the glass. I looked crazy, like I *just* stepped out of the crack house. My mascara looked like it was running a marathon; my eyes were bloodshot, and dried snot was caked on the corner of my nose. One of the sales clerks/make-up artists/divas saw me and "tsk tsk" me.

"Hon, are things really that bad?" he asked.

"I need a tissue."

"You need a lot more than that, honey. Take a seat."

His expert hands repaired my face and painted a new warrior's mask using the hottest spring colors. In return, I picked up my all-time faves, Brick-O-La lipstick and liner to complement. After leaving MAC, the next four hours were a blur. I purchased new shoes from Charles & David, went into Mimi Maternity and quickly came back out, spent way too much time in the food court and made my dreams come true by purchasing a pound of Godiva chocolate, received a much-needed manicure and pedicure, picked up a few shirts and a skirt from Bebe, walked by Baby Gap and tried to imagine something coming out of me fitting into those cute little hats and booties. The only things I had been good at giving birth to so far were receipts.

The drive home landed me in the middle of rush-hour traffic. My phone had been buzzing all day with numbers I didn't recognize. So, I ignored it. I kept the top down and sunglasses on. I made a quick stop at Ralph's before pulling into Tara Hill. There was a gaggle of paparazzi outside the gate I came out of this morning. I entered the main gate unnoticed.

Once inside the condo, I dropped everything on the floor and put away a few groceries. I carried a pack of Oreos, the Godiva chocolates, two separate pints of Starbucks Caramel Macchiato ice cream, and an ice cream scooper into the bedroom with me. Spoons were for sissies. I placed them all at the bedside before going to the bathroom to take a long hot shower. Letting the water wash away the makeup and my tears.

I dragged my laptop into bed and cozied up with my new best friend, Google. I wouldn't be notified by Google Alerts until the morning, so I searched under Diego Rivera, and I cross-referenced searches with Rivera Financial. As I ate, I dropped some crumbs on my laptop. It was after nine on the East Coast. All the major outlets had a story about the misadventures of Diego; they were carrying it from a Reuters story that had been filed. Seeing it in black and white really pissed me off. Diego should have been the one to tell me. He obviously knew enough in advance to split town. I blinked back tears of frustration as I read.

The story referenced his victims on "Swindler's List." It mentioned the raids on his house and office. $26 million was a low estimate as the Feds were still crunching numbers to assess the total damage. Apparently, Diego went to the Madoff school of investment because none of the money he collected from clients was invested in anything other than his personal lifestyle. When the money ran out, he subsidized his lifestyle with phony loans from the bank on properties he didn't own. The Feds seized his *yacht* and *mansion* in Miami, where he had eight luxury cars, including Jags and Bentleys. They froze his assets. I searched our names together and found nothing. Yet. Not that it mattered. Circles were small, but they intersected in Los Angeles, and everyone that knew me, knew him. We were the couple that partied together. From movie premieres to clothing line debuts, we were there. Inevitably, he would pick up a new fan, making his client list read like a gossip column full of boldfaced names. Now, instead of a full-court press for a defense, he let his absence speak for him. In the court of public opinion, they would find him guilty quicker than you could say social media suicide.

My heart wanted to believe he was innocent, but my head and hormones argued that if he were, he would be here, vociferously fighting for his reputation. The pragmatic voice who's seen and heard it all and wrote the press releases to prove it, had witnessed way too many women left in the crosshairs after their men were found to be behaving badly: Jenny Sanford, Elizabeth Edwards, Hillary Clinton, Dina McGreevy, Elin Woods, Sandra Bullock, Maria Shriver, and the list went on. New names were added daily. The public didn't know whether to cast them in the role of co-conspirator, enabler, or victim. Instead, they languished with a scarlet "W" that preceded their names. They were now known as *Wife of Disgraced High-Profile Cheating Husband of the Moment*. All of their previous accomplishments were momentarily overshadowed by his indiscretions. Everyone always wondered, how could they not know? Had to admit, every time I heard one of those stories, I thought the same thing. Was positive that she knew but chose not to see the flashing warning signs, screaming, "Danger! Danger! Cheating man in your bed!" What signs had I chosen to overlook? Although this was deeper than public humiliation over a philandering partner... millions of reasons deeper. Walsh said I needed a lawyer.

I closed that webpage and logged onto my work email to see if they had shut me down yet. They hadn't. When I saw an email from Triad, my heart caught in my throat. The hairs stood at attention on the back of my neck. I prayed it was just a note confirming our meeting tomorrow. I clicked.

Due to a prior conflict, we will need to reschedule your interview. We'll be in touch.

My stomach twisted and lurched. I tapped out a quick reply, letting them know I'd be available on Monday. Or Tuesday, Wednesday, whenever. Just give me a time and I'll be there, and please send all future correspondence to my Gmail account. Being fired would only be palatable if I landed another job immediately. Forget ego, I was drowning in lifestyle debt, and only a fat, steady paycheck could keep me afloat. Where were a pair of ruby red slippers when you needed them?

I fell headfirst into a dreamless sleep, easily awakened by my phones. My cell and landline were ringing. The room was still bathed in gray shadows. It was only six in the morning. I looked at the Caller IDs on both and groaned. When would they understand the concept of different time zones? I chose Justine over my mother, the lesser of two inquisitors.

"How are you doing? Have you spoken to Diego? Does he know about the baby?"

"Horrible, no, and no. And before you ask, I don't know what I'm going to do, ok?"

"Don't worry, it's all going to work out."

"How can you say that?"

"Because these things always have a way of working themselves out."

"'These things'? So pregnant girlfriends with married boyfriends accused of stealing millions of dollars usually come out of things just fine? Good to know. And here I thought my life was over. So, I shouldn't even panic over being unemployed? Glad I spoke to you this morning."

"What? What happened?"

"I was fired yesterday over peanut brittle; who knows? Listen, I don't need optimism right now. If you're not going to sink to new levels of self-pity with me, then I have to speak to you later."

"I'm going to come out there, ok?" Justine said, instantly making me feel guilty. Like her life wasn't busy enough. Work, two kids, and a husband.

"No, don't. I'm just having a moment. Damn hormones. Look, I'll call you later."

"I'm worried about you. Are you going to be ok by yourself?"

"I'm not by myself. I have plenty of friends to lean on. I'm fine."

Justine reluctantly got off the phone, but I knew the price I would pay would be an intense grilling the next time we spoke. My mom wouldn't be so easy to get off the phone; that's why she went to voicemail. It would be a double whammy from her. She'd have twenty questions squared about Diego and would still want to know about the progress of her anniversary gala. The invitations should be ready. I'd have to check my mailbox to see if they had arrived.

The lump in my throat expanded, threatening to cut off all oxygen. The enormity of my loss started to close in on me. I had been consumed with Diego to the exclusion of everyone else. It had been just us in our own little cocoon. He was the one person I could usually go to for help in this type of situation, but now he was the situation. Never saw that coming. Break-ups were different. You had time to prepare; usually, one or both parties were tired of the other. It limped along until someone had the guts to pull the plug. This? No warning. Sucker punched. One day, life as I knew it no longer existed.

If I weren't a publicist at Savage Rhythms, if I weren't Diego's girl-friend, who was I supposed to be when I'd forgotten how to be anything else?

I sat up in bed. Wait, when did I become *that* person? I was always the one with a plan. It's been only five days since I'd last seen Diego, and I felt so unmoored and adrift without the anchors of our relationship and now, a job. How did that happen? Who had I become when I wasn't looking? I knew, in relationships, you had to sacrifice certain parts of yourself in order for the "me" to become a "we." Compromises were made. You couldn't take two singles and expect them to become a pair without some type of casualty, but how could it be that I was falling apart after five days? Had I grown too comfortable in the idealized version of us? I felt like I needed a search and rescue mission to reclaim my inner Elle because she would know what to do.

I turned off my cell and put the ringer on mute on the landline. I threw the covers over my head. There was no place for me to go. Never been fired before. *Let go*. I felt my energy seep out of my pores like sweat. Diego never texted me back. Maybe he didn't get it; maybe he still didn't know he was going to be a father for the first time. Or maybe I didn't know he was going to be a father for the third time. Either way, we needed to talk. All I could do was wait for him to call me.

ten

THE END of April slid into May, with the first few days being dry and hot as we suffered through a heat wave. At least, that's what the news said. I spent much of the time huddled in bed with the curtains drawn. I was so tired and drained; I slept as though in a coma. Chunks of time evaporated as I spent my few waking hours eating and peeing. Still no word from Diego. I was waiting to hear from him as though he could snap his fingers and everything would be fine.

Initially, I had been living off Oreos, delivered pizza, and bottled water, since the ice cream had been licked clean the first night. Gigi, our housekeeper, took pity on me and made a grocery store run that included a large supply of tissues. She also cleaned Diego's house and knew I was a basket case because of what was happening.

One morning, a sudden burst of loud voices and heavy footsteps roused me from my sugar-induced semi-coma. My eyes shot to the clock on the nightstand. It was 11:37. I stumbled out of bed, searching for a weapon. I grabbed one of my Jimmy Choos with the heel pointing away from me. My six-inch stilettos could cause some serious damage if I stabbed someone in the neck or eye if I didn't vomit first. I walked down the hallway and bumped into Blake. He caught my arm in mid-swing.

"Whoa! Take it easy, Slugger. What's wrong with you?"

"I thought you were trying to break in."

"I left you a message telling you I was coming by on Monday to pack. I brought some extra boxes for you."

I yawned. "Oh, right. I forgot."

"You alright?"

"I'm cool."

His eyes traveled over my pillow, matted hair, and wrinkled shorts and shirt. He looked like he had just come off the tennis courts at a private club with his Nike warm-up pants and tank top.

"Right." He walked into his room, grabbed a few boxes, and slid them my way.

I hurried to my room and closed the door. Macy, one of Nikki's executive assistants from the office, called me while I was checking my voicemail messages.

"Girl, where have you been? I've been calling you like a fool! Where are you?"

"I'm home. Where else would I be?"

"Meet me at Tony Roma's at Universal City."

"Now?"

"There's some stuff going down. Just meet me over there, 'kay?"

Driving from Culver City to North Hollywood was not on the agenda, but the need to know what people were saying about me in the office overrode all else.

I threw on some yoga pants and a loose-fitting tee and left. Battling my way up Overland took forever. I listened to my voicemail messages. A few editors and producers I knew called for exclusives about Diego, wanting to trade our professional relationship for a scoop. I'd rather have my wisdom teeth extracted with no drugs before I sat down for any interviews. A driver in front of me slammed on their brakes, and I punched the horn a few times to voice my displeasure. The road was filled with stupid drivers. Traffic. Potholes being repaired. After exhausting my vast supply of curse words, I finally pulled into the parking garage at Universal. By the time I got to the restaurant, I was exhausted. I didn't see Macy in the lobby; I peeked into the dining area and saw her at a table. Her long braids were tied back in a ponytail. I sat down in front of her and watched as she sipped on a Blue Romarita with Blue Curacao. She wore her usual utilitarian uniform of jeans and a t-shirt. A half-eaten platter of baby back ribs sat in front of her.

"You hungry?" she asked.

"Does Weight Watchers even have enough points to cover the cow you just devoured? Where's the menu?"

Macy flagged a waitress, and I ordered the gulf grilled shrimp skewers. My mouth was watering as I said the words. I sipped the glass of water she left on the table.

"Girl, how can you come to Tony Roma's and not order the ribs?"

"Easy. I just did. What's so important that I had to meet you all the way over here?" I stifled a yawn from a soul-sucking exhaustion. I wanted to go home and crawl back into bed and just sleep.

Macy leaned in close, one hand clutched around a rib. She dropped her voice, and I could barely hear her over the clatter of plates and glasses and lunchtime conversation.

"You will not believe what's been going on in the office!" Macy was such a drama queen. What could have happened? "The office is tripping! Cameron's masters for the new CD are missing."

"Seriously?"

"And the track is on the radio, with that rapper out of the ATL, Strykker, rapping on it."

I snapped my fingers. "I think I heard it on the radio. I just couldn't figure out why I knew it. That's Cameron's *Missed You* track, right?"

Macy fell back into the booth and smiled. "Yup, and guess who they're saying took it?"

"Who?"

Macy looked at me.

I was raising my glass and missed my mouth. Cold water spilled all over my face and neck.

"You're kidding, right?" I grabbed a few napkins and dabbed my shirt. For the second time in less than a week, I was left hanging while waiting for the punch line. "*I* took his masters? Please. Who's saying that? Helene?"

"No," she answered with a pause, so pregnant I thought I would give birth at the table. "Cameron."

"Cameron? Seriously?"

"Casey said he had the masters in your office the other day, and Rob said that you took some CDs when you left, and you were real funky about it. And Veronica said that you and Cameron were in your office with the door shut, and something went down, and you came out all angry and yelling at her. Oh, and Dana's like you threatened her, telling her she'd be sorry."

"Veronica's a moron, and Rob? What the hell? I was just fired. How am I supposed to act? What's with all this he-said-she-said bullshit, anyway? Should we break out in song and dance and just call it *High School Musical 4: Wrongful Termination*? So, what I took my CDs? The masters are usually on a thumb drive. How would I even have access?"

"Don't shoot me. I'm just telling you what I heard. Besides, we've been trying to get at you all week, but you've been ghost."

We were interrupted as the waitress set a steaming plate of food in front of me.

"I was busy. I do have a life outside of the office. Not like I'm just lounging around in bed the entire weekend. So, what is everyone else saying? Do people really think I did that?"

"Elle, I know you wouldn't steal Cameron's masters, and I'm sure everyone else knows that too... but..."

"But what?"

"Well. Disgruntled employee. Revenge. You could get a lot of money for those masters. Dana thinks you know you wouldn't be able to win a lawsuit, and this was a faster way to get the money and..."

"And what?"

"And all that's been going on with Diego."

My heart started doing the rhumba as it made its way to my throat. I was hoping no one in the office had watched the news, gone online or read the papers, or dealt in any type of gossip.

"It was in the trades all last week."

"First *GMA*, now this. What did it say?" Note to self: Google Alerts are only effective if you log into your email account.

"It was on *GMA*? Dang, I missed it." Off my appalled look, she shrugged none too apologetically. Everyone loved to watch a good train wreck; I just wasn't used to being the only passenger on that train.

"Here," she said as she grabbed a copy of *Variety* from her purse. She tossed it on the table. Diego's face stared back at me from the front page. A half-smile teased his lips as though we were sharing a private joke. Except it felt like the joke was on me. It took a moment for the jumble of lines to register as words.

I read the brief article three times. It was a rehash of the Reuters story. Each time, the air in the restaurant seemed to get a little drier. Phrases like *arrest warrant, Securities and Commission investigation,* and *swindler to the stars* leaped out at me. Besides Cameron, he had a few A-list actors, directors, athletes, and singers. Those were just the bold-faced names. He had deep ties in the industry, his client list grew from word-of-mouth. My very big mouth included. My ring and necklace felt heavy from the potential guilt of reaping the rewards from someone else's misfortune.

Macy looked at me as though I would fill in the blanks. I shook my head. If this had been anyone else's life other than mine, I'd be able to devise a publicity plan and execute it flawlessly. I dug into the grilled vegetables, plucked a plump shrimp off the skewer, and popped it in my mouth. I closed my eyes to savor the moment. The confluence of tastes on my tongue was a heavenly respite. Before I knew it, I was scraping an empty plate. I wanted more. I wanted simple acts to complete, so I wouldn't have to think about anything else.

"I don't understand why Cameron would say I stole his masters."

Macy looked disappointed I wasn't going to say anything about Diego. She pouted as she said, "I don't either, but he is, and that's a problem. Oh, and Helene is afraid for her life. She's thinking about getting a restraining order against you."

"She can restrain my foot from going up her ass 'cause that's what she deserves."

Macy laughed. "Right, right."

"This is one of the few jobs that I know where you willingly go into work knowing that you will be shit on. If an album tanks, it's not because it sucked or because the artist blew off the press day I set up. No, it has to be because I'm incompetent and a moron. I'm supposed to pull magazine covers out of my ass, knowing good and well the artist doesn't deserve an inch of space. I gave them blood, sweat, and tears every day, and this is the thanks I get? I *should* sue."

When a waitress walked by, Macy tapped her glass and nodded for a refill. I wanted to order a chocolate martini so bad; I just needed something, anything, to take the edge off the day. Something to make the brightness recede into a warm and fuzzy motif.

"You not getting anything?"

"No, I'm just going to nurse my glass of water over here."

Macy studied me for a minute, pursing her lips. "So, how are you doing?"

"I'm alright. Going to look for another job, I guess." Macy was quiet.

"What?" I asked.

"Elle, no one will hire you right now, especially Triad, as long as people are saying you stole Cameron's masters. I don't know how, but you need to take care of that."

I didn't even ask how she knew about Triad; I just prayed she was wrong. Macy paid for lunch, compliments of Savage Rhythms. She put her hand on my shoulder before she left and said, "I'm here if you need me." I could only nod my head.

On the drive home, I navigated the ever-present traffic. Thoughts spiraled, looped, and somersaulted off into nothingness. I wished I were back in the safety of my bed cave. I took Sepulveda down to Manchester and headed west. A few lights later, and blissfully, those were all green, I pulled in front of Wendy Warren's office, our real estate agent. A cubbyhole with a receptionist inside greeted me as soon as I opened the door. Looking down at her phone, I saw all the lines were blinking, and a non-stop low ring permeated the air.

"I'm here to see Wendy."

The receptionist put a long finger up with an impeccable French manicure. She was either fresh out of high school or right off the heels of a Botox treatment. She glanced at me after she had corralled all the calls to their appropriate recipients.

"Do you have an appointment?" She was extremely chipper. Immediately, I felt a vein in my forehead throb.

"No."

"Oh." She paused. She pressed her lips down in consternation like this hadn't been covered on training day. It was Botox; she couldn't frown if you scared the crap out of her. Finally, she chirped, "And you are?"

"Elle. Nixon. Is she available?"

"Oh, you're Elle! Wow! I should have recognized your voice!" she giggled. "I know this is so totally, whatever, but my boyfriend has this really tight demo... this is so lame; people must do this to you all the time. But do you think you could give this to someone at the label? Ya know, maybe someone could listen to it and sign him or something, ya know?" She pulled a CD out of a drawer and slid it over. "They're on YouTube, so check them out. They have like over 100,000 views."

"Sure. I'll listen to it and see what I can do." I glanced at my watch. "Do you think Wendy has a moment for me?" I smiled a smile that matched hers in brightness. I didn't want to tell her they needed at least a million hits before anyone cared. It was so easy to slip back into the facade of being in control, being a plastic person with a plastic life and plastic, recyclable problems. Being shallow and vain and worrying about whether the shade of my $1100 shoes matched my $400 purse, I longed for the bullshit nature of it all. The uncertain hairpin turns my life had taken were more than I could handle. My plummet from grace gave me new problems to fret over: unemployment, no insurance, and defamation.

The receptionist spoke in a low voice into her headset and then beamed at me.

"She'll be with you shortly. You can have a seat."

"Your ladies' room?"

"Down the hallway and to the right," she said as she reached into her drawer and pulled out a key attached to a large neon pink metal square.

I was glad to be out of there because I sensed the onslaught of conversation, and I didn't think I could stomach smiling one more nanosecond. The hallway seemed never-ending. The faster I walked, the more the corridor lengthened. I reached tentatively for the bathroom door as though it were a mirage. I almost sighed with relief when my hand landed on something solid and cool.

I felt more like Harriet the Spy than Mata Hari as I looked in the mirror and tried reapplying my lip liner and gloss. My hand shook so much it looked like a second grader put on my makeup. So, I washed my face. Stripped away the armor. I have to do this. I still felt a stab of guilt. Diego and I were an island of two, wrapped up in our own world. He didn't talk much about his family and didn't have any close friends. I didn't have anyone to call to see if they had heard from him. How could he have a wife when he made me believe it was just us against the world?

I walked back into the corridor and called my dad. He had left several messages.

"Hey, Pops."

"Where are you?"

"Just running around doing some errands."

"You've been running around all week? We left you a few messages. Justine called and told us about Diego. Are you ok?"

I made a mental note to curse her out next time I spoke to her.

"You know how it is..." my voice trailed off. I slumped down to the floor and drew my knees to my chest.

"Call your mother. I had to stop her from sending the police to check on you. You know it's tough for her this time of year."

"It's tough for all of us, don't you think?"

"Well, you're getting too old to just up and run off and not tell anyone where you are. What if something happened to you?" How he managed to make me feel extremely guilty and like a wayward 16-year-old in less than five seconds made me shake my head in disbelief. I was a grown woman.

"Dad? Hello?"

"Elle?" His voice came through crystal clear.

I rubbed the phone against the carpeted floor. "We must have a bad connection. I'll call you later."

I closed my eyes and leaned my head back against the wall. Evie would have been 39 on our birthday. Even though we were four years apart, people often mistook us for twins when we were younger. She died when I was 10, and sometimes during unexpected moments, I could feel the weight of grief on my back, stalking me. I'd learned how to rearrange my life to accommodate it. We all did.

Back in the waiting room, my eyes fell on an issue of *Essence* magazine. Chantal Chambers' face stared back at me. I got her that cover. I helped to turn her from a run-of-the-mill R&B hoodrat into a pop princess. I had to pitch my ass off to get the rags to interview her. And this was the thanks I got? I had an artist in just about every magazine on that table.

I couldn't sit on the chairs. Uncomfortable and hard, they bred anxiety. Not good for the waiting. I paced the small room. Abstract art and motivational posters made up the décor.

Finally, the door swung open, and Wendy waved me into the inner sanctum. Portable headset on; she was still on a call. Her footsteps were like rapid gunfire as she strode back to her office. By the time we got to her corner office, which was only 10 feet from the receptionist's desk, she had completed two calls and left a message for someone to call her back.

She took off her headset as she leaned back in her chair. She crossed her legs in one graceful motion and pulled up her calendar on the computer.

"Did I totally just lunch and forget that we had a meeting?"

"No, no, I was in the neighborhood," the lie was stuck in my throat. It was like rat poison, you added water to it, and it swelled, blocking off the air. I coughed.

"Would you like some water?" she asked as she buzzed the receptionist.

"Thanks. I'm just getting over a cold, and my throat has been scratchy."

"Oh." She pushed her chair away from me and swept her eyes over my appearance. The receptionist knocked once before entering and handed me the water.

"Like I was saying, I was in the neighborhood, and I knew I was going to have to call you anyway, so I just decided to stop by. We're looking to buy a small condo." I hoped and prayed she hadn't read the papers and was clueless about Diego's newfound popularity.

All thoughts of contagion washed away from her face as she leaned in closer to me.

"That's great, Elle! Do you have a specific property in mind?"

"No. We're just starting to look. It'll be a rental property. I just want to have a pre-qualification letter ready for the agents when we look."

"You guys make the cutest couple."

A dry chuckle got stuck in my throat; I thought I would choke on the tight smile that seemed stamped on my face. Wendy was the realtor du jour. I recommended many of my artists to her, used her several times myself to rent a spot, and turned Diego on to her. She had helped him purchase the house in Tarzana.

"Ok, give me your social. I know I have Diego's on file."

All business, Wendy spun around in her chair and pulled up my credit history.

She kept her face neutral as she read my report. "It's good you two are buying this together; your debt ratio is too high to really qualify for anything on your own. Even with the bailout money, the banks are holding onto their dollars. If you can get a loan, the deals out there are great. Diego's income will help even things out. Although honestly, it might be better to keep you off the loan application."

She printed out a copy of my report and handed it to me. "You need to think about clearing up some of that debt, though. You know, if you ever want to buy something on your own."

She clicked on a file, and Diego's information popped up. His application for the house in Tarzana had been scanned in. Leaning over, I knocked over my water bottle, which spilled onto her lap.

"Oh jeez! I'm sorry." I looked in my purse for a tissue.

"Don't worry about it," Wendy said as she excused herself and hurried to the bathroom.

She left the door partly open. I grabbed a yellow stickie and a pen from her desk and quickly copied Diego's information off the screen. Date of birth. Social security number. I was working on previous addresses when I heard the surefire strut of Wendy approaching. I shoved the paper into my purse and leaned back in my chair. She had a roll of paper towels and was dabbing at her sleeve and skirt.

"I'm so sorry. Must be the cold medication. I've just been so clumsy lately."

"Don't worry about it. I'm a mess without my Red Bull in the morning."

Her phone lines were lit up like Times Square on New Year's Eve.

I followed her glance and stood up. "You know what? You're busy. Here I am, just popping in. Just email or fax me the pre-qualification letter when you get a chance."

I gave her a business card and left. Once she got wind of the news, I'd doubt she'd fax me the time of day.

eleven

EGGSHELLS. My nerves were just as fragile. The slightest misstep would send hairline fractures snaking their way across me. They would splinter off and travel around me like a roadmap... leading me to a nervous breakdown. My mouth was dry and itching. Darkness surrounded me. I had fallen asleep as soon as I came home and awoke to that dusky, netherworld feeling. Was it morning? Was it night? Finally, after turning on the television and finding an episode of *Extra*, I realized it was only 7:30 pm. I ordered a pizza for delivery from Pizza Hut even though it was just a block away. It was hard to believe that it was just a few weeks ago when I was at the airport waiting for Diego. It was the *before*, when things still had the possibility of being normal.

At 2 a.m., I was still wide awake. How long had it been since I had Diego's warmth radiating like an electric blanket? Enveloping me like my mother's kisses, letting me know all would be right with the world as long as I didn't stray too far. Felt like forever. I had rummaged through my hamper and found a t-shirt of his, still steeped in his scent. I wore it like a cloak of courage. I'd always been a night person, and Diego was an early morning-got-to-be-the-first-person-at-the-gym-when-it-opens type. Some nights, after making love, after the double time of my heart had slowed to a lazier pace and his breathing became longer and more rhythmic, I would watch him sleep.

Always on his stomach, his game face gone and in its place, a vulnerable boy, mouth slightly open. Some nights, the low rumble of his snoring was like a lullaby; other nights, I wanted to put a pillow over his face and hold it. My heart would feel so full of tenderness because I wanted that now to be our forever. A moment where we were as close as two people could be, take that moment and extend it, so we were always a part of one another. And now we were. Our baby. It didn't just roll off the tongue. It felt as real as saying I have four breasts. Would the baby have his smile? My eyes? His penchant for running at the first sign of trouble? Icy fear snaked its way into my thoughts. What if I couldn't protect him or her? I found out early on, no matter how much you loved your children, sometimes it just wasn't enough.

I also wasn't naïve enough to believe you could ever really know someone. Everyone had secrets. I had my own skeletons buried in designer shopping bags hidden way back in my closet. But if what they said was true about Diego, was I carrying the child of a complete stranger? How could I not see this coming? I worked around bullshit every day in the entertainment industry, where no one was what they seemed. Always. People inflated their accomplishments to match their egos like they were buying Tic Tacs. No big deal. How did I fall in love with a con artist? Wasn't I smarter than that? Wasn't he better than that?

I swung my legs over the side of the couch. The credit report that Wendy had given me sat abandoned on the table. I wasn't in any rush to claim it after spending a mind-numbing hour going through it. My phone was on the table as well. Still vibrating. Nothing from Diego. I didn't answer any of the calls. I wasn't validating the rumors or the truth. Let people think what they wanted until I had time to figure out what type of spin I was going to put on it. So much for the mantra I had always preached to my artists: *get in front of a scandal. You have to control the story.*

His earthquake had triggered a tsunami in my life. Sure, I'd quit a few jobs, but I always had something lined up. Life had always carried me along. I would stay somewhere until something better came along. Men. Apartments. Jobs. Things would just happen according to my plan; I never had to work too hard to *make* them happen. Now I was fired and considered a thief. An unwed, knocked-up, debt-ridden, unemployed thief, to be exact. I could only imagine how that conversation would play out with my mother.

I shuffled into the kitchen and ate the last two slices of the supreme pizza. I had gas, and I was belching like a sailor. This was the time I needed to be alone. I looked at my credit report again. It was trifling, just like Blake said, and for a moment, I hated him for saying that but even more so for selling this place. Just one more thing I had to worry about. I had my VIP access revoked from the club of the working poor before I even knew I was a member.

I turned on my laptop. Finding Diego. I had to start somewhere, and getting his social security number was a good start. Before Diego and after my last two substantial relationships, I dated a private investigator for a hot second. He once said during one of his many drunken philosophical rants—and there were many—that as long as you had a birth date and a social security number on someone, you could find out anything you wanted. Well, I wanted to find Diego, and online or offline, having $19.99 could solve many problems.

According to the myriad of infomercials, if you didn't enjoy iron-ing, Mr. Steamer could magically make your clothes wrinkle-free; just toss him in the dryer. If you wanted to lose weight and learn the moves of a stripper, there's a DVD for that. And if I wanted to fill in the missing pieces of my boyfriend's life? For $19.99, I could buy his credit report from all three agencies and police records online.

Hard to believe a few weeks ago, we were planning a trip to Rio and had looked at the hotels and flights. Within a matter of minutes, his credit and police reports were emailed to me. I scanned the information quickly. A part of me really didn't want to know. A very large part of me wanted to hold on to the fantasy that he was innocent. This was all just a mistake. I had to know, though, so I pressed on.

For an additional low, low price of $24.92, I discovered quite a few fun facts about Diego previously unknown to me. Diego Rivera owned two homes in Miami and apparently died in 1989. He didn't utilize any credit until six years ago. I stared at the death certificate that was emailed to me.

I wanted to be anywhere but here. For the first time in a long time, I wished I were on the track with my dad in those early mornings when the only thing that mattered was the little hand on that stopwatch. Life was so simple then.

My father. Wade Nixon. Always push, push, pushing. I still hear that annoying shrill of the whistle slicing through the thick, silent morning air. Those mornings where everything was painted a muted gray in the pre-dawn hours. At the high school track field, he would train me. The crisp chill of dew-soaked grass would send goosebumps spiking along my arms. The silver whistle worn on a chain looped around his neck would gleam as a beacon on a field bathed in fog. My head would be filled with nothing but the sound of my heart pounding and my feet crunching against the ground as I tried not to watch him watch me.

"C'mon Elle! You can do better than that!" he would bellow. Staring at his god, the stopwatch.

Always he said, "You can do better." Whether I placed first in regionals or first in state, my time could have been better, I should have been faster, or my dismount was sloppy. Always something. Those early mornings on the drive to the field, he would tell me, "Never settle, Elle." We would leave the home he had lived in since before he met my mother to go to a high school he had attended and now coached part-time. He had been a big track star with Olympic dreams derailed by a career-ending injury. So, he followed his father into dentistry, took over the practice, and settled into married life with my mom. They had met in dental school. Instead of fame and glory, it was crooked teeth and bad breath every day. As the last child standing, my feet were lost trying to fill his impossibly large shoes. At 14 years old, I was 5'8", all arms and legs. I had the talent; it got me several four-year scholarships, but not the drive. Since I'd rather shop than sweat, it translated into a frustrating duty to try to live out his dreams. Right now, I'd trade anything for the simplicity of it all. I only needed to run faster so everything would be okay.

I closed the laptop. I didn't want to read anymore. Didn't want to think about the fact that for the past three years, I'd been sleeping with a dead man. I racked my brain trying to come up with an explanation; any reason at all, someone would need to assume an identity. I couldn't come up with anything I hadn't already seen in the Jason Bourne series.

It reminded me of that kid's book, *Where in the World is Carmen San Diego?* Even if I could spot him, it wouldn't be him. I wanted to call someone to help direct the building hysteria somewhere else. Shame quickly stamped out the desire. How could I explain that I never had a clue?

I grabbed some boxes Blake had left behind and headed to my closet. What I wanted to do was go back to bed. To sleep away all the tomorrows until today was nothing but a distant memory. It hurt to even think about how I would survive the next few months if Diego weren't here, pregnant or not.

I was able to put one pair of shoes in a box before I stopped and leaned against the wall to survey my trappings. All this stuff. The right shoes. The hottest dress. The must-have purse. Even my damn belts were high-end. And what did it mean? What if I wasn't a good mother? What did I know about motherhood? I didn't even like kids. How was I going to do this on my own? No job. No insurance. No savings. No place to live. Diego's corporation owned the house in Tarzana, and all the assets were frozen and soon to be liquidated. I couldn't go back there.

Diego couldn't help me if he was in jail, and even if he didn't go to jail, there was still the little issue of his wife. I walked over to the box I had packed at the office. I went through it again. I didn't find a thumb drive of Cameron's masters anywhere. How was stealing his masters supposed to benefit me? I pulled out the bobbleheads and set them on the end table by the couch.

"We're going to get through this, right?"

They nodded in unison, giving me a little hope.

I grabbed my cell and dialed Cameron's number. It was disconnected. He changed phone numbers like some people changed their underwear. I called Casey.

A loud bass bump bumped in my ear when Casey picked up. "Yo."

"Casey, it's Elle. I need to speak to Cameron."

Silence.

"Come on Casey, you know I wouldn't steal his masters. I need to know why he's saying this. So put him on the phone."

"I'll have him call you." The phone went dead. I sat there with the phone in my hand, my mind reeling. I could be a lot of things. Shallow. Bitchy. A selective perfectionist. A pang of hurt blossomed in my throat. I would never jeopardize the career of my artist by stealing masters. Wouldn't Cameron know that after almost two years of working together? Or maybe he was also thinking you can never really know a person.

It was almost five in the morning when I found myself driving to Diego's place. A litany of maybes came along for the ride. *Maybe he would be there. Maybe I would find a clue, something the Feds missed, that would help me understand. Maybe. Maybe.* Hope evaporated like a fair-weather friend when I opened the front door and found a house wrapped in stillness. It was like walking into a scene that had been paused on a DVD. Stray papers were orphaned on the ground. The home office was stripped of its computers and files. Drawers were left gaping open, robbed of their contents.

I dragged my fingers through my hair. *What was I doing here?* I sat down on the steps and looked around. He was slumming in this house with its four bedrooms and two bathrooms, compared to the lifestyle he was purported to have in Miami. Mansion. Fancy cars.

Who was this man I had so freely given my heart to, the father of my unborn child? There had to be something, a relic from his past life. No one was that good. He had to have a souvenir. Where would it be? I pushed myself off the step and headed up to the bedroom. Had to start somewhere. He had a large walk-in closet. I began pulling stuff out of the drawers and flinging it on the floor. I worked my way methodically through the house. I searched for false bottom drawers and checked behind pictures for a wall safe.

The annoying buzz of a helicopter, which could be like ever-present elevator music depending on what part of town you lived in, interrupted my thoughts. It sounded like it was directly overhead. I had just flipped over a painting in the hallway, looking for a wall safe, when I noticed an envelope taped to the back.

At the same time, a disembodied voice via bullhorn blared into the house. "Diego Rivera, please exit the house. You are surrounded."

My heart stopped for what felt like a full minute. How could he have gotten in here without me noticing? Slowly, it dawned on me; that they were here for *me*.

"Holy crap."

I peeked through the curtains of the front window and saw half of LAPD assembled on the front lawn, with guns locked, loaded, and pointed at the house. *All this for fraud?* I slipped the envelope into the waistband of my pants and lowered my shirt over it.

I tried not to hyperventilate as I swung open the front door. Arms raised, I yelled, "He's not here! Please don't shoot!"

Some nosy neighbor had reported seeing lights on in the house. Three hours later, after being taken away in cuffs and interrogated by Walsh and friends, I finally had a lawyer. Jade DeVereaux wasn't a criminal defense attorney; she was my business lawyer, but she would do in an emergency.

"Just stay away from that property, Elle. If they catch you there again, they'll hit you with trespassing and tampering with evidence. Diego's considered a fugitive, and if you know anything-"

"I don't!"

"You better not, because you're looking at obstruction of justice if you do."

She left me with a business card of her associate, who was better accustomed to handling "these matters."

I called Blake to pick me up from the station and return to Diego's to get my car. I couldn't wait to get home and see what, if anything, was in this envelope.

Blake dropped me off and then headed to Arden's with promises of coming by in the morning with more boxes—and questions.

I sat inside my car, pulled out the envelope, limp with my sweat, and opened it. Inside was a class ring and a small key with a number. Like the type to a locker. ED was engraved on the back of the ring. "Class of '92" and "Monroe High School" were etched on the sides.

* * *

Blake came by in the morning and started hauling away some furniture. Life as I knew it was being dismantled all around me. In between grilling me over yesterday's indiscretion, he stayed on me about packing.

"Have you even started?"

"Yes, Blake. I worked on my closet last night but ran out of boxes. Don't worry, I'll be out of here before you close, damn. Don't ask how I'm feeling." I hoped he didn't look in the closet; I'd only packed one pair of shoes.

I quickly closed my door as we walked to his room.

"Sorry." He tugged at his twists. "You a'ight?"

"Fine."

He looked at the boxes stacked against the wall. "What's all this stuff, anyway?"

"Shoes. Purses. You can never have enough." Aspirationally speaking, they were empty right now.

"If I were you, I'd put all that up on eBay. You probably have a down payment in those boxes."

He picked up one of my Manolos abandoned in the corner and whistled. "Look at this, doesn't even look like it's been worn."

"Grammy night last year," I remembered with a slight smile. So buzzed after the last after-party, Diego and I made out in someone's bedroom. The rock, rock, rocking of the waterbed made me seasick all over the cashmere comforter. We ran out of there like naughty school kids, and we were halfway to his house when I realized I didn't have any shoes. Made him go back to the party, sneak back into the room, and get them.

"You think I can make some money off this stuff?"

"Hell yeah, you can sell anything on eBay. I heard some lady in Germany was auctioning her kids."

After Blake left, I grabbed the yellow pages and sat on the floor in the living room. He had sold the couch. I needed a storage unit for my stuff until I could figure out where to live. I mentally ran down the list of friends I could crash with - a short list.

I knew a lot of people but didn't have many friends. Macy would probably do it if she had the space, but she had two roommates and a boyfriend who was practically living there. The only person who would be a remote possibility was Freddie. What I paid for in wedding gifts and bridesmaid dresses should amount to at least one month's rent and some goodwill.

The phone rang as I was getting dressed.

"Elle, it's Lucy from Dr. Madison's office. I need to schedule a follow-up visit."

I sank down onto my bed. "Oh."

"We'd like to see you once a month." I could hear her flipping through the charts. "You're nine weeks, and you're due on December 13th. Can you come in next Wednesday?"

My brain had locked up, and I couldn't say anything.

"Ms. Nixon, are you there?"

"I'm here, sorry. Um, let me get back to you, ok?"

"Are you looking at other options? Do you need me to refer you to someone?"

"Um, I don't know."

"You don't want to wait too long. You need to start your prenatal care."

I spent the rest of the day running around trying to stitch together a Plan B. I rented a small storage unit. Talked with one of the guys who did the website for Chantal. He agreed to take pictures of my shoes and purses and upload them to eBay. I would write the descriptions. I also grabbed an apartment rental guide and made a few calls to record labels in search of work. No one has called me back yet. Suddenly, I was persona non grata. I couldn't even get past the flunky who answered the phone. I imagined a hashtag on Twitter #whyEllesucks. Overnight, the phone calls, texts, and emails stopped. Invites evaporated.

It was almost 7 p.m. when I made it over to Freddie's apartment. Big, loud, and proud was how Freddie loved to describe herself. She traded a small town in Jersey for the bright lights of Los Angeles. We were kindred spirits when it came to hanging out. No party was too small as long as it had an open bar. Before Nigel and Diego entered the picture, we ran the streets like each social event was a religious experience. Whether or not we were on the list, we always got in.

Like so many in Los Angeles, our friendship was based on convenience. So caught up in our own spheres of life, we would only notice one another if we rotated too closely. We'd catch up at parties, random lunch dates, and through mutual friends. No real effort was ever made. It just happened. Because it was so easy, it made our friendship seem "meant to be." I knew nothing about her day-to-day life, or much about her past, only what she shared. Without Diego to lean on, I realized just how alone I was in the city. No one to confide in.

Freddie lived in the lower unit of a duplex on Olympic Boulevard on the outskirts of Beverly Hills. Just close enough to see how the other half lived, yet segregated by the stretch of constant traffic running down Olympic. A moving barrier letting you know you had a better chance of being mowed down and flattened by a speeding car than getting a taste of the gated good life.

The sound of a jazz song through the door soothed me. I leaned on the doorbell and knocked for added effect. I was tired. I stifled a yawn and was getting ready to reach for my cell when Freddie opened the door.

"What took you so long to answer?"

"Elle, this is not a good time. Come back tomorrow or something," Freddie said in a dramatic whisper. I was tempted to look stage left to see who the hell she was talking to.

Freddie tried to close the door, but I stuck my foot out to prevent it from closing.

"Freddie, you know I just wouldn't roll up here on your doorstep unless it was important."

"Well, can't it wait? At least an hour or two?"

"Why? You and Nigel doing the nasty? I promise I won't listen." Like that was going to happen. I was convinced Freddie was a beard for Nigel.

I pushed past Freddie, dropped my purse on the table, and headed over to the couch. I noticed for the first time that Freddie was wearing a robe, and her hair sported that tussled, just-made-love look.

"Hey, babe—who was at the door?"

My neck swiveled to catch the voice attached to a towel-clad man. It wasn't Nigel. He was a pretty, perfect metrosexual type. Perfect teeth. Perfect hairless body. Eyebrows perfectly arched. Mani and pedi more recent than mine. I was jealous. Not because he was with Freddie, but because his grooming habits were impeccable. I felt like Mr. Snuffleupagus from Sesame Street standing next to him.

The three of us stood frozen for a second, as though posing for a picture.

"Brad, Elle, Elle, Brad." Freddie made the introductions as though we had bumped into one another at the coffee shop.

"Nice to meet you, Brad." I shook his free hand; he was using the other one to keep his towel closed.

"You too. Hey, weren't you a bridesmaid at Freddie's second wedding?" He pumped my hand vigorously.

"Yes. You were there?"

He leaned against the breakfast bar. "Yeah. I was one of the waiters. Freddie gives a great party. Are you the one who does casting for NCIS?"

"No. I do publicity."

"For who? Actors? Cause I got a part in the play that's running at the Geffen and-"

"Brad baby, don't you have to be somewhere?"

Brad looked up at the clock on the kitchen wall. "You're right. I gotta split." He grabbed Freddie's face and kissed her on the mouth before hurrying into the bedroom.

"So, what's so important?" Freddie asked as though nothing had happened.

"You are too wild. Aren't you supposed to be getting married in a few weeks?"

Freddie shrugged her shoulders and dragged her fingers through her shoulder-length hair.

"I'll be back." Freddie disappeared into the bedroom.

I picked up the remote lying on the couch and flipped on the big screen television. Freddie reappeared fifteen minutes later, clad in a loose-fitting dress and a cloud of perfume. She walked Brad to the door, "nice meeting ya'," he called before disappearing. They talked outside for a few moments before Freddie came back in.

"You look like hell."

"You look like you've just finished fucking."

"Maybe if you hadn't been banging on the door like you lost your mind, that would be the case."

"Damn, Freddie. Who was that guy?"

"He was a waiter at my wedding reception. Before this gets into 20 questions, tell me why you're here."

"I'm not up for 20 questions either... I um-" I opened my mouth to continue, and nothing came out. Freddie looked at me, waiting. I drew in a deep breath, hoping the fresh air would kick-start my brain and get my mouth functioning again. Nothing happened.

"Look, is this about Diego?"

"Huh?"

"I know you had nothing to do with it. I don't blame you." Her voice was muffled as though I was submerged in water. Everything slowed down, my breathing, my heart. My world was collapsing on itself.

"Blame me for what?" I didn't even recognize my voice at this point.

"For him running off with our investment. I gave him $15,000. Not a lot by his standards, but for me... He told me he could triple it, so we could have the honeymoon of our dreams," she said. "I still haven't told Nigel I lost the money, among other things."

I stared at her blankly.

"What? Isn't that what you wanted to talk about?"

"I didn't know. I'm so sorry. I-I-I came here because Blake is selling the condo, and I need a place to crash for a little while."

"Oh." There was so much surprise and confusion in that one syllable. We sat in silence, trying to corral our thoughts until finally, Freddie said, "What's a little while?"

"Until I find another place. A week maybe?"

Freddie studied me for a moment, eyes narrowed, and lips pressed together. I could see the wheels turning in her head and a burning curiosity coloring her eyes. Timing was on my side for once. She couldn't ask me about my issues if I couldn't ask about hers.

Finally, she couldn't resist and asked, "Did he hit you?"

"What? No! Diego would never touch me like that. I haven't seen or heard from him since... It's just... complicated."

"Yeah, I know what you mean." She nodded her head. "The couch pulls out into a bed."

"Thanks. I appreciate it. And I'm sorry. I didn't know."

Freddie left to meet Nigel. They were going to pick up his mother from the airport.

I sat in the car after I left Freddie's apartment. The sun had abandoned our parcel of the sky long ago and dipped below to greet the other side of the world.

I took stock of what I knew. Other than my name, it wasn't much. I felt betrayed by love. It had incapacitated my common sense by distracting me with pheromones. Made me see a king in a $3000 suit when he was just a naked emperor all along. He was holding his stuff together with gum and spit, just like the rest of us. Although I knew that if he were here and told me everything would be all right, I'd believe him. In a heartbeat. Was that what love did, made you believe in the unbelievable? The fact remained, he wasn't here. I was left to draw my own conclusions.

By the time I composed myself enough to drive home, I was exhausted. It was the kind of exhaustion where you had to keep moving, or you might not get back up again. Ever. I made myself walk over to the mailboxes before going inside. I pulled out a thick clump of bills and a note from the post office telling me to come and pick up a package. Probably the invitations for the anniversary party.

As soon as I stepped in the door, my home phone and cell started up again. I checked the ids for both, and it was the same person calling.

"Girl, what's going on with you?"

"Hi Déjà." The third Musketeer from my high school days. She was the excitable yang to Justine's calming yin.

"Don't 'hi' me! I have been leaving you messages. Why am I seeing your man all over TV? I'm on Travelocity right now, looking up plane tickets. Me and the kids are coming out and keeping you company."

"Whoa! Slow down. Now is not a good time for you and your brood."

"C'mon, you know when things are hectic, you need your girls around you."

"Look, I'm just walking in. I can't talk right now, but I promise I'll call you back."

"You sure? Cause we can be out there like tomorrow. What's the weather like?"

"I'll call you later."

I hung up before she could complain. I knew she would be pissed. I just didn't have the energy to give voice to the words that were my nightmare. Instead, I started going through the mail. Everything seemed to be due at once. Car insurance. Lease on the car was up. My credit cards, Bloomies, Visa, American Express, Discover, and MasterCard. All due.

Sure, I could pay all of my bills this month... maybe next month, but after that, if I didn't get a job... I threw the papers on the coffee table and dragged myself down the hall to my bedroom. I sat on my bed and stared at all the creature comforts I could no longer afford. How did things spiral out of control? How could I pay for the therapy it would take to straighten out any kid I would bring into the world in the middle of this mess? I fell backward onto the bed. My eyes stayed propped open. I grabbed the ring, which was on the nightstand. My analytical mind sluggishly kicked in, and I weighed the pros and cons of everything as I twirled the ring slowly. *Who are you?* More importantly, what was hiding behind the door that only this key could open? The number 207 was printed in small black letters on the side of the key.

twelve

SOMEHOW I EXECUTED my tasks one by one. I packed. Moved everything to a storage facility. I searched for Monroe high school on the Internet and tried to search the records of graduates with the initials ED. Rented a mailbox on Robertson Boulevard. Shut off my phone and had the phone company leave my cell number as a forwarding number on the disconnect message. I went on a few job interviews. The only reason I got the interviews was for the curiosity factor. By now, more details about Diego's alleged crimes were coming out. Diego was still missing, and his list of clients kept getting longer. I became a natural target.

Most days, I didn't even answer my phone. Reporters. Former co-workers. Friends. Everybody wanted to rubberneck at the wreck I was calling my life. I was sleeping during the day and prowling around the remains of my life at night to avoid the paparazzi. I had Google Alerts in my email inbox daily, with a link to a photo of me, usually looking stressed and broke, on one of the gossip sites. As expected, I got my new title, "embattled girlfriend of disgraced financial adviser." It rolled off the tongue so much easier than vice president. I stopped reading the comments on the articles after the first time. I didn't have thick enough skin. The consensus seemed to be that I should have known. Should have done something. It was tough reading things about me written by people who didn't know me, didn't know us. Yet, they felt comfortable enough to call me a greedy bubblehead and to hope I rotted in prison. Nice. It made me wonder if those who knew me, did they see me that way as well? Whatever happened to innocent until proven guilty?

Instead, I followed the escalating war of words between Strykker and Cameron playing out in the blogosphere, yet another disaster I was somehow responsible for. Some hip-hop blogs had sniffed the winds of malcontent and were fanning the flames. Strykker's camp said it was his song first, while Cameron remained adamant that the track was stolen.

Despite it all, my pregnancy kept progressing. For the first time since ever, I had boobs. My trips to the bathroom were frequent, and I was sure I was wearing a groove on the hallway floor. I still didn't know if Diego knew he was going to be a father. I didn't want to make this decision alone, and I was running out of time. I was mad at myself for missing him. Love and hate were so intertwined that most days, I just felt an ache, and the pendulum could swing in either direction about how I was feeling about him.

I thought things couldn't get much worse until the lease was up on my car. I drove it back to the dealership to turn it in.

"Marlon, I've been leasing cars from you for *years*. There's no type of deal you can work out with me? I'll take a cheaper model. Just give me something."

Sitting in his glass-enclosed office while other prospective buyers "ooohed" and "ahhed" at the cars on the showroom floor made me feel like the star act in a freak show. It's *Broke Girl*—she has the ability to make men, jobs, and money disappear instantly!

"I'm sorry Elle, you've always had a job whenever you came into lease a car. I can't do anything if you're not employed or have some source of income." Marlon tapped his fingers on his desk. Gone was the fake camaraderie, the "anything for you Elle." Now his eyes tracked the potential commission checks walking by as his colleagues swooped in and helped customers.

I gripped the edge of his desk. My chipped manicure was on full display, but I didn't care. *How was I supposed to get around in LA without a car?*

"How am I supposed to get home?"

Marlon pointed me in the direction of the bus stop, and I found myself outside the dealership on Figueroa, walking northward bound. LA's downtown was a work in progress. The city was making the push for the live-work-play downtown theme, but it was still quite grimy and dirty outside of the immediate multi-million-dollar radius of the Staples Center and LA Live complex. Carts full of undeterminable stuff were parked under the underpass. Their owners shielded by ratty blankets that acted as makeshift barricades. Sometimes a pair of feet clad in busted sneakers could be seen poking out from behind them. Were they, too, once full of self-importance as they chased after shiny, bright objects? Did they see the fall coming? Did they feel the snowballing effect and decide to just give up? I hurried by them, wondering how many were like me during their "before" and if I would end up like them in my "after."

The only bright spot in my life was my eBay auctions. I wound up taking my shoes and some clothes to one of those companies that put your items online for a percentage of the sale because the guy who did Chantal's site was taking too long. I needed money now. So far, I had made $3,000 off high-end shoes and dresses, and not all the auctions were over. The mundane aspect of packaging and mailing the items helped to keep me from eating myself into another two sizes. As it was, my slacks were already fitting me like hot pants.

I managed to get out the invitations for the anniversary party. That was an albatross around my neck; every RSVP call from family was more of a cursory exploration of how far I had fallen. I was as close as they would get to a Hollywood flame-out, and talking to me provided them a little solace. No matter how bad things were for them in Podunk, wherever, it could be worse. They could be me.

When I arrived at Freddie's courtesy of the Santa Monica bus number 12, I knew I would be staying there longer than a week. Without a job and dwindling funds, I had no prospects for apartments, my life had effectively come to a screeching halt, and I didn't know where to look for the reset button.

* * *

A dull ache inched its way along my back, steadily working toward my neck. Freddie's couch looked cute in the living room but wasn't meant to be slept on. It was narrow and hard. Pulling it out as a couch bed was even worse. The mattress was so flimsy; I had imprints from the springs etched in my back after the first night, so I stopped pulling it out. As I squeezed myself into the crevice to keep from falling off the edge, I could feel a pair of eyes boring into my skull. At least I wasn't waking up to one of the cats sitting on my face again.

Freddie cleared her throat. I peeled the pillow off my head and turned to look at her. I was eye level with her knee. It was connected to a leg that was connected to a foot that was impatiently tip-tapping on the floor. I turned over slowly. If I did it too fast, I would be on the floor.

"Hey Freddie," I yawned and rubbed my eyes. "What time is it?"

"It's 3:30 in the afternoon."

"Are you serious?" I sat up slowly and tentatively rose. I didn't want to alert my morning sickness that I was available for a visit.

"Why? Are you late for something?"

"There's a 'Hoarders' marathon on." I shook out my blankets in search of the remote control.

"Elle. We need to talk."

A sudden urge swooped down on me, and I had to hurry to the bathroom.

"Oomph!" I said as I made a mad dash. I ran into the bathroom and slammed the door. Freddie was sitting on the edge of the couch when I came out. She had folded up my blanket and placed it on the chair.

I sat down on the floor and leaned against the couch. My eyelids felt as though weights were tied to each individual eyelash. I could barely keep them open. Another yawn slipped out, leaving me feeling even more deflated.

"What's going on with you, Elle?"

I opened one eye, and even that was a struggle. I hadn't mentioned I was pregnant. Freddie probably thought my weight gain was from depression. That's what she always blamed hers on.

"You've been here for 17 days and haven't moved off my couch."

"Who's counting, right?"

Freddie smiled grimly. "It's not like I don't want you here—"

"But?"

"But I'm moving in with Nigel," she paused. "Since I lost our investment, we can't afford two households. We might as well consolidate now."

"Oh." I just sat there for a moment. My brain was on lockdown. "When?"

"Next Friday."

My eyes popped open. "Next Friday? But don't you have to pack or something? You're going to be ready by then?"

"None of this stuff is mine. I'm just subletting this place. Girl, all I have to do is put my clothes in some suitcases, and I'm done. And there's one other thing..."

"What?"

"Don't take this the wrong way, but it's probably best if you're not at the wedding."

"But I'm the maid of honor," a slight indignation crept into my voice.

"Was. I asked Tina."

"Oh, well, ok. I guess."

"It's supposed to be about me on my wedding day."

"For the third time, but who's counting?"

"And having you there would be too much of a distraction with this whole Diego thing. I'm sorry. Look, I have to take care of a few things. I'll see you later."

A sigh of relief escaped my lips, and I laughed. As maid of honor, I was bestowed the honor of wearing a hideous gown not fit for bridal party or beast. As ugly as it was, it no longer fit. My happiness was short-lived as the sting of rejection settled in. I closed my eyes. I only meant to rest for a minute, think about what I was going to do. Not like I had a lot of options, so I didn't have to think very long. I woke up three hours later on the floor. I walked into Freddie's bathroom and looked in the mirror. Besides hair gel and Scrunchies becoming my new best friends, I was changing. I turned sideways. The small lump in my stomach, discernible mostly after meals, was growing. I imagined it saying in a Glenn Close voice, a la *Fatal Attraction*, "I will not be ignored!" My hand rested on my stomach. I didn't think I could go through with it, not now, not with the way things were.

I was too afraid to move forward, but things were moving along without me. And if I put an end to things... would I be haunted by illusions of an alternate life? Dark dreams about *what if* stalking me in the night? Going through with the pregnancy terrified me even more. I was paralyzed in a tempest of self-doubt and self-pity. I splashed cold water on my face to stop the never-ending debate in my head. The clock was winding down, and soon I wouldn't have a choice.

An hour later, Macy called me on my cell and invited me to an album release party in Hollywood. Reluctantly, I agreed to go. I didn't have anything to wear. I sold most of the good stuff, and the rest of my clothes were starting to make me look like a pork sausage. I checked Freddie's closet. She had clothing sizes from 10 to 22, everything from her binge-eating break-up gear to her new and improved fad-diet-of-the-moment wardrobe.

I took a top from her collection and a skirt from mine. Macy was picking me up at 9. Ever since I gave back the Audi to the dealership, I was bumming rides from folks. I wasn't in a position to buy a new car. Never in my adult life had I been without a car unless I was traveling and didn't feel like getting a rental. Not having a car in LA was an exercise in patience when dealing with the bus and its passengers.

I sat outside on the steps and waited for Macy. The colors from the sky were fading fast. Traffic was an ever-present stream of motion. Macy pulled up to the curb 20 minutes late. I stifled another yawn as I got into the car.

"Watch broken?"

"Traffic."

I gave her a scowl. I had used that line so many times because it always had the possibility of being true.

She kept glancing at me sideways. "So, do you have anything to tell me?"

"What?"

"How far along are you?"

"What do you mean?"

"Girl, please. I can tell."

"What? Am I showing? Is it that noticeable?"

"No, no, you look... nice."

"No. I look like shit, and I feel like shit. I have morning sickness all damn day, and the moments when I'm not sick, I'm tired as a dog. Who the hell said pregnancy was supposed to make you glow?"

"Well, aren't you the poster child for safe sex?"

I just stared out of the window. I was complaining, but I didn't know what I wanted. If Macy could tell, probably so could everyone else. This bit of news wasn't for public consumption.

Strykker's song came on the radio, and Macy turned it up. Off my look, she said, "What? It has a catchy hook." She started singing along.

I jabbed the off button, and silence filled the car.

"Do people still think I stole that song, and it somehow winded up in Strykker's camp?"

Macy shrugged, not an easy feat to do while wearing a seat belt. She wouldn't look at me.

"Do you think I did it?"

"No. But something's going on. If you're being set up, gotta wonder why..."

As the distance closed between the club and us, I began to have second thoughts.

"Turn the car around," I croaked.

"Just let go and have some fun. Everybody already knows about Diego, whether or not you go out. And who cares about Cameron? Strykker's track is better."

"Are you trying to make me feel better?"

"C'mon Elle, it's time you stopped hiding and show your face."

"Who are you, Dr. Phil? I don't; I can't do this. Just take me home."

"You did nothing wrong. The more you stay out of sight, the more people will think you were in on it."

My hands were slick with sweat and shaking. I knew Macy meant well, but she wasn't the brightest bulb, so why in the hell would I listen to her? This was not the night to go hang out and have fun. Diego had been on the news non-stop. His disappearance only fueled the story more. I didn't want everyone pointing and staring at me. Or have my picture taken. The absolute last thing I needed was for it to get out that I was pregnant.

I just stared out the window for the rest of the drive. I had resolved myself to knowing he may never come back. Even if he were to show up on my doorstep tonight, the man I thought I knew, thought I loved, I now was confronted with evidence that he never existed. Innocent men don't run. They don't just disappear off the face of the earth. They don't have a dead man's social security number. They just don't stop calling and erase you from their lives as they started over fresh. I fell in love with a fantasy. He was never real.

thirteen

BODIES WERE STACKED in the club like breadsticks in a basket. Pregnant or not, it was a tight squeeze. I sat at a table in the corner, hidden in the shadows, and nursed an iced tea. Macy would come back periodically, each time covered in more perspiration as she shook her groove thang on the dance floor.

"You should come on out! This DJ has it going on, girl!" Her eyes were slightly glazed over, and the looseness of her limbs and words told me I wasn't going to let her drive me home. I think for the first time, I was going to be a designated driver. When had life slipped away from me? I watched as women flitted in and out of social circles. Felt the bump bumping of the bass and slightly swayed my body to the music. I stayed rooted to the chair, too self-conscious about my tacky ensemble to want to see or be seen.

No one ever mentioned how many trips to the bathroom you had to make when pregnant. It got to the point where if I didn't get up, I was going to pee on myself. On my way to the bathroom, I saw Cameron and a pack of his cronies filing out of a side door.

"Cameron!" My voice cut through the music and stopped him in his tracks.

He turned around and looked at me. Gave a slight nod to his crew to keep walking.

"Wassup, Elle?" he asked, his bedroom eyes giving me the once over.

I felt a jolt of indignation and a blast of energy as I walked up to him.

"What's up? You run around telling people that I stole your masters, and you want to know what's up? What do you think?"

He grabbed my arm and pulled me outside. I snatched my arm out of his grasp. "What the hell is wrong with you? Don't you ever–"

"Let's talk in the car."

He took long strides, leaving me breathless as I tried to keep up. His security discretely followed us as we walked half a block to a short, one-way side street where his hulking black Hummer punked the other cars and dominated the street.

"You don't valet?"

"Nah. Don't need fools watching the door waiting to see if I'm coming or going."

We got in the truck, and he started it up. Etta James' "At Last" filled the air.

"How could you tell people that I'm a thief?"

"Shit went down, and I had to do what I had to do. Know what I'm saying?"

"No, I don't know because you're not saying anything specific."

Cameron jiggled his leg up and down, checking the rearview and side mirrors like he was keeping a constant vigil. He was making me nervous.

"You need some money or sumthin'? You lookin' like times have been hard."

"Thanks to you."

He reached into his pocket and pulled out a thick wad of money. I glanced at my side-view mirror and saw a dark car with the lights off, creeping up on us slowly. As the car inched past us, the driver's window rolled down, and I saw a flash of silver and a gun. I grabbed Cameron's arm and yelled, "Oh My God!"

There was a rapid popping sound and an explosion of glass. Money and chunks of the window rained down on us as we tried to crawl into the back seat. It seemed to last forever as a thousand prayers leaped off my tongue.

I don't know how many times they fired the gun before the screech of tires sounded, and we were plunged into a sudden silence that hung tenuously in the air. My heart was thumping jackrabbit crazy, and in my mind, maybe out loud, I kept saying *we're-alivewe'reok,we'realivewe'reok.* Over and over. But in that moment before, I made all kinds of bargains and promises with God. No matter how bad life was, I didn't want to go out like this. Spare us, I begged. All three of us. In the moment after, time stopped, and we were in a vacuum where all the noise and air were sucked out. Then it burst, and a melee of sounds assaulted my ears. Police sirens. Screams. Etta. Moans. My side hurt as a hard pain traveled up and around my back. Cameron was draped across me like a shield. His breath was hot and raggedy as it burst in my ear. I struggled to sit up and move him off me. He whispered a moan. Blood was everywhere.

"You're bleeding!" My words tumbled out, as jagged as the shards of glass around us. I felt as though I were moving in slow motion as I looked around to find something to stop the blood from spurting out of his shoulder.

"So are you," he said. I looked down and saw a red mosaic spreading across my shirt. I hated the sight of blood, but adrenaline kept the darkness at bay.

Shaking the glass out of my hair, everything I touched was sticky. The metallic taste of iron was in my mouth, and its heavy stench hung in the air. Suddenly the doors opened, and hands pulled me out. A sea of faces swam before my eyes as waves of nausea threatened to overtake me.

When things like this happen, people always say they felt like they were watching it from outside their bodies. Not me. Every jostle and poke seemed to electrify my nerve endings. I was placed on a stretcher and lifted into an ambulance. A piercing pain on my side snatched my breath away. Questions were thrown at me. What happened? What's my name? Where did I hurt?

"I'm pregnant," I told an EMT before he put an oxygen mask on my face even though I was breathing just fine. Club goers had spilled into the alley as police and security tried to control the scene. Camera phones were waving in the air as people tried to snap pictures, even though they had no idea what had happened. Cameron disappeared into another ambulance.

The barely controlled chaos of a hospital exploded around me in the emergency room. The attendant yelled I was pregnant as they wheeled me into a room. Someone wrapped a wide black belt around my stomach and velcroed it together. It was hooked up to a monitor. A whoosh whoosh sound came through loud and clear.

"What's that?" I asked.

"Your baby's heartbeat," a nurse answered.

My breath caught in my throat, and tears welled in my eyes. It was so steady and willful. There was somebody inside me. And it became real. Not a situation. Not some problem.

No, the actual problem was trying to figure out why someone would want to shoot me. Was someone trying to get to Diego by getting to me? $26 million stolen could cause someone to get very angry. The next few days were a blur. Two bullets had grazed me, one in the arm and one in the back of my shoulder. I also had a few cuts from the shattered window. I was kept in for observation because of the baby.

The Feds and police streamed in and out of my room like I was giving away free coffee and donuts. They peppered me with questions. They posted a guard outside of my door as a precaution. Life as I knew it no longer existed. I was stripped of my identity, professionally and personally. Instead of Elle Nixon, publicist, party girl, and extreme shopper, I was the girlfriend of disgraced financial planner Diego Rivera or woman in the car with platinum-selling rapper

Cameron and the scariest title of all... unemployed, unwed mother-to-be.

Nurses were in and out of my room, checking my blood pressure, temperature, and baby's heart rate. In those moments when I was alone, I realized I could have died. No matter how depressed I'd been about my life and Diego, I knew I wasn't ready to go. Not like that. So many unfinished conversations, milestones not achieved. Thoughts about the shooting hounded me, causing sleep to become a distant cousin. Its absence left me plenty of time to think about what I needed to move on. Answers. For me. For our child.

I also had to figure out medical answers for us. I sat there gnawing on a pen, perfectly flummoxed by the patient forms a nurse had given me to fill out. They wanted a dossier on the father's medical history. I looked at the list of genetic mines that could befall our child. I had no idea if Diego's side of the family had high blood pressure or was prone to a rare chromosome disorder. Hell, I didn't even know his real name; how could I know his blood type? He was an unknown value; it would be a crap shoot what our baby would inherit. Even artificially inseminated women had a better grasp of what they were getting in the gene pool than I did.

Because I was over 35, I was also confronted with a host of "what could be wrong" scenarios with my pregnancy. I was introduced to mind-numbing phrases such as *Chorionic Villus Sampling, first-trimester screening*—which shouldn't be confused with the *Quad Screen* or *Triple Screen, Trisomy-18* and *Trisomy-21*. I had the sickle cell trait, and if Diego did, there was a one in four chance our child would be born with the disease. I could find out with a CVS, but it was invasive.

I used the rotating nurses on duty as an encyclopedia of information. I would badger them every time they came into my room. Nurse Clara saw the panic rising behind the glazed look in my eyes and was able to break it down for me in simple terms.

"Look, if you want certainty, you can do a CVS now or an amnio in your second trimester, but both are invasive, and they do have a small risk of miscarriage."

"How small a risk?"

"It's about .6% or one in 1,600 pregnancies. If you just want a risk assessment, do the screening, and you can decide from there if you want further testing," she told me.

My first instinct was to quiz everyone and see what they would do, but something happened to me in Cameron's truck. Even though I had strong control freak tendencies, there was nothing I could do about odd number chromosomes and sickle cell traits. Except bargain, beg, and plead with God, and I could also throw in cajoling for good measure.

I just knew I loved this baby, whoever they turned out to be. I knew whether she or he had six legs and four eyes or 10 fingers and 10 toes; I would love them. If the tests couldn't provide preventative treatment... then what was done was done.

* * *

"Are you sure you're ready?" Blake asked for what had to be the 20th time.

"Yes already, let's go. It's been two days too many. I hate hospitals."

He answered his phone, which was vibrating nonstop. "Ok, we're leaving now," he said, "Macy's out front, and it's crazy out there."

I was stuck in a wheelchair as a nurse pushed me down the hall. I had a plastic bag full of my bloodstained belongings on my lap. Inside my purse was a sonogram. A 12-week-old blob that only the technician could distinguish but would morph into a baby over the coming months.

Checking out of the hospital was pure pandemonium. I was persona non grata no more, thanks to my *Boys In The Hood* episode with Cameron. Besides *Access Hollywood, E! Entertainment,* and *The Insider* wanting to speak with me, I was also popular with the DA's

117

office as they tried to solve yet another high-profile crime, and now I was involved in two. It took maybe five seconds for some hungry intern to figure out that the unidentified pregnant woman (so much for patient confidentiality) in the car with Cameron was also the girl-friend of the Hip Hop Madoff.

Fortunately, Macy was double parked right in front of the hospital. Blake wheeled me a few feet, and it felt like we were going into the eye of the storm. The oxygen was sucked out of the air, and it was just massive flashbulbs going off, one after the other. It was a convergence of paparazzi like no other. It wasn't all just for me; two starlets were scheduled for C-tuck (lipo and C-sections) later that day. Their voices coalesced into one long, roaring sentence, lobbing questions at me faster than a tennis match with Venus Williams.

"Where's the money?"

"Did someone shoot you because of Diego?"

"Elle, how's the baby?"

"Did your boyfriend shoot Cameron?"

"Where's your boyfriend?"

"Who's your boyfriend?"

The crescendo of voices rose into a fever pitch as they speculated if I was seeing Cameron. It would be a love triangle that ended in a hail of bullets by the time their shows went on the air. I kept my head down and didn't say a word. I knew the drill. There was no need for me to speak because I wasn't pushing or selling anything. Besides, I had nothing to say. Lately, I seemed to be the last to know.

Cameron had checked out of the hospital the day after we were brought in, convinced that he was a sitting duck if he stayed longer. He had been hit twice, once in the chest; one went clean through his shoulder. I suffered only a flesh wound, and it hurt like hell. The doctors didn't want to dope me up with anything heavier than Tylenol because of the pregnancy.

Blake helped me into the backseat. I slumped into it and closed my eyes. I'd done the paparazzi stroll plenty of times; hell, I even knew some of the shooters out there. Probably paid half of them at one time or another to shoot my artists, but this was different. I was never the target.

I wanted to stop by Diego's house on the way from the hospital. Blake and Macy were quiet in the front seat as we turned the corner onto his street. In the middle of his block sat his house, surrounded by a chain-link fence with a heavy-duty padlock on the front. Agent Walsh had agreed to meet me there so I could get some of my things.

Macy and Blake waited for me in the car while Walsh let me in. Entering the house felt like walking into a tomb. It didn't feel like home anymore. I hurried up the stairs to the closet to grab a few pairs of shoes and my favorite jeans. I scooped up my spare contact lens solution and Dermalogica products from the medicine cabinet in the bathroom. Walsh tried to act like he wasn't watching me as I slipped a photo album into my bag and grabbed a framed photo of Diego and me in front of the Trevi Fountain from Diego's bedside.

I trailed behind Walsh as we walked downstairs.

"Do you have any leads yet?"

"No, not yet. But ahh, just so you know, Coogan's missing."

"What? Since when?"

"A few days ago. He was free on bail and had an appointment to meet with one of our agents, and he didn't show."

"Do you think he had something to do with this?"

Walsh paused, his hand on the doorknob. "Honestly? No, I think he's afraid of being next, but you be careful."

"What do you mean? Do I have a target on my back?"

"We're investigating the possibility of a link between Mr. Rivera and organized crime. He may have been laundering money for one of the families. That's all I can tell you for now."

"My life could be in danger, and you're just now telling me that the mob could be after him? After us? Amazing. Do you even care about anything other than bringing Diego in?" I didn't wait for an answer. I left. Somehow, I had become an expendable factor in this equation. The sooner I got out of town, the better.

Macy and Blake were quiet when I got back into the car. I closed my eyes and forced myself not to look back at the house. I didn't know when I would see it again, if ever. That part of my life was over. Not that I had time to dwell. I was at the epicenter of two scandals and a potential co-star for a lost episode of the *Sopranos*. Who was gunning for me? Coogan? The mob? I knew nothing about Diego's business, so why come after me? Unless it was to teach Diego a lesson. The thought chilled me. People had been killed over $20 and 40 ounces of liquor. Millions of dollars upped the stakes.

Macy was taking me to a hotel, and the next day I would be on a plane homeward bound to New Jersey. Home. They say you can never go back, and I've never wanted to, never needed to, until now. Hopefully, there, I would be safe.

fourteen

GETTING out of LA had been hard. Deciding to go back home to Mariner's Pike, New Jersey, had been harder, but I was caught in a maelstrom of police questioning and the media stalking me and had nowhere else to go. Everything about Mariner's Pike reminded me of how far I had fallen. It was like someone just kicked the ladder from underneath me and launched me into this never-ending free fall.

They had dubbed Diego the Madoff of Hip Hop, even though his clients spanned from Hollywood directors to non-profits to music producers. Somehow, I had been painted as his ride-or-die chick, the floozy who had set up the marks. Since I wasn't talking, the media made up what they didn't know. Some ass had sold their soul to TMZ, and pictures of Diego and I in the Caribbean were on the site with the headline "Living La Vida Ladron." Arrows highlighted my necklace and ring, inferring that they were ill-gotten gains. I had always liked to be the center of attention, but not in a felonious type of way.

I had to stop answering my phone. The same editors I had pitched my artists to were now calling me, asking for exclusives about Diego *and* Cameron.

Now I defined myself by what I'd lost. I used to be a publicist at a record label. I used to be a size four. I used to have a boyfriend named Diego Rivera.

I'd become an algebra equation, $(x-y) - (a+b)=z$. I am now who I am by subtracting what I used to be and adding a few unknown quantities of what I will become. Just like home.

Mariner's Pike, pop. 12,700, used to be the place to be back in the day. Way back. Like beginning of the 20th century way back. It was a haven for the old film stars who wanted to vacation on the Jersey Shore. It was their East Coast Monte Carlo, a playground for the rich and famous. Now its dilapidated buildings dotted the shoreline like ugly blemishes. Reminders of what should have been. Half-finished projects, abandoned buildings, and gutted-out buildings, all symbols of various promises made by politicians and developers who vowed to restore Mariner's Pike back to its original glory.

The last time I lived in my parents' house, cell phones were the size of a briefcase. I marched out of there proud and defiant, vowing never again to live under the despotic rule of daddy. I had served my 18-year sentence and planned to make the most out of my parole. I went away to UCLA, a university all the way across the country. Now, only to return with bitter disappointment from the experience of a life unhinged.

As I waited for my plane to board, Agent Walsh sat beside me. I didn't try to hide my scowl.

"You've got to be kidding me... You're like an embarrassing rash that just keeps popping up."

"Thanks. One way to get rid of me is to help me find your boyfriend," he said.

"Nothing's changed since yesterday. Still clueless." I opened up my magazine and stared at the pages as though there was a map to Diego drawn on it.

"You will contact us if you hear from Diego, correct?"

I sighed and closed the magazine. "You know more about him than I do. I don't know what you want from me. Do you want to hook me up to a lie detector, water board me? What's it going to take to get you off my back?"

"I realize how you must feel, but-"

"No, you don't. You have no clue how I feel. How could you? This is just your job. I don't get to go home and not think about this until the next morning when I get to the office. It's my life. So don't feed me the tired platitudes you say to those left behind to deal with the aftermath. Just save it for someone who didn't spin bullshit into gold for a living." It came out in a forceful rush, surprising both of us.

"This is not just a job. This is what I do, and right now, I want to bring Mr. Rivera in safely. The longer he's out there, the worse it gets for him." He leaned in toward me, his steely blue eyes holding my gaze.

"Oh great, you're the obsessive type. Have you checked his credit cards? Is he back in the country? You told me about his wife, but what's his real name? What exactly are you doing to find him? And Jeffrey? How could you let him get away?" I went back to my magazine.

Walsh kept his face neutral as he pressed his lips together for a moment. "I can't get into the details of our investigation. The only thing I can tell you is his real name... Eugene Daly. And that stays between us."

"Of course."

People hurried to their gate, babies cried in the background; it was the usual pandemonium in the airport. My flight was going to be full; every seat in the waiting area was occupied. I processed these sights and sounds while my brain chewed over the name Eugene Daly. So, the ring was his. Which caused a batch of new questions to populate my mind. How did he become Diego? Why? Did he really love me? Did he mean to steal the money? Eugene Daly sounded like the polar opposite of Diego Rivera.

"Can you tell me anything else about him? About the name he chose?" I finally asked, hoping for a morsel. Anything. I needed more if I was going to be a laptop detective.

"No. I'm sorry. The longer he stays away, the harder it's going to be for him when he comes back. Will you tell him that?"

"What makes you think he'll contact me?"

"He will if he hasn't already."

"Do you think I was in on it?" I felt like I had to keep a poll.

"No. It doesn't appear that Daly funneled any funds through your bank account."

"You reviewed my bank records?"

"Yes."

I tried not to think about what other aspects of my life they poked and prodded. "Can you make some type of statement that I'm not a suspect? The media's having a field day with me."

"Maybe your boyfriend will come bail you out, not let you take the heat for him."

"I'm bait?"

"Look, you seem like a nice lady caught up in a bad situation. Cut your losses and move on."

"Easy for you to say. I'm moving in with my parents."

Walsh leaned forward and dropped his elbows to his knees. He laced his fingers behind his neck. He looked at me, and I saw sadness coloring his eyes.

"Growing up, my father always stayed one step ahead of the law, petty crimes, scams. My mother was always right behind him, dragging my sister and me along from city to city. So no, it's not easy for me to say. That's hard-won first-hand experience. Do you want that for your child?"

"Low blow, Agent Walsh." My face burned as the images in the magazine swam before my eyes. I took a deep breath and tried not to think about his words.

Agent Walsh handed me another card before he left. I would be able to wallpaper the nursery with his cards if he didn't cut it out. Some bedtime story for my little one. *Yes, honey, and when your dad was on the run, probably acquiring a new wife and identity, this nice agent provided me with plenty of business cards for the Quantico motif.* I didn't even want to think about how he knew I would be at the airport. I almost couldn't wait to get away from the prying eyes and surveillance here... to go home and live under the prying eyes and surveillance of my parents.

I rested my hand on my stomach, a dull throb pulsing in my shoulder. My arm was in a sling, and falling asleep. The bandages made me itch, and I wanted to take a nap.

The flight back to NJ was long. Left me plenty of time to think. Too much time. When I closed my eyes, I was back in Cameron's truck. The iron stench of blood was suffocating. The sound of my heart pounding in my ears like the boom boom of a marching band on speed. I'd never been so afraid in my life. A warm trickle of urine raced down my leg, and I didn't care. The fear of death had erased all pride. It wrapped around my heart, squeezing until I thought I would pass out from not knowing if someone was going to get out of the car and finish us. On the floor in the back, Cameron covered me like a blanket. Surprising. He always gave off a serious every-man-woman-and-child-for-themselves vibe. I needed to speak to Cameron. I had too many questions and no way to get the answers. Those who knew refused to be found.

I half-heartedly flipped through one of the rags I purchased at a newsstand. *Worst Celebrity Break-Ups* was a tagline on the cover. Chemistry was a bitch. It sold us a false bill of goods. Made us believe he was Mr. Right when really he was Mr. Right for Right This Second, with no warranty or guarantee.

We always remember the first kiss, the first touch, the last hang-up, and the final "fuck you" hurtled at a retreating back. Everything else in between was a blur, like the sands of time trickling down the hourglass, counting down the moments until all we had left of one another were the memories.

Our countdown began in Jamaica. A cool island breeze kissed away the pearls of sweat that glistened on our backs while I tasted the Cristal on his tongue and the saltiness of his body. He wrapped his arms around my waist and pulled me close as he buried his face in the crook of my neck. Legs entwined, stomachs pressed together as though sealed with glue. "I love you Elle." It fluttered from his lips with such a satisfied swoosh that it tickled my ears. So quickly and so unexpectedly. It was like glimpsing a rare butterfly at the end of autumn. Blink, and it's gone, leaving you to wonder if you ever saw it at all.

As I thought about it more, I realized that many of the circumstances surrounding the first utterance of those three words by the men in my past usually involved sex and/or alcohol. Chalk it up to one of many red flags I overlooked. Did it take a drunken wild night to invoke the "L" word? How come a man never realized he loved me as we hunted around for the car in a parking lot after a date? Or while sitting in traffic?

My ankles had swollen to the size of a small car from being cramped in coach for five and a half hours. I walked the aisles so much that passengers started giving me drink orders.

I called my dad when we landed and asked him to meet me at the baggage claim. I staggered off the plane in Newark, looking like a Project Runway assignment gone wrong. Very wrong. I could get away with it in anything-goes-Uggs-in-the-summer Los Angeles. Not in NJ. I tugged at the belt of one of Freddie's flamboyant frocks, on loan after the zipper broke on my jeans. I didn't know whether to pee or eat. Both urges were so strong. I was tempted to buy a Snicker's bar at the newsstand so I could inhale it on my way to the restroom. By the time I made it to the baggage claim, my father was standing by a cart, waiting for me to point out my suitcases.

His lanky frame was ramrod straight, capped off with a tight salt and pepper fade. Disappointment was stamped all over his face as he took in my appearance before giving me a stiff hug.

"You have a good trip?"

I frowned. "It was too cold on the plane. They barely fed us. And my ankles make me feel like I should be eating peanuts and doing circus tricks."

Dad just shook his head. "You sound just like your mother. Got to complain about something."

"Can't blame me then. I'm genetically predisposed to complaining."

"Considering your situation, you should watch your mouth. That's probably what got you in trouble in the first place," he said, a frown tugging at the corners of his lips, making his laugh lines deepen like creases in a piece of paper.

His tone made my stomach contract. I felt like I was 12 years old and being scolded for mouthing off to a teacher. I kept my mouth shut. I didn't want to get into an argument so soon, but I wanted to say if you knew anything about biology, you'd know my mouth had nothing to do with the trouble I was in. Well, it may have been essential in foreplay... but that was another story.

Some genius coined the term "boomerang" to describe an adult child who returned home to live with their parents. After only 10 minutes, I knew it was a surefire recipe for a nervous breakdown.

"Did the rest of my stuff get here?"

"Some boxes came yesterday. I placed them in your room."

"How many?"

"Three large boxes. How many more do you expect?"

"Two. Where's mom?"

"She had a migraine. She was still in bed when I left."

Translation: she was so mortified that not only was her adult daughter knocked up by an alleged fraudster, it was being broadcast all over the free world. She had taken to her bed in shame. Forget the fact that people lost their retirement or college funds for their kids. I was pregnant by a fugitive with zero chance of getting married. She would wisely use this quiet time to strategize how to make it all sound respectable to neighbors and relatives.

We were silent on the long drive home.

"You been taking care of yourself?" Dad asked as he glanced at me.

"Well enough," I answered. I looked out the window at the

hulking smokestacks lining the parkway as we sped through Elizabeth.

"Have you been seeing a doctor?"

"Funny thing about being in a hospital, everywhere you look, there are people in white coats..."

"You know what I'm asking."

"Do you think I'm that irresponsible not to have seen a doctor?"

He didn't say anything. The small car was so full of unsaid words from past and present conversations that I thought I would suffocate. Nothing else was spoken until we arrived in Mariner's Pike.

Home sweet home. It was in the middle of a semi-quiet street that had seen better years yet wore its pride earnestly in the neatly trimmed yards and rows of middle-class homes. 1841 Neptune's Way. Back in the 20s, it was a summer cottage for the minor stars. Six blocks away from the beach—not exactly prime beachfront property, but it was the house I grew up in.

fifteen

MY MOTHER SWEPT me up in a hug, almost crushing my spine. More than a few years had passed since my last trip home, yet time was still on her side. Not much had changed about her or the house except for a fuller look to her face. She kept her silver hair cropped short, and as usual, her eyes missed nothing.

Whenever I did manage to make it home, I was always surprised by the assault of before and after memories. Evie was everywhere in this house, but I had just as many memories of being in the house without her. In her absence, our family was like a fine piece of china that had been broken and glued back together. The fissures and cracks were masked, but not if you knew where to look.

Numerous trophies still lined the shelves in the living room, a shining testament to a skill that had become useless to my father and me. The same beige living room set I used to curl up on with a corded phone and trade three-way gossip with Justine and Déjà was still there, sans plastic slipcovers.

"You look tired, let me make you some tea," my mother said.

Even though I didn't like tea, and she knew I didn't like tea, I was going to be drinking tea as soon as the water in the kettle boiled. "Drink tea to heal your soul," was a refrain I often heard. She wasn't so much New Age-y as pragmatic. The parents of her dental patients either loved her or hated her because she didn't play nice. She spoke her mind. "Makes no sense this baby needs eight fillings, and he's only five. I will report you to social services if you don't take better care of his teeth and stop feeding him all that soda and candy," she had no problem reprimanding.

Sitting on the couch waiting for my tea, I knew none of my answers would be satisfactory. I would have had more fun during the Inquisition than dodging the multitude of questions my mother fired at me. Needless to say, both Dr. Nixons were very unhappy with my current state. Finally, at the end, my mother's answer to everything:

"If you would have just gone to medical school like we suggested and settled down with a nice doctor-" she began.

"Seriously? I'd be divorced and still paying off school loans. I'm tired. I love you, and I'm going to assume for the time being you still love me," I said as I gave them both a peck on the cheek before I headed upstairs.

I had to pass the pictorial montage of my childhood that lined the wall along the stairs. Pictures of Evie and me from kindergarten to junior high school with all the goofy, awkward stages in between, from braces to bras, were all on display. There should be some statute of limitations on embarrassment.

"When are you going to put some new pictures up?" I called down.

"I guess I have to put some up of my new grandbaby," my mother answered. "Put your stuff away and come down for dinner."

My mouth was watering for some baked mac and cheese or some other special dish she may have conceived for my homecoming. I dumped my jacket and purse on my bed without even turning on the light or opening the blinds.

No mouthwatering aromas greeted me as I entered the kitchen. I looked around and saw a colorless mound adorned with veggies in the center of the table.

"It's a tofu casserole," my mom said.

"Did your mom mention we're vegan now?"

"What?"

"We're not hardcore vegans yet, but we're not getting any younger, and with your dad's high sugar and high blood pressure, we have to change our diet," my mother said as she scraped sautéed spinach onto my plate.

"No ribs, pork roasts, meatloaf, or roasted turkey on Sundays?" My stomach folded in on itself with hunger. "You could have warned me," I whispered to my dad.

"Funny, I felt the same way when I saw on the news that you were pregnant," he whispered back. "You outdid yourself Olivia, can't wait to see what you cook up for tomorrow," he said loudly to my mother.

* * *

I woke up angry and stiff. Don't really remember any dreams; I was left with the residue of frustration clinging to me. I had been in bed for so long that I made a permanent depression in the small twin-sized mattress. I wanted to relegate thoughts of Diego to the back of the closet, like a dress that was out of season or shoes that no longer fit. Instead, he loomed front and center like the anticipation of a sample sale.

When I used to think about our relationship back when it was then and not now, I saw it in a series of picture-perfect glossy post-cards. Diego and I on a sunset-stained beach in Maui. Diego and I sailing to Paros Cyclades in Greece. Diego and I drunk in the back of the limo going home from a Grammy Awards after-party. We lived the good life, and I had no clue that stolen money subsidized it. Looking back on it, it all seemed so shallow. All I had were two-dimensional memories with a stand-in from Central Casting for a boyfriend. Everything about him was a lie, and I never noticed.

Funny how things evolved. It went from me to we to us to he, him and his. He is so selfish. I don't understand him. This is his fault. He, he, he, he. Ha hahaha. Cracking up like a lunatic. The dissolution of sanity never happens all at once. They say art is in the details. Well, lunacy starts out with the small, ordinary thoughts that spiral out of control, like viral marketing. Next thing you know, you're howling like Eddie Murphy's *Raw* is looped continuously in your head.

A loud knock on the door startled me out of my thoughts. "Come in!"

My father strode in and dropped his car keys on my nightstand.

"What's this? You're bequeathing me your prized possessions already?"

"Go to the store and pick up some milk, and here's a list of stuff your mom needs."

"You're lactose intolerant."

"It's good for the baby. You need it."

I looked at the scrap of paper he dropped on the bed. Kale. Squash. Tofu. Zucchini. Eggplant.

"You're kidding, right? Can't you get this stuff? You're already dressed."

"You have to get out of this house. Been locked up in this room too long now. Who you hiding from?"

"Everybody." I turned over on my other side and pulled the sheet up to my chin. The same posters I had hung so lovingly in high school, now yellowed, stared back at me. Prince and Michael Jackson seemed to be saying, "Get your fat ass out of bed. We're tired of looking at you."

"Pick up my prescription from Walgreens while you're out. Money's on the table."

He closed the door behind him. I was left feeling like a frustrated woman-child yet again. Which wasn't that hard of a stretch, seeing as everything in my room was exactly how I left it. Banana clips, Wet 'N Wild nail polish, curl activator, and stuffed animals littered my dresser. A bunch of wallet photos lined the edge of my mirror. My cell phone chimed. I threw out an arm and groped the nightstand, knocking over the keys. Finally, I heaved myself into a sitting position.

It was Detective Moran from Mariner's Pike PD. The LAPD had asked him to follow up with me about the shooting; he had a photo line-up to show me.

"I told you, I didn't see anyone."

"The memory is a funny thing Ms. Nixon; seeing these pictures might trigger something."

I hung up after agreeing to meet him tomorrow at the local police station in Mariner's Pike.

Barely here a week, and already my problems were following me from California. I tried calling Casey, Cameron's manager, but his number was disconnected. Just like I felt. I had no idea what was going on with Cameron, the masters, if he knew who tried to shoot us. I grabbed my robe and headed to the bathroom to take a shower.

I still needed to find an OB/GYN, find a job, and figure out what life would be like after the baby. At this point, I had cobbled enough money to pay for medical expenses. I could afford a drive-thru vaginal birth. Or, if I stayed in the hospital, it would have to be a la carte; maybe I could bring my own meals and meds with me. At the end of the day, it all came down to dollars. I didn't have enough, and Diego had too much of someone else's.

An hour later, I was driving past rows of cookie-cutter bungalows with neat little postage-stamp lawns. In a matter of blocks, I was at the ShopRite debating whether to get the Hohos or the Yodels. I had just tossed them both in the cart when I heard my name.

"Elle? Elle Nixon? Is that you?"

I looked to my right and saw what could only be a former classmate of mine. Even though weight and time were generously distributed across her face, I could still see a shadow of the instigating teenager I once knew.

"It's me, Beverly. Beverly Thompson, now Beverly Mason," she smiled a wide, phony smile and flashed a tiny, microscopic chip of a diamond. I wasn't sure if it belonged on her finger or behind her dog or cat's ear in case they were lost. She checked me out from head to toe.

"Oh... Bev. How are you?" I asked. Her cart was blocking mine, forcing me into extended small talk.

"I'm fine! How are you? I heard on the news that you were in the car when that rapper was shot, and I told my husband, 'I know her!' What are you doing back in town?"

"I'm on the run, and you just blew my cover." Her eyes widened. "I'm kidding... obviously," I said. So stand-up wasn't an option for me.

I missed the anonymity of living in a sprawling city. Small towns were gossiping hotbeds, sitting in judgment of everyone while carefully keeping their own skeletons stacked neatly in their closets.

"Oh, of course. Well, my husband and I are having a house built in Jackson, and my husband just got promoted to VP at Merrill Lynch."

"Does your husband have a name? Or is he just known as 'my husband'?"

Bev shifted from one foot to the other. A look of impatience was creeping into her tone. "Ronnie. Ronnie Mason. He was a year ahead of us."

"Really?" My eyebrow shot up like my eyelashes were on fire. Odd coupling. He was homecoming king, and I don't think she ever went to the prom. Hmmm. We've been out of school for 17 years. Would bet that her oldest kid was 16 years and nine months old.

"What does your husband do?"

"I'm not married."

"Oh... I'm sorry... I just... because you," she trailed off.

"Yeah, well, no." I was finally able to maneuver my cart around her.

She followed me down two aisles as I continued to shop and even stood behind me in the checkout line. I got to hear all about her fabulous life with her fabulous husband and her fabulous kids. We were never friends in high school, so her sudden interest in me was dubious at best.

We were in the parking lot, and as I was walking to my father's car, she pulled out a key fob and pressed the alarm to disarm a Mercedes SUV, about 15 years old, parked five cars from the Chevy.

"What have you been up to?" she finally asked as she looked from my stomach to my ringless ring finger.

"Too much to tell you now. Give me your number so we can do lunch or something."

She wrote down her number. As she stood there waiting for me to write down mine, I said, "Let me take this call. We'll catch up later."

"But I didn't hear your phone ring."

I pulled my phone out of my purse and started talking as I unloaded the bags from the cart to the trunk. I smiled and waved her away.

I was pushing the cart back to the rack when I heard my name again. I groaned. This was why I didn't want to go out. The town was too damn small. Who was I going to see next? My first-grade teacher?

I turned around with a scowl on my face.

"I thought that was you, Smelly Ellie." The voice belonged to a tall, well-built man with a beautiful smile.

"Lucas? Lucas Chavers, is that you?"

sixteen

LUCAS USED to have a crush on me in junior high school. Because he only came up to my nose and was below sight level, I never gave him the time of day. I was too busy enjoying the only perk of being on the track team: socializing with the boys on the track team. Now he stood before me, all grown up, while I looked like a hot mess in flip-flops, a pair of sweats, and an oversized t-shirt. My hair was thrown back in a sloppy ponytail. When did I stop caring about what I looked like?

"Some little birdies told me you were back, but I didn't believe it," he said, shoving his hands in his pockets and rocking slightly on the balls of his sneakers. He had definitely filled out, no longer the scrawny kid with stick-thin legs. Now he was all broad shoulders housed in a t-shirt that flaunted muscular pecs and biceps, with perfect white teeth flashed in a teasing smile, framed by a neat mustache and soul patch.

"Let me guess, Déjà? Her mouth's like a pair of wings, always flapping. Well, it was good seeing you. I'm sure we'll bump into each other again," I said as I walked away to my car.

"I hope so," he called after me, his voice holding the hint of a promise.

I felt his eyes on me. I swore once I got the wireless hooked up at my parents, I would only shop online and would never, ever leave the house.

That night after dinner, my mother came upstairs to my room. My suitcases and boxes, still untouched, were shoved against the wall.

"So, what are we going to do with you?"

"Don't start. I've only been here a week."

"Yes, and you've been in bed the whole time. It can't be healthy for the baby or you. And what about our anniversary party?"

"I know, I know."

"Life isn't over for you Elle; it's just beginning. So quit mourning and get to living."

"Yeah, well, your life isn't imploding around you, is it?" I immediately regretted saying anything. I wish I had a spare foot I could just keep in my mouth. She had battled much worse, and she still managed to be there for my dad and me every day.

She was unruffled as she said, "But my child is suffering, and one day soon, you'll understand. It hurts to watch our children struggle. We want the best for our kids."

"Your best and my best have never been the same, have they?"

She chuckled and sat down on the bit of space left on the bed. "No, but it doesn't mean I don't want to see you happy. You feeling sorry for yourself and moping around is not the Elle I know or raised."

"How did you do it? I mean, I know it's not the same, losing a child and what Diego has 'allegedly' done but... how did you get out of bed every day?"

She paused a moment, choosing her words carefully. "I always thought if something were to happen to Evie, it would be because of her sickle cell, and I would have time to prepare myself. But it didn't work out that way, did it? One morning it was life as usual, and she left the house and never came back.

"I made a choice, Elle. It wasn't easy, but I had a child and a husband who also needed me. I did what had to be done. And so will you. You're much stronger than you give yourself credit."

She was right, but I didn't need "right;" I needed understanding or at least a willing guest at my pity party. I retreated to where it was safe. My bed. No one gunning for me. No paparazzi. Sleep and long naps seemed to be my only way of escaping. Long, dreamless naps. Long dreamless nights where I didn't have to account for Diego's behavior or my ignorance. Not even Evie could find me. I didn't exist.

* * *

I woke up feeling tired. I'd tossed and turned all night, worrying about the photo array. I'd had more contact with the police these last few weeks than I had in my entire life, except for that time when I dated that cop right out of college. Oh, the things you can do with handcuffs...

I'd decided that today was the first day of the rest of my pregnancy. I signed up for emails that delivered week-by-week developments of my baby. My baby was now the size of a lime. Afterward, I went for a walk on the beach. If I didn't exercise, I was going to look like Jabba the Hut at the end of nine months. The baby, my ever-present companion, and I walked along the water's edge and enjoyed the solitude. It was late June and only a matter of time before the tourists became unwelcome fixtures on the boardwalk and beach. I walked to where the old Funhouse used to be and then turned around.

Back at home, I logged on to the neighbor's network so I could get online. It was beyond me that people kept their networks open without a password. I had Diego's wife's name, Estella Rivera. They were married six years ago. First, I went to Google images to see what she looked like. Hundreds of pictures came up. My phone rang, startling me. The caller id showed it was Justine.

"What's up?"

"Come have lunch with us. I played hooky from work, and Déjà's off today."

"Where are you guys?"

"Swifty's."

"I don't know. I have some stuff I need to do around the house..."

"Elle, what's going on with you? You've been back almost two weeks, and I haven't seen you. Every time I call, you say you're busy. I'm not taking no for an answer. You better be at Swifty's by one, or else we're coming to your place and kidnapping you."

"Have you and my parents been talking?"

"What?"

I sighed. "Never mind. I'll be there."

I got directions for Swifty's from the Internet, then put my laptop on sleep and swung my legs over the side of the bed. My belly was getting more pronounced. It was wider. I couldn't wait to feel the first kick; so far, all I'd felt was gas. I wondered about the little person who had taken up residence in my tummy. Would Diego be around when I had the baby? Was he going to be a part of our baby's life? Would we have to watch *America's Most Wanted* to catch updates on him? "Oh, look honey, he's been spotted in South America." Worrying about the unknown stressed me out more than anything else. I couldn't even think about giving birth (and the prospect of an episiotomy) without breaking out in hives.

I would be four months at my next appointment and could find out the sex of the baby. I'd also have to decide whether to do an amniocentesis to see if there were any problems because of my age. Although, after speaking with the nurse back in the ER, I was still leaning toward not getting one.

I took a quick shower. The hot water turned cold about two seconds after I got under it. The drive to Swifty's was a short one. I saw Déjà and Justine already seated outside.

When I got to the table, I was caught by surprise in a group hug.

"Where have you been?"

"Ohmygosh! You look huge!"

"Déjà!" Justine scolded as they released me, and we all sat down.

"What?"

"You don't look that big, honey. You look fine," Justine reassured me.

"I meant bigger than the last time I saw you," Déjà said with a smile.

It seemed like in no time at all, we had slipped into the roles we had back in high school. Justine and Déjà were chatting like it was circa 1990, ignoring that the better part of a decade or two stood between us and our glory days of high school. I suddenly realized I missed my girls. We were inseparable back then.

Justine was still tall and slender and always put together. She was often mistaken for the substitute teacher instead of a student when we were in school because of her no-nonsense attitude and laser-sharp focus. Even back then, she knew she wanted to be an actuary. Déjà was short and exploited her brick house with skimpy window dressing. Back in the day, we used to call her Opal from *All My Children* because they shared the same fashion sensibility. I noticed she had held onto her love of spandex. She had dyed her hair blond, and it was raging in an out-of-control Afro. I was the only one out of character.

We ordered our food, and the conversation circled lazily around the local goings-on. Good news traveled fast, but in small towns, scandal traveled even faster than the speed of light.

It was the type of day that seemed wasted on Mariner's Pike with its royal blue sky that looked hand-painted with a playful hot breeze that skipped across our table, tussling napkins in its wake. Our view consisted of empty storefronts and traffic. No delicious eye candy strolling by, only a few abandoned dogs scrounging around for scraps.

"A toast," Justine said as she raised her glass, "to friendship."

"To friendship," Déjà and I repeated, our words mixing with the melodic clink of champagne flutes tapping against one another.

"I'm glad you moved back home," Justine said before taking a sip of her mimosa.

"Yeah, welcome to the Baby Mama Drama Club," Déjà added as she turned up her glass.

"Speak for yourself. I'm *happily* married, and my kids are almost grown."

"Whatever. Then I guess it's just you and me holding it down in the drama department," Déjà said to me.

"You chasing after your babies' daddy is causing all the drama in your life. You guys break up to make up and forget to use any birth control."

Déjà shot Justine a nasty look before catching a passing waiter's eye and raised her glass to signal a refill. "Steve and I have our issues, but we are working them out; thank you very much."

"Working them out? You better be glad he dropped those charges for assaulting his girlfriend. You'd look like a pumpkin in one of those orange jumpsuits."

"Leave your earrings on the table and let's take it out back," Déjà teased.

I rubbed my stomach; it was itching like it was on fire. I was religiously spreading cocoa butter on my bulging belly, hoping it would scare away the stretch marks. It just made me itch even more. Justine and Déjà traded good-natured barbs. They were polar opposites. As much as Déjà was freewheeling and over the top in her emotions, Justine was a closed Ms. Manners. She and her husband lived an upper-middle-class life while Déjà struggled to maintain a toe-hold in the middle class as a single mom of three. I neutralized them and balanced them out. Or at least, I used to.

"The food's great here. How long has Swifty's been around?" My plate was spit-shine clean of an order of biscuits, grits, eggs, sausage, and bacon. I was contemplating adding another order of grits.

"Swifty's opened the year after we graduated from high school. What's that, seventeen years?" asked Justine.

"Damn, that's a long time ago," Déjà said as she took a sip of her drink. "That's about the last time you came back for a visit, right, Elle?"

"C'mon Déjà, you know Ms. Hot-Shot publicist to the stars doesn't have time for little nobodies like us," Justine said.

"You think she thinks she better than us?"

"Probably. You see how it took her a whole week to meet us for brunch."

"Stop it, you two. I haven't felt like going out. You know how it is," I protested, my voice trailing off. I tugged on my shirt, feeling self-conscious.

Justine squeezed my hand lightly. "You know we're here if you need us."

I leaned back, closed my eyes, and let the humid rays of the sun wash over my face. Already my hair was plastered to my head, and sweat had dissolved my makeup. It felt nice to sit outside and not worry about being photographed or watched. I felt relaxed until Déjà asked, "So why did you move back to this dump? What happened to your baby's daddy?"

Justine must have kicked Déjà because she gave a yelp and glared at her as Justine rushed to say I didn't have to answer and tried to steer the conversation elsewhere.

"Déjà, you've seen the news. Diego 'allegedly' stole some money, and he's wanted for questioning. I haven't heard from him." I put up air quotes with my index and middle fingers around "allegedly."

"Allegedly? Girl please, he ain't coming back. Is he going to kick you down a mil? I heard that he - OW! Heifer, if you kick me again, I will take you out back for reals."

"How are you managing?" Justine asked. "Do you need any help with anything?"

"Right now, I'm just trying to figure out how I wound up here. I had it all planned out, and this wasn't part of it. I thought I was doing everything right. Went to the right school. Got the right job. Thought I met the right guy."

"You did everything right but a background check. That probably would have told you right there something was up with him."

"We're sorry. I know it's probably the last thing you want to talk about," Justine said as she shot a look at Déjà.

"You know I love you guys. I'm sorry I haven't been in touch, just trying to figure it all out."

"We've all made mistakes. Just give your baby all the love you can," Justine said.

"Oh please, why don't you get her a Hallmark card? They have sappier sayings," Déjà said. "This is what you do - I don't care where he's hiding - if he's in the mountains, you hire a Sherpa. Or if he's in the desert, you get a guide and a camel. Track his ass down and make his ass pay."

"And how do you spell Déjà? T-R-O - temporary restraining order," Justine said.

I laughed for the first time in a long time. It was nice things hadn't changed, although that would be impossible, wouldn't it? We'd all gone off, grew up, and made our lives, yet it was so easy to slip into the roles we were assigned long ago. Playing a "type" was much better than facing our real selves. At least it was for me. We went our separate ways afterward.

I sat in the car long after they were gone. I wanted to head over to the police station about as much as I wanted to get maternity clothes from Target, which I would have to since I had outgrown my wardrobe.

The drive to the police station was a short one. Everything was two giant steps apart in Mariner's Pike. It was considered rush hour if there were more than three cars waiting at a traffic light. The squat brick building next to the high school hadn't changed much since I was a kid.

I waited in the lobby for Detective Moran. I was surprised to see a youngish guy loping in my direction. All teeth with a goofy smile, Detective Moran escorted me to a room in the back. It was small with a table and two chairs. No two-way mirror, though. He seemed more suited for hospitality; I could easily see him in Bermuda shorts on a cruise ship telling the seniors all about shuffleboard.

"Thank you for coming in, Ms. Nixon," he said as he pumped my hand vigorously.

I winced slightly. My other shoulder was still tender from the gun battle, and sudden movements would cause spikes of pain to erupt.

"I'm not sure what help I can be. I told everything to the detectives in LA when I saw them at the hospital. And everything happened so fast," I closed my eyes. I could hear the shots being fired and the shattering of glass. Moran's warm pat on the hand startled me.

"I know. It was pretty traumatic, from what I was told. Usually, the best statements come from witnesses right after the crime because everything is still fresh in their memory. So, it may be a long shot, but I have a photo array that the LAPD sent, and hopefully, our perp will be in it. Just take your time, no pressure."

His voice was so soothing; he made me want to pour my guts out to him. I wondered if he did any therapy on the side.

He spread out a six-pack photo array—two rows of three mug shots. Glares, dead eyes, and empty gazes peered back at me as I went through each row. None seemed familiar.

I pushed the photos away from me. "I'm sorry, all I saw was a gun, and then we ducked."

"Would you mind telling me what happened?"

"I just did."

He smiled patiently. "I know, but if you could start from the beginning, and take your time. Sometimes the biggest clues are in the smallest of details."

He had such a kind face, so earnest with large puppy dog brown eyes. I took a deep breath and steadied my voice. "We were at the club when I saw Cameron. I needed to talk to him, and he didn't want to do it inside the club, so I followed him to his car. He was fidgety, checking the radio station and looking at the rearview mirror. He made me nervous. I remember turning my head, and I saw a truck, like a large SUV, approaching. It was dark outside, and the truck was dark, like black or a dark blue. An Escalade, I think. It was big, but not as big as the Hummer we were in."

"You saw the truck approaching. Could you tell if it had been parked somewhere?"

"No. The headlights were off; I think they came on just as he pulled up next to us. As the driver's side window rolled down, a gun was pointed at us, and I saw," a memory teased me. A flash of silver. I closed my eyes to hold on to it. "A smile. The driver had a full platinum grill. I totally forgot that. How could I forget that?" I opened my eyes. "But when he smiled, I saw platinum on his upper teeth, and some type of diamond was in one."

Moran smiled. "Do you think maybe you could sketch out what tooth the diamond was on?"

"Sure, I guess. I mean, I can try. I took a couple of art classes in college, purely electives. I'm no Frida Kahlo, but I exhibited one of my pieces on campus."

"I'm sure whatever you do will be fine."

He tore off a sheet of paper from his notebook and slid it across the table with a pen.

I closed my eyes and returned to that night, trying to see the smile in the dark, the way the streetlight bounced off his teeth. I've always had a memory for faces and killer smiles. I finished and slid the paper back to him.

"That's great. I'll pass this along to LAPD."

"I hope it helps. What do you guys think happened? Are there any other witnesses?"

"None that will come forward. From my understanding, your friend, Mr. Cain, isn't talking to the police, only through his lawyer. He hasn't been that helpful at all."

"He's no friend of mine."

Moran raised an eyebrow slightly but didn't push. "Well, it's going to be difficult to solve this case unless someone talks, but your sketch may be the thing that breaks it wide open."

"Do you think it's random? The shooting, I mean."

"I've never been to California, but from what I've been told, random drive-bys are very rare in West Hollywood."

"True. Do the police think maybe it has something to do with Diego, and um, what's going on with him?"

"No. I think they're looking at Mr. Cain as the intended victim."

I exhaled hard. "What?" It felt like the giant target on my back loosened a little.

"I don't have any details, but it is one theory they're looking into."

"Well, will you keep me posted? Let me know if they catch the guy?"

"If anything happens, I'm sure LAPD will contact you. They'll need you to come back and testify."

Great, one more thing to add to my bucket list: testify as a witness for the prosecution at an attempted murder trial. Goes right up there with dating a married fugitive and having a baby with him. I was on a roll.

seventeen

IN THE MIDDLE of the night, I awoke with a start. I thought I heard a noise. My shoulder throbbed. Stupid Tylenol. It took away the physical pain for the most part, but did nothing for the loud voices in my head. I got up and did a check of all the locks and windows. My heart slowed down once I made sure everything was secure. I hated feeling this way, but until they caught the shooter, I didn't want to find out that I was the real target after the fact.

I passed Evie's room, now the office my parents shared. I paused at the doorway. Instead of the desks and chairs, I saw how it used to look, as a mirror image of my room, posters wallpapering the wall, and shoes, clothes, and purses competing for floor space. I went from being the baby sister to an only child in what seemed like the blink of an eye. I don't think I'd ever loved as fiercely or fought as fiercely with anyone other than Evie. A part of me still ached from her absence.

Trying to fall back asleep was futile. I opened my laptop and continued my quest for Estella. I searched property records in Los Angeles and found none. Then I searched in Miami and found seven. None of them matched the two addresses I had for Diego. I copied them and booked a flight to Miami, departing in three weeks. Gone was the expense account when I could leave at the drop of a hat, and cost didn't factor into the equation.

It was crazy and irrational to spend money looking for my boyfriend's wife, but so far, the ring was a dead-end, and trying to find the lock that fit the key was next to impossible. It sounded even crazier when I said it aloud in my childhood bedroom. I had no clue what I would do if I found her. Big if. Or even why I felt like I had to find her. I had no idea what she looked like or if she would even admit to being married to Diego. All things considered. I just knew that with so many gaping holes in this puzzle, which oddly resembled my life, I needed to plug in answers whenever and wherever I could. I had no luck finding anything on Eugene Daly, no surprise there since I didn't know where he was born or his actual birthday. So I researched Diego Rivera. He had died in a car accident while away at college. I found his older sister's name in an article about his death, Constance Rivera of Trenton, NJ, about an hour and a half south of Mariner's Pike. I sent her an email asking if she would meet with me. Long shot, I knew.

I was on the phone with the registrar's office at Harvard as soon as they opened to find out if my Diego really graduated from there, as he claimed. He had the whole Harvard get up. He had proudly displayed his MBA on the wall and often wore a Harvard hoodie or cap. My heart ballooned in my chest and threatened to deflate, leaving me breathless when she said no such student had graduated from Harvard during the year I had specified. I couldn't help but wonder, how far did his scam go?

The house was still quiet when I left for my usual walk along the beach. A few tourists had already staked their claim in the sand and were preparing for their daily bake. For the most part though, I still had the beach to myself. Walking along the water's edge, I let the ocean play hide and seek with my feet. What did I do to deserve this? Everyone in the northern hemisphere knew I was pregnant. Diego must know as well. Why hadn't he called?

Yesterday was the annual sandcastle-building contest. There

were castles, mermaids, and all sorts of creations dotting the shoreline. Before I could think, I took my foot and swung it, demolishing a turret on impact. And it felt so good. I kicked the other half and stomped on it for good measure.

"Ha! Hope you had insurance for the unexpected pitfalls in life," I said to the non-existent royal inhabitants of the castle.

I needed him. I wanted to enjoy my pregnancy and worry about stretch marks and heartburn, not if I would be indicted for conspiracy after the fact or something crazy. I didn't want to ache for Diego while simultaneously hating him for not being here. For running away. For making me much stronger than I ever wanted to be. I just wanted things to go back... maybe. Ignorance wasn't bliss. It was the seventh level of hell once the wake-up call arrived.

"Arrrgggghhhhh! Why are you doing this to me?" I stomped on another castle, feeling the cool sand crumble beneath my toes. I was Hurricane Elle.

"What are you doing?"

Lucas's voice snatched me out of my thoughts like a splash of cold water. He appeared before me wearing a white t-shirt and black warm-ups. He jogged in place as he talked to keep his heart rate up.

Ankle deep in the remnants of some kid's hard work, I smoothed my hair down and said, "Nothing. Just out for a stroll. What are you doing out here so early?"

"I always come out here to run in the morning before it's taken over by kids and sunbathers, and I thought I saw you doing some type of dance or something. You working out?"

"Yes, my prenatal exercise routine." I kicked the sand for show.

"You look upset. You want to talk about it?"

"No. Not really."

He pulled a white towel hanging out of his back pocket and used it to dab his face.

"Ok, see you around."

He continued jogging. I watched him for a moment, his figure getting smaller and smaller before I headed home.

* * *

"Oww! Not so hard!"

"You got all tender-headed when you moved to L.A." Déjà said. "You should be happy that I'm scratching up my fingers in this tangled nest of yours. You shoulda let me put a relaxer in."

"No thanks. Last time the hair on my sides fell out for how long?"

"Girl, please. That's ancient history, and I've gotten better, alright?"

I cut my eyes in the direction of her 'fro and asked, "Who can tell?"

A big screen television dominated the small room and was blaring while her three kids, ages 2, 5, and 6, were running wild in a free-for-all. I was sitting on the floor in her living room as she sat on the couch; she was parting my hair to put it in cornrows. It was mutually decided that I had been rocking the gel-slicked edges and ponytail for too long.

"You should just cut it all off and go natural. You have the perfectly shaped face for it."

"Really? You think so?" The changes to my body spawned insecurity about my appearance. I devoured the compliment whole. I didn't feel April fresh with a glow. I felt October musty, with perpetual armpit stains from sweating all the time. I was always hot and hungry. The only good thing was that the humidity kept my thighs from chafing. Everyone always said the second trimester was the best because the morning sickness went away, and you got your energy back. LIARS.

"Girl, nothing you can do with long hair but wear it long. Let me cut this mess for you. You'll look too cute. Steve Jr.! Jolie and Tyra! Sit your butts down and act like y'all got some sense. Go on in your room or something with all that noise."

"But mamma!" Steve Jr. whined.

"I don't want to hear it. Go!"

The three slunk off into their room, looking like wounded

150

puppies. A few moments later, they were shouting and laughing even louder than before.

"Oww! Take it easy." My neck was hurting from keeping it bent as she combed through it. I was tired of looking at Déjà's beat-up pedicure and well-worn carpet. "Ok, fine, cut it off. But first, I have to pee."

"Again?"

"You want me to hold it and get a urinary tract infection? You want to put my baby's health in danger just because you're in a hurry?"

"Shut up and get your big behind into the bathroom." A flying brush sailed past me as I stepped over, coloring books, dolls, and trucks scattered haphazardly on the floor. Déjà's tiny two-bedroom house reminded me of an overstuffed couch. Oversized furniture sucked the space out of every room while knick-knacks, toys, and plain old stuff competed for floor space. The super sweet scent of incense and crushed cookies filled the air. Even in the bathroom, I felt claustrophobic with all the hanging plants and shelves brimming with beauty products, toilet tissue, and magazines. I barely had any room to turn around.

"Elle! Cameron's on the phone!" Déjà yelled from the living room.

"What?" I opened the door, and she was standing there with my cell in hand.

"It was ringing, so I answered it."

I took the phone from her and closed the door in her face when it became apparent she wasn't going anywhere.

I perched on the edge of the bathtub. "Hello?"

"Yo Elle, how you feelin' kid?"

"Been better. How are you doing?"

"Yo, I had to raise up out of there. I ain't letting nobody come back and finish the job. Took a hit to the shoulder, and another one hit me in the chest. Thought I was gonna die up in that piece."

We were silent. It was ironic how the only person in the world who could probably understand part of what he was feeling was me. The nightmares, being jumpy every time a car backfired, wondering, "Why was I spared?"

"I'm going to be at the Hudson in New York. Come up and see me next week. I want to talk to you. It's important. Don't tell anyone, though."

"You know I wouldn't leak those tracks, right? That's my reputation, and I have nothing to gain by doing that."

"Next week, we'll talk," and then he was gone.

Déjà practically fell in the bathroom when I swung the door open.

"That was Cameron for real? His voice is sexy! Is he tall in person? I heard he checked out the hospital the day after he got shot. Is he ok? What was he calling you for? Is he your baby's daddy?"

"Déjà! Enough with the 20 questions. No. He's not the father. And even if he were, I wouldn't tell you. Whole damn town would know before I even left your house."

Déjà pointed me to a chair in the kitchen as she pulled out a pair of clippers and scissors from a drawer in the bathroom, complaining the whole time.

"You changed, Elle. We used to be girls; we were tight and could share everything. Now, you act like you don't want to be around nobody. You want to be all snooty. We never see you..."

"Did you just call me snooty?"

She laughed.

"What kind of word is that? Yeah, I've changed, but so have you. It's called life." Déjà raised the scissors, and I asked, "Are you sure you know what you're doing?"

"Yes, of course, I cut little Steve's hair all the time. You'll be fine."

Her hands moved quickly, and my shoulder-length hair drifted to the floor. A part of me started having second thoughts as I watched it pile up.

"Look. Of course, I've changed. We're not kids anymore. Doesn't mean I don't still love you guys. Things are just different. That's what people do. They go away. They experience new things, you know?"

"No. I don't."

She turned on the clippers and trimmed the back and sides of my hair so it was close to my scalp. A loud crash sounded from the bedroom, and I felt Déjà's hand jerk across my head.

"Damn," she said under her breath.

"What?"

"Huh? Nothing, just wondering what the kids got into now."

I grabbed a mirror, and I thought I was going to cry.

"You shaved off half my hair!"

Déjà stood back and viewed me from a frame made of her two thumbs touching and her index fingers pointing in the air.

"Maybe it's just a little crooked. I can even it out."

She turned on the clippers, and more tufts of hair drifted in front of me. She handed me a mirror and walked out of the kitchen.

"You shaved off all my hair!"

"Honey, you look like a million bucks. You have the type of face that can wear any style," she yelled from down the hall.

"Then why did you give me a new one? I could have kept the one I came here with."

"It's only hair. You act like it's not going to grow back."

"Who has to walk around looking crazy until it does?"

"You look fine. Steve's coming by to pick the kids up for the weekend," she said as she put their overnight bags by the door.

The doorbell rang just as she finished. Steve Jr. raced to the door with Tyra and Jolie following. It was a flurry of limbs as three pairs of arms and legs wrapped themselves around any available body part. The kids kept up a chorus of "Daddy! Daddy!" as Steve made his way in.

I'd never met Steve; he didn't go to high school with us. He wasn't bad looking, although he had skinny legs, lost in those over-sized shorts that looked like big gauchos on men. Mauchos. Not a good look if my forearm was bigger than his leg. Déjà was just a vessel because the kids were carbon copies of him; paternity would never be an issue.

"This is my girl from high school, Elle. You may have seen her on TV; she was in the car when-"

"Déjà!" I gave her the side eye. "Hi Steve, nice to meet you."

"Nice to meet you," he said as he stuck his hand out to shake mine. He had a firm grip and an easy smile. Watching Déjà watch him, I knew she wasn't over him.

"Doesn't her hair look cute? I just cut it."

Steve Jr. came up to me and gave me a hug. "She cut my hair the night before the first day of school last year. Worst first day of my life. It'll grow back; it just takes a long, long time."

"It looks ahhh, it's um, nice. It brings out your eyes," Steve Sr. said.

I went to the mirror over the hall table and gazed at my shorn and still uneven hair. I was almost bald.

"You busy on Sunday? Think your mom will watch the kids?" he asked as he moved to the door. Jolie and Tyra were still holding onto his legs and were giggling up a storm.

"Nah, after what they did the last time, my mom said I had to find someone else from now on."

"Oh yeah, do you think your girl will watch them?"

"What girl?"

He looked at me and said, "Her, Elle."

I was still wondering, what was it they could have done to make their own grandmother ban them from the house?

"Would you, Elle?"

"Sure, I guess. I mean, if you really—"

She squealed, "Thank you!" and turning to him, demanded, "So what's up? Where are we going?"

"Out to dinner if that's ok with you."

After he left and for the rest of the night, Déjà speculated about what he could want to talk about. She grabbed my hands and squeezed them. Her eyes rippled like dark pools of hope, her face was stripped of its usual wisecracking veneer, and a childlike vulnerability was in its place. "I think this is it. Me and Steve been through so much, you know, but I think he's ready to settle down and be with the kids and me."

Justine texted me, and I told her to stop by Déjà's and hang out with us for a while. While waiting for her, Déjà made the pitch for me to work in her kids' clothing and accessories consignment shop. She opened it a little over a year ago, just outside of Mariner's Pike. Business was picking up, and she needed an extra set of hands. I told her I'd think about it, like I had other offers on the table. Justine showed up bearing a bottle of sparkling apple cider. She paused at the threshold of the door.

"Where's the assault from your little ones?" she asked.

"Steve came and got them. He gets them every other Thursday through Sunday, and..." she paused dramatically, "he invited me to dinner on Sunday night. Elle's going to watch the kids."

"That's nice! Whoa! What happened to your hair?"

"Déjà cut it for me. What do you think?"

"Oh, well, um, what do *you* think about it? That's what's important."

"You hate it? Do I look bad?"

"No, no, you look wonderful. It's just drastic, is all. You look great in any style. It's just that, um..."

"What?"

"Don't start nothing Justine; you know her hair looks fine."

"Listen, all I'm going to say is be careful of making certain decisions when you're pregnant. When I was pregnant with my youngest, I let my hairdresser talk me into getting finger waves. You know that was barely hanging on in popularity when Salt n' Pepa wore that style back in the 80s, so you know I looked crazy. But wearing your hair natural looks good on you."

I ran my fingers through what was left of my hair; it felt soft and fuzzy. "It'll just take a little getting used to, I guess."

"It's fine. Let me shape it up for you and even it out. And you'll probably need some help. I'll come over on Sunday and help you out with the kids. They can be a handful," Justine said, quickly changing the subject as we walked into the kitchen.

"Leave my babies alone. They're just rambunctious like all kids."

Déjà disappeared into her bedroom for a moment.

"Rambunctious, my big toe. Her kids are like *Bebe's Kids*, only wilder."

Déjà returned with our yearbook.

We spent the rest of the night laughing at the photos. Déjà and Justine gave me updates on our former classmates. I told them I saw Lucas in the parking lot at the grocery store.

"I haven't seen Lucas in ages," Déjà said.

"Me either. What's he been up to?"

"Oh. He said someone told him I was back in town. I just knew it was you Déjà, seeing as how keeping secrets isn't one of your strong points."

"Wasn't me. I thought he lived in DC or Virginia or something," Déjà said.

"People always move back for one reason or another," added Justine.

Disassembled lives packed up and returned home, I couldn't help but think. I couldn't wallow too long because we fell headfirst into a pool of warm memories punctuated with howling laughter. My role back then? I was the one who always wanted to leave. I wanted to be anywhere but there because everywhere else seemed more exciting than Mariner's Pike. In the yearbook, the caption under one of my pictures was "the one who got away..." Mike Nealy was looking at me with love-struck eyes, and I had a disinterested look on my face. I knew I wasn't going to get trapped into a dead-end relationship with a small-town boy, not when the big city was beckoning.

Pointing at Mike, I asked, "Whatever happened to him?"

"Oh Mike? He's like some big millionaire living in Rumson. He sold some internet company or something."

"Wasn't it Twitter?" Déjà asked.

I almost spit out my cider.

"No silly. I forget the name, but he was looking good at the reunion a few years ago."

Justine walked me to my car after we polished off leftover ziti and apple cider.

"What do you think Steve wants to talk to Déjà about?"

"Who knows with those two? Could be anything. I just don't want to see her get hurt."

"They sound more on again/off again than a stripper's clothes. I hope it works out for her." I grabbed her hands. "Thanks for offering to help me out on Sunday. I don't know the first thing about kids except they're small and loud."

"You've been around kids before... right?"

"Yeah, like passing them by on the street or in a store. None of my friends in LA have kids, and I just don't come into contact with them. Thank goodness for age limits at the club," I joked, although, on the inside, I was kicking myself.

Justine shook her head. "Déjà's kids will wear you out. But don't worry; if you can survive them, everything else will be a cakewalk. Before I forget, Theo and I are having a cookout for the fourth of July. Come over, okay?"

I promised I would. Justine seemed like she was in the throes of stable adulthood. The husband. A house in the suburbs. The kids. It made me miss my old life. My mind was an empty shoebox when trying to think about my new life with the baby. Alone.

eighteen

DÉJÀ WAS PRACTICALLY GLOWING as she sprayed on some perfume. I had been watching her prepare for her big date for the past hour. Instead of her usual spandex-themed ensemble, tonight she wore a simple black dress with a pair of pumps.

"You look beautiful."

"I still don't know what he wants to talk about. I'm hoping he'll want to move back in. Maybe we can get a bigger place together. Sucks to try to sell this place in this market right now, but-"

"Girl, slow down! Get through dinner before you start planning the rest of your lives together."

She squeezed my hands, and I gave her a hug just as the doorbell rang. A nervous Steve fidgeted on the doorstep. The kids gave him a lukewarm, just-been-dropped-off-this-morning reception. Only Tyra, the youngest, barreled into his legs as though she hadn't seen him for months. He had traded his Mauchos for more age-appropriate khakis and a white shirt. He whisked Déjà away in a matter of moments, and three sets of eyes turned to me in their absence.

"I'm hungry!" wailed Tyra while Jolie and Steve Jr. engaged in a shoving match.

"Didn't your mom just make you something to eat?"

"I want cereal!"

"Me too!" Steve Jr. and Jolie said, momentarily forgetting their beef.

"Alright. Let's go to the kitchen. Where does your mom keep her menus?"

"Menus for what?" asked Steve Jr.

"To order out? How else do you guys eat?"

"Mommy says there's a baby in your tummy," Jolie said as she grabbed my hand.

"Yes, there is," I answered, tussling her little Afro puffs.

"How did it get there?"

"Um, hold that thought."

I went into the living room to call Justine; she needed to get over here *now*.

"I'll be there soon if I don't maim Amara first," Justine said from her cell.

"Hurry up, they want to eat, and they're asking questions. What am I supposed to do?"

I found a bag of chips and sent them into the room with it and a remote control for the TV. Five-year-old Jolie dragged out a Barbie Glam vacation house (or so she said) to the middle of the room and said, "Will you play with me?"

I lowered myself to the floor, and she handed me a Barbie doll with chopped-off hair.

"Here, you can be her. That's Venetasiatic."

"Thanks. I'm going to call her V for short."

Jolie plopped on her stomach and started undressing another doll.

"Why do you think there's a toilet in the bathroom? It's not like she's going to use it during one of my games. That's just weird."

"Well, suppose V caves into peer pressure and goes out on a night of binge drinking, and the next morning she has the worst headache. She's got to puke somewhere."

The doorbell rang, saving me from further explanation. So much for my teachable moment. Justine had arrived and brought along her 12-year-old, who played with the kids in the back room while we talked. I overheard Jolie asking Amara, "What's binge drinking?" as they walked into Déjà's room.

Justine left around nine after the kids were in bed. Of course, she neglected to tell me they wouldn't stay in bed. Five trips to the bathroom, three requests for water, and a steady chorus of "but I'm not tired" almost sent me to the closet to hide.

"Ok, rug rats, we're going to have a fashion show."

Steve Jr. was less than enthused in the beginning but warmed up to the idea when I told him he could be the host. I let him pick out runway music while I helped the girls get ready. Much to their delight, I painted their nails and added a little lip-gloss to their lips. We ransacked Déjà's closet for clothes.

Steve Jr. announced the girls and turned up the music as they sashayed down the pseudo runway, which was basically a bunch of pillows on the floor.

At the end, around eleven, we collapsed in Déjà's bed. I read them books until they fell asleep. Two-year-old Tyra was the last holdout, big brown eyes drooping but refusing to shut.

Looking at their freshly scrubbed faces, wearing an innocent countenance, I felt... less scared. I had to disentangle myself from their tiny arms and legs to get out of bed and wait for Déjà in the living room.

It was almost 2 a.m. when I heard the key in the door. After a few minutes, when Déjà didn't walk in, I got up to investigate. I found her sitting on the front stoop with the keys still in the front door. I sat down beside her. She was hunched over and looking off into the distance.

"I'm tired, Elle."

"Me too. Your kids did not want to go to sleep."

"No. I'm tired. I feel like I've lived at least a hundred lives and ain't none of 'em been kind."

"Girl, we all have our hard days. My stretch marks have stretch marks. I'm going to look like a damn zebra when this is all over."

Déjà shook her head. "At least you got out. You've been somewhere. You've been somebody."

"Are you calling me a has-been?"

"No, I mean, you've seen and done shit I wouldn't even know to dream about. This is just a setback for you." She waved her hand around. "This shit here, this is my life. Every day. So what, you fucking slipped down a few rungs on the ladder of success. At least you know you'll be back out there."

"Déjà, don't talk like this. What happened?"

She laughed, a small tight laugh that seemed to spiral downward and disappear. "I was listening to Sade talking about how she wouldn't want to go to heaven if he were hers. I feel that way about Steve. And some days shit is just so fucking hard, and I would give anything, not to be here, not to be me. Can you believe that? I'd give up heaven for a man and would waltz into hell and not be here for my babies."

I grabbed her hand and held it. I didn't have any words, didn't know what type of spin to put on it. Even as we sat side by side, I could feel her drifting away from me. When she turned to look at me, her eyes were so empty that they made her face unrecognizable.

"I gave him everything. We have three babies together. And still, he goes back to that bitch."

I breathed a sigh of relief. We were back in familiar territory—trifling asses. I could list a litany of reasons why Steve was a loser and no good for her until the sun came up four days in a row.

"Forget him Déjà. He doesn't deserve you."

"He makes me feel like I don't deserve him."

"Rule number one, don't ever believe that how a man makes you feel when he's screwing you is how he feels about you. He's the one who cheats and doesn't treat you right. We all get caught up." I couldn't help thinking about my trip to Paris and how that seemed like some made-up fantasy.

"But I love him."

"I love Diego. And look where we are now. I'm 35, pregnant, and living with my parents. Love isn't supposed to hurt like this. Not when it's right."

"But it's all I have."

"No, it's not! You have me. Your family. Your kids. And one day, you're going to find that man who believes you're special, and he will treat you like a queen, not like a seat filler."

"You saw that episode on Oprah too?"

"Yeah, but I think it could really happen. Maybe."

I let the silence build between us as I scratched my stomach with my nails bitten to the quick. Who was I to counsel anyone on the ways of love? I realized I knew absolutely nothing about love. Déjà leaned forward with her elbows on her knees and waited like Steve would come and undo whatever foulness he had dumped on her.

Finally, she exhaled and said, "I thought he would propose to me tonight."

I leaned over and squeezed her shoulder. "I'm sorry."

"He took me out to the Outback, and I'm sitting there all nervous because I know he wants to say something. I can't even eat. We're making this stupid small talk, not even fighting like we usually do. It's different. It's nice. About mid-way through dinner, he clears his throat, and I'm like, 'oh my God, this is it.' He tells me that Jackie's pregnant, and he's going to marry her because he wants to do the right thing. What happened to doing the right thing three kids ago with me? Now it fucking looks bad?"

Déjà sat there, so quiet and so still, I realized I'd been holding my breath. When she started talking again, her voice was so low that I wasn't even sure she was speaking to me.

"He should be marrying me," her breath hitched in her throat before she could go on. "I have his babies. I love him more than anyone else will ever love him. He went on about some bullshit about Jackie being great with the kids and him wanting more time with the kids. It was all 'Jackie thought this' and 'Jackie thought that,' I could see what was happening. It was like they were just cutting me out of the picture, like I didn't exist anymore. She was taking our family. Those are my kids. He was my man. I just want to be with him, to be like it was. I just want him to love me back. What's so wrong with me that he won't stay?"

The red and blue swirl of police lights washed over our faces as two police cruisers slowly pulled in front of the house.

"Oh, come on, don't tell me they're here for us? Were we disturbing the peace?" I turned to ask Déjà. She looked at me with a broken smile as she smoothed down her hair. Then she stood up with her hands in the air. I watched in horror as the police approached us.

"What's going on? Déjà, what the hell did you do?"

I watched a police officer turn Déjà around to handcuff her. The light from the house illuminated deep dark splotches splattered across her dress like a Pucci print. I tried to push myself off the stoop as they read Déjà her rights. My knees became flimsy pieces of pipe cleaner, and I had to sit back down.

Before they pushed her head down so she could get in the back seat of the car, she turned to look at me. "Take my kids to my mom's. Make sure they're alright."

nineteen

I CAME HOME with the sun. My dad was sitting in the living room watching the morning news when I opened the door. The newspaper was splayed across the kitchen table in front of him. A few new worry lines seemed to snake their way across his forehead.

"Where have you been? Not right for you in your condition to be out all night," he saw my face and stopped. "What happened?"

My back was hurting, my feet were swollen, and it felt like a long walk from the front door to the couch. I immediately sunk down and closed my eyes for the first time.

"Déjà was arrested for vandalism and some other stuff. She trashed Steve's car." That was an understatement, but I couldn't even begin to get into the details. It was the Fourth of July, so she would have to spend the night in jail.

I only had time for a quick catnap. I had promised Justine that I would come by for her cook-out.

* * *

Justine and Theo had purchased a home in nearby Glenwood, an upscale suburb with a gated community. I could hear the music as I approached the backyard. Slow jazz. Typical. The men, mostly husbands, had self-segregated to one side where they talked about cars? Sports? The women dominated the large table. A few new boyfriends were at the table, probably hoping to make a good impression. They looked longingly at their more experienced comrades.

I didn't recognize many of the faces, which was just as good. I was tired of strolling down memory lane. I wanted to be incognito and just sit in a corner with a plate of barbecue ribs and some mac and cheese, and just eat like a feral child. The tofu buffet at our house was getting old quickly. Unfortunately, Justine intercepted me and steered me to the table, and introduced me to everyone. Most of the guests were co-workers. Theo, short and bespectacled, came over and hugged me before he went back to handle the grill.

Her daughters, Lena, 15, and Amara, appeared briefly before disappearing inside. Everything seemed so... normal. The bourgeois dream. Justine snaked her arm around Theo's waist as she whispered in his ear. They shared a private joke. They seemed perfect together. He was laid back and countered her take-charge personality.

In the kitchen, I told her about Déjà's escapades. She just shook her head. "Déjà just can't let Steve go. I don't know what to do with her."

"You sound just like my mom. There's nothing for you to do. Sometimes you just have to let things run their course."

I drifted back outside and found myself sitting next to two co-workers in a heated conversation.

"Girl, when I saw on the news that he was a brother, I was like, WHY?"

"I know, I do financial planning, and it's hard enough to get clients to trust me, and then he does something like this..."

I glanced up from my plate of potato salad and grilled chicken. The two were well dressed, conservatively so in long flowery skirts, prim button-down blouses, and flat sandals. One bucked the trend by wearing large hoop earrings.

"He gets to that type of position of power and then screws it up for the rest of us." She punctuated the end of the sentence by waving her short, manicured nails to encompass the whole backyard as if Diego—who else could they be talking about—had some type of personal responsibility to every person there.

"And what about that girlfriend that claims she knew nothing about what he was doing?"

A lump of potato salad caught in my throat. I had to cough to get it out. They both glanced my way.

"I know; how dumb do you have to be? I'm so tired of these women covering for their men. I mean, who's that desperate?"

It only took a second for the shock to wear off before I responded. "Wait a minute, who are you to call someone 'dumb'? You don't know their situation. She's not a financial anything. What is she supposed to do, audit his books every night?"

Justine appeared out of nowhere and said, "Hey, can I see you in the kitchen?" as she touched my elbow lightly and guided me inside. I'm pretty sure puffs of smoke were billowing from my ears as we passed a few couples on the couch in the living room.

"Did you hear them?" I asked as soon as we were alone.

"They didn't mean anything by it. You know how people always have an opinion on something."

Theo poked his head in the doorway, "Hey hon, do you-"

"Not now, Theo," Justine said. He ducked back out.

"Ok, but we're not talking about some random topic like when is it ok to wear white after Labor Day. This is my life. Were you going to step in and say something?"

"And say what?"

"I don't know. How about 'shut the fuck up because that's my friend you're trashing, and she's sitting right next to you?'"

"You want me to cause a scene in front of my co-workers? Over an *off-hand comment?* They'll probably be talking about whether Nicki Minaj's ass is real or if Charlie Sheen is bi-winning or just plain crazy. It's just... idle gossip."

I let out a deep breath that had been pent up for too long. I stared out the kitchen window into the backyard as people laughed and ate. A few brave souls were dancing and trying to pull their reluctant partners up. It felt like the sum of my entire experience had been reduced to a little blip of idle gossip. I could be picked apart and tossed aside. They didn't know me. They didn't know us. The irony wasn't lost on me that I traded in gossip for a living, sharing tantalizing tidbits with editors to curry favor for my acts. I never felt bad. This is what celebrities signed up for. Fame and fortune went hand in hand with scandal and condemnation. But I didn't sign up for this. Infamy was a lot less fun than fame, especially when it was pro bono. I swallowed a lump.

"Do you think I should have known? Or that I was in on it?"

"Of course not! How could you even ask me that?"

There was a nanosecond of hesitation in Justine's answer. I heard it. I knew. Even she wondered, how could I not know?

"But?"

"You can't keep running from this. You have to let him go and move on. You're going to be a mom, and Diego's chosen his path."

"Running? What are you talking about?" I spun around her immaculate kitchen, waving my hands to encompass the high-end stainless steel appliances, Betty Crocker-ish breakfast nook, and the overall domestic bliss that radiated from the goofy his and hers aprons they were wearing. "You're married to Mr. Domesticated over there flipping burgers with your 2.5 kids." As if on cue, their golden retriever, Goldie, trotted into the kitchen. "Not everybody is as lucky to have love come in such a neat package. Sometimes it's fucked up and ugly, and it breaks your heart into a million different pieces. I love Diego and I'm pregnant with his child. Those feelings just don't disappear overnight just because..." Because he lied, cheated, was married to someone else, and stole millions of dollars.

"Elle, just -"

"Forget it. I'm going to go because I don't want to cause a scene and ruin your perfect little party."

I drove home, turned off the engine, and sat in the car. My parents had gone up north to have dinner with college friends in town. I didn't want to go into an empty house with nothing but vegan leftovers, so I walked over to the beach. I put my feet up on the railing and watched as kids dug for seashells and played in the water. Their shrieks and whoops filled the air. Suddenly, a soft-serve vanilla ice cream cone appeared in front of me.

"You look like you could really use this," said Lucas as he sat down next to me.

"What are you, a beach bum? You're always here."

"I could say the same about you."

"Touché."

"You're sitting in the best seat in the house for fireworks. It's also my favorite place to come when I need to think."

"Or after a jog?"

We ate our ice cream in silence. It was just what I needed.

"What has you out here looking all surly?"

"Ha! Surly. It's stupid. I said some things I probably shouldn't have said to Justine."

"You and Justine have been road dogs ever since I can remember. You guys will get over it."

"I guess. Enough about me and my sorry problems. What about you? How come you're always trolling around at the beach? Don't you have a girlfriend?" I teased.

We spent the next hour trading first-date war stories, and I think he had me beat. I laughed so hard at one point that my ice cream nearly came through my nose.

"Maybe you shouldn't try online dating anymore," I said after I was able to control myself.

"You're probably right, but I'm a glutton for punishment."

Darkness was staining the sky, and the beachcombers had long ago packed up, making way for those coming to see the Fourth of July fireworks. We watched in silence as brilliant blues, reds, and sparkles lit up the sky in a display of patriotic pride. Bittersweet memories paraded by of long-ago summers when we would come out as a family to watch.

"I should probably go. Thanks for the ice cream and conversation," I said when it was over.

"Anytime."

Lucas walked me back to my parents' house. He stopped at the foot of the stairs and watched as I let myself in. I waved to him before I closed the door.

* * *

Even though my baby was only the size of an avocado, I felt like I was carrying a belly full of baseballs. It was hot and humid, par the course for East Coast summers, and I was drowning in pools of sweat from sun up to sundown. At least the warrior's grip of nausea was easing up some. I was feeling butterfly flutters in my tummy, and it wasn't gas. It was actually the baby moving! It underscored the fact that soon something with eyes and a tongue would emerge from my body.

The waiting room wasn't that crowded. Only one other mother-to-be was there when I signed in. It was my first visit with Dr. Afton, and I couldn't stop my foot from tapping against the leg of the chair. Déjà had recommended Dr. Afton, swore by him. He had delivered all three of her kids. I knew from my pregnancy update emails I could find out the sex of the baby during this visit.

After I did a weigh-in, blood pressure, and limited chit-chat with the nurse, Dr. Afton finally entered. He was a big bearded man and kept the conversation short and cordial. He seemed more suited to being outside doing construction work rather than examining my lady parts. Why did I listen to Déjà?

He pulled in a machine and spread cold jelly over my stomach. The moment I had been waiting for, boy or girl? My nerves were a little raw.

More than anything, I wanted Diego to be there and just as

excited and nervous as I was. Although lying on the table, I would settle for the receptionist from my parents' practice, the mailman, anyone; I just didn't want to hear the news, any news alone. But I was.

The images leaped to life on the screen, silencing me. I wasn't sure what I was looking at, but it was alive and moving. I thought I could make out little fingers, but the doctor informed me that was my son's penis. It was a boy! I was going to have a little boy.

Once I was dressed, I went to Dr. Afton's small office and sat in an overly masculine leather chair. His wall was a testament to his skill. It was lined with rows and rows of fatigued-looking parents, and newborns with their eyes squeezed shut. He also had a few shots of him kayaking and rock climbing. He stroked his salt and pepper beard as he outlined the pros and cons of getting an amnio. I didn't feel as though he was talking to me. Instead, it was as though he was delivering a standard spiel at me about my age and high-risk pregnancy.

"According to the ultrasound though, my son," I relished saying that word, "appears to be healthy."

"Yes, everything looked fine. But the ultrasound can't detect chromosomal disorders or genetic disorders. You mentioned you carried the sickle cell trait?"

"I do. But you wouldn't be able to do anything if we found out something was wrong, right?"

"Correct. It's just information for you to have and to prepare you in case there are issues."

I left his office and drove over to Déjà's store, *Déjà's Baby Booties*. Inside were racks and racks of clothes from infant to toddler, strollers, jumpers, swings, and toys, lots of toys. A play area with a plastic slide and a miniature kitchen kept Tyra and a few other little kids busy. Jolie and Steve Jr. were at camp. I was surprised to see it so neat and orderly, considering her house looked like hobos lived there.

"This is really cute! I'm so proud of you!"

"Not too proud to roll up your sleeves and help a sister out? I can't afford to pay you much, but I'll give you the BFF discount on merchandise, and trust me, you will need a lot just starting out."

"Of course, I'll help out. But first, I want to shop. Where's your boy section?" I asked with a smile.

"You're having a boy?" Déjà squealed and gave me a hug.

I whipped out my ultrasound picture. She told me about a place I could go to get a 3-D image of the baby. The technology made it crystal clear, but it was an additional cost I couldn't afford. I was paying for everything out of pocket. Maybe I had been too hasty to turn down the COBRA health insurance alternative offered by my former job.

Déjà showed me how to work the register and how to take in items for consignment. Her shop received a steady flow of traffic from parents and caretakers buying and selling their things. It was in an upscale neighborhood where the $1,000 Bugaboos were parked right alongside the $10 umbrella strollers. I received a crash course in all the junk new moms supposedly "needed." It sounded like I'd need arms of steel just to schlep this stuff around.

My head was spinning with the myriad of options for car seats, strollers, carriers, baby bags, breast pumps, nursing bras, and bottle warmers, and this was all for portability during the first six months. Then there were the questions of jumpers, swings, walkers, cribs, mobiles, developmental floor mats, baby monitors, and the list went on to the moon. Where was I going to store all this stuff once I figured out how to pay for it?

The sonogram was a truce between my mom and me. True to form, she had it custom framed and hung it on the wall. She was getting excited about her grandson. I often arrived home to find cute little outfits for boys on my bed or notes on my pillow with names like Connor, Brent, and William.

He would have to have my last name. What would be the point of giving him Diego's real last name? Seeing how Diego Jr. was out of the question and I wasn't exactly feeling Eugene as a name for a little baby. On paper, Diego would have nothing to show that he was ever involved in the process.

My parents offered me a job at their practice doing filing. Nothing glamorous, but it was an opportunity to get health insurance, so I took it. I could work in the evenings.

We were smack in the middle of the dog days of summer, and Hades was about the only place I could imagine that was hotter when I headed into the city to meet Cameron at the Hudson. I almost didn't want to see him in case he, too, would be the bearer of bad news, in which case he could keep it to himself.

I was thankful for small blessings; the paparazzi hadn't found me or didn't care enough to look for me. The last thing I needed was for my picture to be in the news. On the train ride into the city, I had plenty of time to ruminate. How do you make a way out of no way? It was like going off-roading in a VW Beetle. I was trying to figure out the answer to the riddle that's currently my life. The key was there. I just didn't know what door to put it in. Literally and figuratively.

In Penn Station, I swam upstream in the human tide of people as I made my way through the tunnels, battling the commuters headed back to Jersey. I needed to take the subway to midtown. The loudspeaker droned incessantly about the arrival of trains on such-and-such tracks, while the ding of the bell signifying the closing doors stressed the electric hum of conversation. It was a shock to my system after being cloistered in the car culture of LA.

Understandably, Cameron had become fast friends with paranoia. He wanted me to text him when I was close to the hotel, and he would meet me in the lobby. I exited the subway and walked up the stairs to reach the street level and was smacked in the face by the suffocating humidity. By the time I reached the hotel, I'd wished I had taken a cab, but funds were tight, and I had to cut back where I could.

The Hudson was the ultimate urban hipster experience where you're plunged into surrealism. In a dark hoodie pulled low over his head, Cameron was at the end of a 30-foot-long tunnel, bathed in chartreuse-colored light and walking toward me. He stopped short and did a double take.

"What did you do to your hair, and what's all this?" he said when we met in the middle. He palmed my belly like a basketball. Being pregnant was an open invitation for people, strangers mostly, to get all in your business. "When are you due?" "Do you know what you're having?" "Is this your first?" Blah blah blah.

"New look for a new me." I wore long, sparkly earrings to amplify the absence of my hair. It was a striking look for me, one that I was starting to love.

"C'mon," he guided me back toward the entrance, where a black SUV was waiting.

"Where are we going?"

"To a friend's spot, it's cool."

I hesitated, considering what happened the last time we were in a car together. A driver was already at the back passenger door and opening it for me, so I said a quick prayer and stepped in. Cameron was behind me.

We snaked our way into traffic and headed downtown.

"What's so important?"

"Not right now. Just enjoy the ride. We'll talk when we get to the spot. Hey, yo, can you put on that Charlie Wilson joint you were playing earlier?"

The driver hit a button on the radio, and a CD started playing. Cameron took off his hoodie and leaned back, closing his eyes.

The cloak and dagger nature of it all was a bit wearing, especially when I realized we were going through the Holland Tunnel.

I shook Cameron's shoulder. "I just left Jersey. I could have met you in Jersey somewhere had I known that's where you wanted to go."

"Just chill."

I gave up reading the exit signs, trying to figure out where we were going as we sped down the Turnpike. As long as they had a bathroom when we got there, I would be fine.

The constant motion had lulled me to sleep, and the slowing and stopping awakened me with a start. When the driver opened the door and offered his hand to help me step down, the chirp of crickets and annoying hum of cicadas filled the air. We were far from the glare of city lights; it looked like a heavy blanket with silver glitter had been tossed over the sky as millions of stars twinkled. I looked around and realized we were in a seven-car driveway.

Cameron headed to an inconspicuous door on the side, probably the servant's entrance.

"Whose house is this?"

"One of my boys."

"Gee thanks, that tells me a lot."

We entered a cavernous kitchen with a granite island that looked like it belonged in a culinary arts school. The kitchen was a testament to stainless steel with its professional double stove and walk-in freezer. The appliances gleamed as though they had never been used. Cameron walked towards a hallway, and to the left was an elevator. Someone was home; I could hear the muffled sounds of a television or stereo coming from somewhere.

The elevator door slid open. It was tiny. Only two people could fit in. We were taken to a lower level, a two-lane bowling alley. Blue and gold lights splashed across the floor and our faces as a disco ball twirled in the air.

"You brought me out here to go bowling? Are you kidding me?"

I sat in a chair attached to a table with a small computer that kept score.

Cameron smiled for the first time. "Relax. I just wanted to get out of the city. I been stuck in a studio all day."

"You relax by bowling? Not by drowning puppies or kicking kittens, since that's basically what you did to my career."

"Elle, I'm sorry about how things went down, but Casey told me he left the tracks in your office. He's been my boy since the beginning. Always had my back." His scowl said otherwise.

He meticulously untied his sneakers, lined them up on the side, and grabbed a pair of bowling shoes.

"People will dog you out in this business. Pretend that they helping you when they really stepping on yo' neck trying to get to the next level," he continued.

He grabbed a bowling ball and strode up to the lane. He swung his arm back, his lean body in perfect form with his left leg crossed behind his right leg. The ball dropped and glided down in a straight line. The sharp crack of pins signaled a strike.

He wore all the accouterments of success: the requisite bling - diamond stud, Rolex watch, jeans that cost more than a plane ticket to Europe, and of course, high-end sneakers. Yet, for the first time, he was without his usual swagger. He sat down on a bench against the wall.

"You can't trust nobody in this business. No matter how down you are with somebody. Even friends."

"Even boyfriends."

"And tricks and hoes."

"You need to leave them hoes alone. They'll get you every time."

"On the real though, I'm sorry 'bout what happened with you and your man."

"Not your fault. Why are you apologizing? You've already got a full plate of crow to eat."

"My dad walked out on my moms when I was a baby. I watched my mom struggle, heard her crying at night. I know how hard it is."

"Cam, I met your dad last year at an awards show. Seems like a pretty nice guy, and your mom did alright for herself." I was using the term "alright" quite loosely. She was some big exec at a food corporation. Once Cameron hit it big, though, she resigned and was in charge of his non-profit and business ventures.

"Yeah, he's all cool now, but I'm a grown-ass man. What can he do for me now?" Frustration aborted his words, but I knew what he meant. The unsaid sat between us, and I could easily imagine my son having those same emotions years from now.

I struggled to think beyond the pregnancy. I could only see as far as my stomach. The hurt carried in Cameron's words reminded me that my baby would grow up one day. This wasn't just my story of betrayal. It would be one our child would tell and retell. It would either be the catalyst that pushed him to excel or the excuse used for his own poor choices.

First, Walsh's walk down memory lane, now Cameron's Oprah moment. I wondered if people were more prone to share when they knew you weren't in a position to judge.

"Now would be a good time to cue in a track by the O'Jays, 'They Smile in your Face,'" I said.

"Back Stabbers!" we sang together.

Cameron laughed. "Your turn."

"What?" I hadn't bowled since the sixth grade. If bowling shoes were cuter, I might have done it more often. Who wanted to be caught dead in those things?

"Are you scared?"

"Of course not." I looked at a rack of six pink and blue bowling balls lining the wall.

"Are you going to elaborate?" I asked.

"Just bowl."

I found the lightest ball. Walked up to the line and dropped it. Gutter ball.

"You bowl like a girl. What are you doing?" His deep baritone laugh filled the air.

He came over and tried to help me with my form. His hands were firm as he guided my arm and told me to release the ball. I knocked down seven pins.

We were silent. I put my hand on his arm, "What's going on with you and Casey? Why did you bring me here?"

Cameron sat down on the bench again. He leaned forward and palmed his head with his hands.

"I don't know who to trust anymore, Elle."

I plopped down beside him and leaned back against the wall. "Don't look at me for any answers cause I've got nothing."

"So you really didn't know?"

"Know what?"

"What that cat Diego was doing?"

"Not a clue." Humiliation and sadness draped themselves across my words. I blinked quickly to stave off any tears.

"Casey gave me a song that was promised to Strykker. Never told me I was rhyming on someone else's tracks. It's all so fucked up. He almost got us killed over that shit."

"Wait, back up. What do you mean 'almost got us killed'? Did this have something to do with the shooting?"

Cameron blew out a long sigh that seemed to last forever. "I think so."

I exhaled as well. It caused a domino effect of maybes. Maybe Diego wasn't laundering money, maybe he wasn't involved with the mob, maybe this was all just a mistake. I tried to focus on the conversation at hand.

"How do you know this? Did you tell the police?"

"First of all, I said, 'I think so,' I don't know anything for sure. It's just the word on the streets, but yeah, my lawyer told the cops about it."

"Look, I know I'm not your road dog from back in the day, but I've known you since you got signed to the label. How could you think I would even do something like that? Without even asking me? You didn't even bother to get all the facts. You just ran with it."

"I know. I fucked up." He cradled his head in his hands as he rested his elbows on his knees. "Believe it or not, Chantal's the one that told me to get my head out my ass."

"Chantal?"

"Yeah, we were in the studio together, and she was like, it's always the one closest to us that do us the most harm. At first, I thought she was just paranoid and talking about that douchebag husband of hers. She told me to look to see who stood to gain the most and that you are too in love with your job to fuck it up over some masters. Can you believe she called me a dumb ass?"

"Wow, sounds like the old Chantal is coming back." Never in a million years did I think she'd have anything nice to say about me, backhanded or not.

"Hopefully."

At the end of the day, we were all players in a Greek tragedy. Money, greed, and lies were tearing us apart. Cameron had made a lucrative deal with an energy bar company; overnight, he went from paid to wealthy. Four years ago, he strutted across the stage to accept his degree in business from UCLA. Now he was flying in private jets, zigzagging across the world, with an estimated worth of over $100 million. Who *do* you trust?

twenty

ON THE RIDE back into the city, Cameron's words bounced around in my head. The bare bones of the tale went something like: Casey was an incompetent boob, in way over his head. With Cameron as his first client, Casey thought he could wheel and deal with the big boys. Strykker's camp approached Casey about having Cameron featured on one of Strykker's tracks. Casey didn't tell Cameron about the track's origins when Cameron wanted it for himself. He acted like he was a big shot and would bully Strykker's camp into letting them have it. Except Strykker's camp didn't take kindly to being punked.

Eventually, all roads led back to Diego, somehow. Diego was like Kevin Bacon, except he was six degrees of trouble. Once his misdeeds became known, Casey used me as a convenient fall guy. The perfect patsy. More words were exchanged between Casey and Strykker's camp, and now the first shots had been fired, which was right around the time Casey spilled his guts to Cameron and confessed everything.

"Me and Casey grew up together. Always had each other's backs."

"Yeah, at boarding school, how hard was that? You guys went to Choate."

"On scholarship," he said defensively.

It was a nice sound bite, but I knew it was only a partial academic scholarship. His mom paid most of his tuition because she could afford it.

"Um whatever, you got in. I've heard about Strykker. He and his crew were beating murder charges while you were playing lacrosse and having all-night keggers. You need to squash this before their aim gets better and they finish what they started."

"I went to Choate, but I came from the streets-"

"-of New Canaan, Connecticut. Let it go. I met your mom, remember? You're smart enough to know that music beefs are good for sales, bad for artists. It didn't work out for 'Pac and Biggie. Why do you think you're so different?"

"I'm not gonna let anybody punk me. They shot at me-"

"This is not your fight. It's Casey's battle. Let him deal with it. Casey can always find another client to manage; you have one career. Don't get dragged into this pissing contest. You've got more to lose."

Our tenuous bond while bowling dissipated into a moody silence as we chewed over our options.

"C'mon, tell the truth, Vanilla Ice's *Ice, Ice, Baby* inspired you, and that's why you wanted to get into music." I busted a few stiff, robot dance moves with my arm to lighten the moment.

"You're funny. Not."

The driver deposited us at 55th and Park, a Scandinavian restaurant. It was crowded with well-heeled customers. Many had probably never seen Cameron's albums or movies and didn't care about our arrival. Over the second course of seared diver scallops, he asked if I would help him.

"Help you do what?"

He shifted in his seat. "You're right. I'm about the music, but I don't want to die over the music, know what I'm saying? Will you help me squash this? Put together a campaign or something."

"Seriously?"

"Yeah, we'll be working together again, just like old times. I'll pay whatever you want."

"No, I mean, seriously as in oh *hell* no! First, you drag me into this mess, destroy my rep, and now you want me to help clean it up? Can't say it better than Whitney, 'Crack is whack.'"

"C'mon Elle. It only makes sense if you do it... after everything that's happened..."

I gave him my best stone face. "I don't know. I have to think about it."

"Look, I don't beg nobody for nothing, but I get it. I'm sorry for believing Casey so easily and getting you caught up in the middle of all this. I thought you were down with Diego, and you two were like Bonnie and Clyde. I didn't know," he paused, "Did you lose your money too?"

I hesitated as my face burned. Truth be told, I never invested with Diego. He never asked, and I never had the extra funds to do so. "What's done is done." I speared a cauliflower and popped it in my mouth.

"Here's a thousand for a retainer. Just take it, ok?"

Cameron peeled off some money under the table and slid a wad of bills in my direction. Who carried a thousand bucks in cash? In my pocket, I only had enough for a subway token and a donut.

"I don't need your guilt money. I'm not some charity case, thank you very much." Already, I was thinking about how that money would be spent. I had a doctor's appointment coming up, and I needed to save for an apartment.

"Are you working?"

"As a matter of fact, I am." Cashier and filing count.

"And that extra weight is because you're pregnant, not some emotional weight gain shit, right?"

"What's your point?"

"Take the money. I fucked up. But on the flip side yo, you're good at what you do, and I want you on my team. I need you on my team."

He flashed a megawatt grin of brilliantly white, perfectly straight teeth book-ended by dimples, a reminder of why he landed the movie roles and magazine covers.

"Besides, you don't want to feel guilty if something happens to me, do you? Then you'd be all like, 'I had the chance to stop it, and I didn't-'"

"Stop. We both know I could do this in my sleep, but do you really want me to? My personal drama might get in the way of trying to get your message out," I hesitated, "and I'm not so sure I want to do this anymore." I finally gave voice to the little whispers that had been growing louder in my head. I wasn't so enamored with my job or who I had become anymore.

He put down his fork and looked at me. Not as the performer or media personality, but as someone I'd only recently met, Cameron - the person.

"Elle, you were right there with me when bullets were flying. I can't think of anyone else who knows what I'm going through and wants to see this go away as much as I do. Will you please do this?"

After I agreed to think about it, we had a nice dinner. Cameron was funny and a voracious reader – of current news, African-American history, and fiction. He held his own on any number of subjects. Unfortunately, I was only up to speed on the *What to Expect When Expecting* series and the gossip rags, so I was limited.

"You know, I've worked with you for the past two years, and I've never seen this side of you."

"Why, cause I'm always coming off as a tough guy?"

"Umm, more like an arrogant prick. You should try being yourself more often. It's nice."

"Nice doesn't sell, you know that. And in this campaign, I don't want to come off as no punk ass either."

It was cool being around the real Cameron while it lasted. He had the driver take me home, and he'd walk back to the hotel. He was walking me to the SUV when a flash of light temporarily blinded us.

A photographer suddenly appeared in front of us and started snapping our pictures. The flash of the camera threw off a scent like blood in the air, attracting hungry paparazzi. A few more were coming down the street. Cameron held his jacket up, blocking me from the cameras as he followed me in the car, closing the door on their frenzied questions.

"You ok?"

"I wish they would just leave us alone," I tried to control the tremble in my voice.

"I'm waiting for them to give us one of those names like CamEll or ElCa or some shit."

"Ha! That's all I need. Are you sure you want to work with me?"

"We been shot at; I'm not scared of some punk ass photographers, are you?"

I shook my head yes, definitely yes.

"I still want you on my team."

My heart was racing. I was far from my comfortable position as puppet master and found living life on the other side of the lens was ugly, no matter how you Photoshopped it. His driver dropped him off at his hotel, and I began the journey home.

Sleeping at night was becoming uncomfortable as the baby claimed more space in my uterus. Gone was the bloated look, and in its place, a roving lump. Usually, I slept like a windmill, flat on my back, arms and legs akimbo. That was no longer an option because of the pressure on my back. A dull ache often visited me in the darkness that I attributed to my hip bones spreading (along with my ass) as my body continued to make preparation for the baby's arrival. That night, I fell into a fitful sleep as I added Cameron's reluctantly given pieces of information to the puzzle. Diego's actions had caused yet another ripple effect across my life. Where would it end?

The soft chimes of my phone announced the morning, which arrived all too soon. It was a text message from Justine. It read, *your date's all over TMZ*. I groaned and pulled the sheet over my head. I didn't want to look, but I had to. My phone started chiming and ringing non-stop as more people became aware of the story. Apparently, it was on a couple of other sites and had made the morning news/gossip shows. I finally glanced at the photos. I came off as a broke Amber Rose while Cameron emanated an open hostility. Our being photographed together only ratcheted up the speculation again about Diego and who took shots at us. Macy texted me the link and a bunch of question marks. I texted back a happy face emoticon, which I knew would drive her crazy.

I couldn't linger and gloat. I had to get moving because my flight to Miami International was in a few hours. Déjà was giving me a ride. She had all three rugrats in tow.

"What are you gonna bring us back from Miami?" Déjà's oldest asked.

"I want a Bratz doll," Jolie interjected.

"What did I bring you when I came from LA?"

"Nothing," they all replied, even Tyra, the baby.

"You're going to get the same thing again. Enjoy."

"Don't be mean to my babies! You will have one of your own running around in a minute. So get used to the noise and the questions." She could laugh again.

The charges against her had been taken out of criminal court and kicked over to Municipal Court because she had used kids' finger paints on his car. It came off with water, lessening the total damage to the car.

"What are you going to be doing in Miami?" Déjà prodded. Yet again.

"Don't worry about me. You should be thinking about how you're going to manage staying out of trouble while you're on probation and thanking your lucky stars they gave you a pre-trial intervention."

"I know, you're right."

"If you put half as much energy into your store as you do into Steve, you'd have a franchise."

"You think so?"

"You've got a great business. You've got to put the time in and grow it."

"What about you? I know you're not going to be my cashier forever. What's your next move?"

"I'm working on it. Don't worry; I'll give you plenty of notice."

She pulled up in front of the Departures terminal for American and put her hazards on as she pulled my overnight bag out of the trunk.

"Be safe in whatever it is you're doing that you don't want to tell me about. I won't take it personally," she said as she hugged me.

I spent a frustrating 45 minutes going through check-in and the security check, where TSA felt up my baby bump and me. More than enough time to second-guess and obsess over things. I had no plans after the baby was born. I felt like I was so mired in the why's and how's of the past that I couldn't move forward.

Miraculously, my flight was on time. Outside at Miami International, my shirt clung to me like a second skin as I stood in line for a cab. Rivets of sweat formed interconnecting networks trickling down my back. I sucked down chunks of humid air and exhaust as I waited. Yellow cabs snaked along in a line, devouring passengers until finally, I could climb in one.

"Listen, I'll give you $75 if you drive me around for the day. I have a bunch of stops I need to make before I head to my hotel. So, turn off your meter."

"It's against the rules."

"David, you don't look like the type that's ever played by the rules," I said as I glanced at his id card on the dash.

He laughed and flipped off the meter. I rolled the window down as far as it would go, letting the hot, gusty wind pour in, hoping it would wash away the lingering scent of stale cigarettes and beer. I leaned back into the hot vinyl seats, and a long sigh escaped. My eyes stayed wide open as I looked out the window.

Why was it that all highways and freeways looked the same? Long gray snakes cutting a swath through the grittier parts of a city. Sure, the cityscapes were different, but traffic was traffic anywhere you traveled. The first address was one of seven for Estella Rivera. I had a one in seven chance that this trip wouldn't be for nothing, but I was striking out quickly.

The first two were dead-ends. One was an empty lot with over-grown brush so high a village of pygmies could hide there. The second address was a liquor store, which only reminded me I hadn't had a drink in forever. I was shocked when we pulled up to an actual house for the third address.

"You going in?"

"Yeah, just give me a second."

I had told no one my reason for going to Miami. We all have secret compartments we're unwilling to unlock for public gawking or even private introspection. I felt I had to come. I had no real reason or jurisdiction other than being a jilted lover.

The delicious part about loving someone and being in love was that you got to see and experience pieces of a person that very few others experienced. We shared our private selves in hopes of finally being understood, of connecting. I was honest with him; I let him in to see the real me, in between waxings and other maintenance, and all I got was some smoke and mirrors. I came here to find and claim a piece of him. Some truth I could dust off and later share with our kid. Our son would probably be the only kid in pre-school with home movies of their dad that included footage from *Dog: Bounty Hunter* if Diego didn't turn himself in soon.

I summoned up the nerve to walk to the front door. It was a modest house, well kept. Manicured lawn with geometric shapes for shrubs lined the front yard, issuing a little privacy for the inhabi-tants. I rang the doorbell, not sure what to expect. I held my breath as I waited for someone to answer.

A young woman with a chubby baby attached to her hip opened the door. She had the type of face that only flourished when she smiled. Could she be the first me? Concern washed away suspicion as she said, "Can I help you? Do you need a glass of water?"

She probably thought anyone who looked as hot and uncomfortable as me couldn't be dangerous. "No, I'm fine, thank you. I'm looking for Estella. Is she here?"

"Are you sure you have the right address? No one here by that name."

"Oh, sorry to have bothered you."

"Did you want to come in for some water? Please?"

I hesitated for a moment. Just because she had a baby on her hip didn't mean she couldn't be insane. I looked back at David and motioned for him to wait. He pointed to his watch, and I shrugged my shoulders as I followed her inside.

The crisp air washed over me, instantly drying the sweat on my face and back as I stepped into the foyer.

"Have a seat," she waved over to a couch in the living room. The house was modern. Simple taste pulled the rooms together with bold colors.

She returned with a tall glass of water.

"I'm sorry if I come off as psycho. It's just that someone's teething, and mommy's losing it," she laughed wryly. She carefully put the baby on the floor. Drool dribbled down a double chin while she sat there looking at me with big, unblinking green eyes.

"My husband and I thought it would be great if I took off a few years, at least until Michaela is old enough to go to school. I've never not worked, not that this isn't work... but you know what I mean, or you will soon," she laughed. "I haven't found any playgroups, and I'm starving for adult conversation that I don't have to type or Skype."

"I'm due in December, and I have no clue what I'm supposed to do with one of those. What did you do before Michaela?"

"I worked at an ad agency. It was crazy. I hated my job and

complained and wanted to leave, and now that I'm gone... I miss it. It's funny; working outside of the home used to be revolutionary, and now staying home to raise a baby is considered a big deal. It's like we're damned if we do and damned if we don't no matter what. So, who's this Estella person you're looking for?"

"It's a friend of my boyfriend's, he's missing, and I thought she may know... something. I don't know. Wild goose chase, I guess."

Michaela started crying, a fussy cry that gradually grew into longer and louder wails. The woman picked her up, and the cries subsided.

"Missing? I'm sorry to hear that. We've been here about five years, and it was a nice older couple that sold us this place."

As I got ready to leave, my hand on the doorknob, I asked, "Were you afraid of, you know..."

"Yes," she answered, switching the baby to the other hip. "Motherhood has this way of making you feel so incompetent, it can reduce you to tears, and in the next minute, it can be so beautiful that you forget everything else. For me, the incompetent moments seem to last longer," she chuckled wryly.

"Does it ever go away, the fear, I mean?"

"Ha. Ask me after she's graduated from college, and I'll let you know."

A look of panic streaked across my face. I was so concerned with the immediate issues of childbirth and being responsible for a baby... I had forgotten about puberty, teen years, and then having to detach myself and send him off to college—my baby!

"Listen, you will make mistakes, but just do your best. I say that with more confidence than I feel, but that's all we have, isn't it?"

"Well, that and prescription pills and happy hour should carry us through, right?"

She laughed. "I'll drink to that once I stop breastfeeding. Good luck with everything."

"You too."

It's amazing the things you admit to strangers. The comfort in releasing a burden, knowing it can't follow you back into the circle of your life. A confession that goes nowhere, but the fact that it's been said is a relief. Everyone kept telling me I'll be fine. I'll be a great mom. But what if I'm not? What if my kid does something horrible because I screwed up? Or because I chose the wrong father? My baby was coming into the world with one strike against him. What if my arms weren't wide enough, strong enough to protect him or her?

We made a stop at McDonald's, where I tried to pick healthy options for the baby. Not that it mattered; I inhaled it in a matter of seconds. If you can't taste the calories, do they still count? Stops four, five, and six yielded more wrong addresses. By the time we reached the last address on my list, dusk was on our heels, and a weary ache followed me around like a hangover.

"So, what are you on, some type of scavenger hunt or something?" David asked in between stops.

"I wish. It would probably be a lot easier." I was kicking myself for not looking at Google Earth before coming out. I could have avoided the empty lots.

It was back to the drawing board if Estella wasn't at this last address.

"We're here," David said, his voice jarring me out of my thoughts.

I looked out the window and saw a McMansion dominating the small lot. It was gated.

"Ok, wait here." It was almost 7:30 pm. We'd been driving around all day, and my bladder felt like it would shatter into tiny wet pieces.

I rang the buzzer, and a curt male voice answered, "yes."

Leaning against the cool brick wall, I said, "I'd like to speak with Estella Rivera, please."

"Is she expecting you?"

I paused. Could this really be the right house? "No, is she there?" I shifted from one foot to the other. Now that I was standing, the pressure was mounting, and I thought I would explode.

"You'll have to come back when you have an appointment, Ms.?"

"She doesn't know me. My name is Elle Nixon."

There was a silence, and then a woman's voice coolly said, "I know who you are."

The gates swung open.

twenty-one

THE DRIVEWAY WAS short and stubby, giving further evidence it was too much house for the land. A pair of marble lions flanked double white doors outlined in gold molding with gold-plated hardware. A door swung open by unseen hands as I approached. Barely able to take in the foyer, I spied a bathroom set off to the right.

Estella was pouring a drink when I walked into the living room, feeling a few pounds lighter. It was painted a depraved white; the walls were bare except for one. A massive abstract oil painting rested against the far wall. My Easy Spirit sandals squeaked on the mahogany floor. Tall and lean, she was Diego's alter ego in a pantsuit. A short pixie cut suggested a sense of playfulness. One that was clearly missing from her demeanor. She had the almond-shaped eyes of a predator and moved with slyness while wearing five-inch Ruthie Davis studded pumps. She seemed like the type that could stab you in the neck with her stiletto and keep it moving. I had to pause for a moment of severe shoe envy.

"I would offer you some scotch, but I imagine bottled water would be more appropriate for someone in your... condition." She brought a heavy crystal tumbler to perfectly painted lips and sipped.

I looked down at the table in front of me, where a bottle of Fiji water had been placed. It hadn't been there a few moments ago. I sat down on the couch, which was as soft as I was heavy. My knees practically touched my chin. It was hard to maintain any decorum when I felt like I was sitting at the kindergarten table.

"So, you're Elle."

"Yes, I am. So, what type of marriage did you have when Diego spent most of his time in LA?"

"No foreplay?" she smiled a tiny smile as she slowly sipped her scotch.

My stomach itched, but I refused to scratch it. It would be like blinking first.

"What Diego and I have, I'm afraid you'll have to get those answers from him."

"Under normal circumstances, I would. How much easier would it be for me to just ask him rather than fly out to Miami and drive around and knock on strange doors all day looking for you? That would have been my first choice if not for the fugitive thing."

"Really? What do you think I could or would do for you? Besides, your inability to contact him is not really my problem, is it? I mean, unless you have a warrant or some other compelling reason, I don't have to talk to you."

"Why wouldn't you? I had to find out from the FBI that my boyfriend has an alias and he's married. And you don't seem to be bothered at all. How many other women have been here before me?"

"You are the first pregnant one to show up at my door."

"There have been others?"

She waved her hand, dismissing my question. "What do you really want to know?"

I pulled a picture out of my purse. It was Diego and me at Freddie's second wedding.

"Is this the man you're married to? Diego Rivera?"

She glanced at the picture.

"Of course it is." A look of realization washed over her face. "Oh, poor thing. You believe he's innocent. Did you fly all the way out here to play Nancy Drew?"

"Well, when you say it with that much sarcasm, it does sound silly."

"Do you seriously think that all this time, the Feds have the wrong man? Some mistaken identity?"

"The Diego I know wouldn't do what they say he's done."

"But you love him, right?"

"Of course."

"You don't even know him."

I was almost taken aback by her contempt, but it was true.

"I accept him for who and what he is, and long after you're gone, I'll still be here," she continued.

She took another sip of her scotch and smiled as though she dared me to contradict her. Frustration simmered throughout my veins, and before I knew what I was doing, I was in her face.

"Where is he? What do you know? Why is he doing this?"

Hands were around my arms, pulling me back. She didn't blink. I could have been asking her the time.

"I could think of, say, 26 million reasons. Why don't you go home and play mommy? If Diego wants to contact you, I'm sure he has your number."

Her hand fluttered in the air dismissively; I was no more important to her than a Sephora store clerk. A short man tried to escort me to the door. On my way out, I took my hand and swiped off the crystal goblet and tumblers along with the bottle of scotch, deriving some small pleasure at watching her eyes narrow as the loud splintering crash filled the air.

"You were left behind, too. If you know him as well as you think you do, then there wouldn't be a need for someone like me, would there? Maybe you're not enough either, and you never will be."

She sat there, unperturbed, and for a moment, I thought I saw a flash of pity in her eyes. I got into the cab and just sat there, stunned. It wasn't exactly how I thought things would go.

"Where to?"

"I don't know. Just... just drive."

This whole time, I knew in my gut that Diego couldn't do something like this. Not the man I fell for, the man I let into my home, into my bed, whose baby was growing inside me. I would have known. I would have seen something. I'm not some naïve waif dazzled by a big dick. I was a grown woman who had seen her fair share of cheaters, liars, ballers, shot callers, and the like. How could I be so wrong about him when it mattered the most?

Watching her, hearing her words, I believed she knew him. The cold realization that my Diego was also her Diego shocked me. Sometimes you only see a man with your heart. The sense of loss cut me just as deep as though I had gotten news of his death. The seven stages of grief converged on me. The emotions were relentless, as though a prizefighter walloped me over and over again. Rage, disbelief, and sadness threatened to consume me as I struggled to breathe, to make sense of the unfathomable. Betrayal tasted like a bitter kiss. I kicked the back of the seat and hit it with my hands. I couldn't stop. Each kick, each punch erupted from somewhere deep inside of me, the wounded girl striking out, yelling "liar!" after each blow. I was flush with warm humiliation; it had taken me months to accept what everyone else seemed to know was a forgone conclusion.

"Hey! Hey! What's going on back there?"

David swerved across two lanes and pulled over to a curb. The multiple blares and bleats of horns indicated no one was happy.

He popped open the trunk and left the driver's side door open as he hurried out of the car. He unceremoniously dumped my overnight bag on the sidewalk.

"Lady, I don't know what's going on with you, but you're crazy. You got to go."

I tried to give him the money, but he wouldn't take it; he left me in a cloud of exhaust as he peeled off. I sat down on a bench at a bus stop. I had no idea where I was or how to get to my motel. I don't know how many cars whizzed by me before I finally waved over an off-duty cab. Once I checked into my candy-colored motel, I went into the bathroom. Hot pink walls with roses etched on the tile.

In the bathroom, my hands shook as I tried to turn on the faucet. I wanted to splash water on my face. A part of me wished that I'd never met him. That I would have gotten into my car and just drove away. Gave him a wrong number. I caught my reflection in the mirror and was shocked. I still wasn't used to the haircut, and my face was filling out. Pain was etched so deeply on my face that I was unrecognizable. The person I used to be was gone and in her place was a bastardized version of me, just trying to keep her head above water. I let go of the sink and clenched and unclenched my fists as the sobs erupted, followed by hot tears that cascaded down my cheeks like lava. I felt just as trapped by betrayal as I was by love. I wrapped my arms around my waist as my knees buckled until I was in the fetal position on the dirty bathroom floor, wondering... *how did I get here?*

I don't know how long I was on the floor. The hunger pains rocked my stomach like seizures, forcing me up.

I took the elevator downstairs to find something to eat. There were a ton of shops and restaurants just outside the lobby doors, but I didn't feel like walking. I ate a dry hamburger at the bar. Another flurry of butterfly wings brushed across my stomach. Feeling more like kicks than flurries. My sudden flare of excitement was quickly muted. Only the bartender was there to share this moment, and he was at the other end of the bar picking his nose and watching a baseball game on the big screen television. It reminded me that this would be one of many firsts I'd have to go through alone. My anger flared again. My happiest moments were also my saddest. There was a life growing inside me. It was exciting and beautiful. I wanted Diego to be there, to make the runs for my ice cream and chocolate-covered strawberry cravings, talk to me late into the night about our hopes and dreams for the baby. Or at the very least, say yay or nay to baby names. At that moment, I felt equal amounts of hatred and love for him. I missed the man who had made me fall in love with him.

Back in the room, a dreamless, deep sleep took over. I didn't wake up until late the next morning. Had to rush to make my flight back to Jersey.

* * *

One evening after working at the boutique, I walked to Ralph's BBQ Joint. It was at the end of the boardwalk, not too far from our house. Small and dark, the air was heavy with the sweet, tangy scent of barbecue sauce. I could feel a little drool trickling down my chin. I'd been craving ribs, and eating a medley of raw vegetables every night wasn't hitting the spot. Sitting at the corner table, with a baseball cap pulled down low and hunched over a Ralphie's special, a slab of baby backs, and three sides was none other than my father!

I stood in front of his table, tapping my foot. It took him a moment to notice me, and when he did, he snatched off the white Ralphie's bib, stained with sauce.

"Ellie, what are you doing here?"

"What are *you* doing here? Vegans don't eat ribs unless they're made of tofu!" I pulled back a chair and sat down. I took one of his ribs. I stripped the bone clean in a matter of seconds. He shooed my hand away when I reached for another one.

"Get your own. I told your mother I was picking up fresh asparagus from the market. I'm on the clock."

"You know if it's two against one, she can't force us to eat that stuff."

"Yeah, then I have to hear about how we're ganging up on her. She's just trying to help us. You know how your mother is. She finds something she wants to fix and puts 200% into it because she does it out of love."

"What'll you have, sugar?" a woman said from behind the counter.

"The daily special looks pretty good." The aroma of ox tails, macaroni and cheese, and corn muffins were calling my name.

196

I was quiet during the few moments it took me to inhale my food.

"How's practice going with the new recruits?" My dad was up most mornings and at the field working with the track team by the time I rolled out of bed.

"Not bad, none of them with your talent. Ellie, you could have gone to the Olympics."

I shook my head. "That was your thing."

"I know. You have to follow your heart, and you did that. I'm proud of you."

"Really?"

"Your old man's no dummy. Being a track star was always my dream. I remember one time at practice, you must have been about 13 or 14, you got so mad at me, you told me you were going to college in California to 'get away from me and my stupid whistle.' Once you set your mind to something Ellie, you get it done."

"How do I figure out what I want when I don't even know who I am anymore?"

"Sometimes it's not about figuring things out; it's about listening and accepting what you already know. You've got more heart and determination than anyone I know—other than your old man. You just have to be still, you'll see."

I threw my arms around him, careful not to get barbecue-stained fingerprints on his back.

"Thanks, Dad."

He gave me a quick hug before going off on his errand for asparagus. I used to think I wanted my old life back, but sometimes, I sensed there was something more.

An email from Constance Rivera, the real Diego's sister, came through while I was at the restaurant. She had agreed to meet me. Now I wasn't sure if I wanted to go. I had my fair share of the truth, and now I wanted my one-way ticket back to ignorance. My visit with Estella still weighed on me as much as the additional baby weight. I don't know what I had expected from the visit, but certainly not what transpired. What I really wanted was someone to confirm my idealized version of the truth, and that didn't seem to happen.

As the week went on, annoyances were packaged big and small, everything from the constant thoughts of Diego that plagued me to hating the way my nose was spreading because of the pregnancy to trying to figure out a more permanent job situation. As usual, I hated Diego, and I loved him. I hated the weakness I saw in his absence with a childish fervor. Hated him for not being the man I needed him to be. I knew life was more complicated than the black or white, right and wrong of the situation. It was colored more by shades of empathy. Right now, though, all that I knew, all that I felt, was that I needed him, and he wasn't here. It took me two days to respond to Constance.

On the day we were to meet, second thoughts plagued me. I sat on the edge of the tub and took gulps of air. What else was I going to hear that I didn't want to hear? Somehow, I scrounged up enough courage to get in the car. During the 90-minute drive to Trenton, I played The Script's "Breakeven" over and over on my iPod. It pretty much summed up my mood. My life was still going along at a steady clip; there was no emergency brake to slow things down. While I was falling apart and putting myself back together every night like Humpty Dumpty, what was Diego doing? Lost in anonymity and starting over somewhere in the Caribbean?

Constance Rivera lived in the same house where she had grown up with Diego. The real Diego. She didn't want to meet me there, though. She suggested a diner right off the NJ Turnpike. This was the diner capital of the country; there was no shortage of choices. The small state was littered with them.

I found a booth near the front and ordered a fruit platter while I waited. I didn't have to wait long. A woman wearing a black blouse and slacks with a Macy's nametag made her way to my table. She sat down across from me.

"Hi, you must be Elle."

We exchanged stilted small talk as we sized each other up. She ordered a cup of coffee. Black. I nibbled on a piece of cantaloupe even though my stomach was clenched in a knot. I tried to relax, convinced the baby had to be feeling the stress.

"Thanks for agreeing to meet with me. I know it must be awkward because your brother died so long ago, but I have reason to suspect another man is using his identity."

"Gene. I know."

I stared at her.

"I've seen you on the news."

She opened her purse and slid a photo across the table to me. It was three young men, arms casually thrown across each other's shoulders, mugging for the camera. I recognized Diego, my Diego, immediately, even with hair. Same cocky grin and assured pose. He towered over the two young men on either side of him.

"Eugene and my brother were roommates in college. He came home with Diego over Christmas break their freshman year."

"Is this your brother on the left?" He looked like a younger, boyish version of Constance. Same caramel complexion, warm milk chocolate-colored eyes. He had a halo of curly black hair, whereas she kept her thick hair slicked back in a tight bun.

"Yes. He was the baby of the family. What do you want to know?"

Why hasn't he called me? Did he ever truly love me? When will I see him again? These were all questions I wished she could answer. Instead, I said, "Anything you can tell me. I just want to know who he really is; I mean, he's the father of my child."

"He was," she took a breath before starting again, "he was driving the car when they got into the accident. We never blamed him. It was a freak accident. There were no drugs or alcohol involved. He dropped out of school shortly after."

"Do you know where he's from?"

"No. I'm sorry. I haven't spoken to him in years. It was just... too hard, you know?"

"What about this guy?" I pointed to the third guy in the photo. "Who is he?"

"That's Dillon. They all hung out together."

"Is he still alive? Do you think I could talk to him?"

Constance told me what she could remember of Dillon. His last name was Martin, and she believed he was from Chicago. They all went to a college in Atlanta. A long way from Boston.

"I wish I could be of more help," she told me as we stood in the parking lot.

"This has been great, thank you."

"I hope you find the answers you're looking for, but... sometimes the answers don't really matter. It doesn't change the truth. What you know inside."

"I'm not sure of what I know anymore."

* * *

The mornings always seemed so full of promise because each held the precious hope that I would hear something. Maybe Diego would surface. Or the police would catch the man who shot us back in Los Angeles. My life was in a holding pattern, and the intended destination couldn't be decided upon until there were answers. I couldn't help but think of his wife, Estella. We were two moons orbiting around the same sun. Every night, I went to sleep with crushing disappointment as a backdrop against my dreams, only to have it evaporate, and the vicious cycle would start again. I had to know what happened to Diego to make him assume a dead friend's identity. Horrible childhood? Running from the law? Or maybe he did it because he could. I grabbed the envelope on the nightstand, pulled out the ring, and slipped it on my index finger. *Who was the man who used to wear this?*

I shook my head to clear my thoughts. I could get lost in my head for hours. I pushed myself up and out of bed and went to my laptop. The house was quiet; my parents had gone to the office. I logged on. I would have to find out which neighbor was quippygirl12 and pay her some money for as much time as I spent using her Wi-Fi.

Facebook was a great way to stay in touch with friends and an even better way to track down strangers. I had a bunch of messages in my inbox that I ignored. None were from Diego, so it didn't matter. I hadn't updated my status or sent out a tweet since I was in Paris. Seemed like a lifetime ago. I found the college in Atlanta and searched the people who liked their page. Dillon Martin wasn't hard to find. He hadn't changed much over the years. I sent him an email telling him I was a friend of Gene's and would love to talk with him. Clicking through his page, I saw he was married with two rug rats. Moved back to Chicago. He didn't update his page that often either. Hopefully, he would log on and see my message.

I pulled out the photo album I had taken from Diego's house for the hundredth time. Most of the pictures were recent. I was hoping to find old pictures that could give me a clue about his past. I stared at the face of the man I thought I knew so well. I loved the part of him that I knew and didn't know how to stop.

A call from Walsh interrupted my thoughts.

Cutting straight to the chase, he said, "I don't have good news. We found Coogan. He committed suicide late last night."

"Does this prove that Coogan was behind it? I mean, is that why he killed himself?" I hated myself for sounding ghoulish. A man had just died.

"I don't know what it proves right now. I just wanted to tell you before you heard it on the news."

It felt as though my heart was permanently lodged in my throat. I knew Jeffrey had an ex-wife and child somewhere, and I could only imagine how difficult the road ahead of them would be. Even though every time I met him, he was an ass, it saddened me to think about what his final moments were like, and then it hit me... *Could Diego? What if?* I wouldn't let my mind travel down that path. I went online to search for stories, but they hadn't hit the web yet. I was relieved in a way. It bought me a little breathing room before a fresh onslaught of coverage began anew.

I had to focus. I had to go into the dental practice to file in a few hours, and I needed to work on Cameron's stuff. Being prideful and poor wasn't my cup of tea. I had decided to take Cameron's job offer. Besides creating a campaign to squash the escalating beef, he also wanted me to plan his album release party. I wanted it to be BIG. It was my way of saying, "In spite of it all, I'm still here, still standing." Even though I felt like hiding in the closet. I grabbed a notebook and pen and started outlining my to-do list for the party.

The next day, I needed to do a walk-through of the venue for the anniversary party. The Biltmore room, an elegant ballroom in the Ospry, one of the oldest hotels on the shore, was located two towns over in Long Branch. I was almost dressed when Déjà sent me a text. She was in a panic; she needed someone to watch Tyra while she went to court. Steve was making a move to get more custody and used Déjà's most recent behavior as a convenient weapon. She would have a hard time refuting the anger management issue if he brought in pictures of his vintage '66 black Mustang. Water-based colors or not, she did a number on the doors with lovely phrases in red such as "dickhead" and "loser." A taxicab yellow covered the front window.

I wanted to watch Tyra about as much as I wanted my toenails pulled off, but I agreed. I picked her up on my way to the venue. Déjà installed the car seat in the back of my mother's car. Tyra climbed in, looking pretty in a pink short set with butterflies on her sandals. She wiggled her little toes for me to show off the pink nail polish.

On the drive to Long Branch, I received a call from Macy. As she filled me in on the updates at Savage Rhythms, Tyra's singsong voice kept complaining that she was hot.

"I'm going to roll down the windows for you; that should cool you off, ok?'

The call served a dual purpose as Macy wanted to grill me about what was going on with Cameron. He had been MIA. Few from the label could get in touch with him. Except for me, apparently. I told her he had hired me as his indie publicist to handle the Strykker issue and album release party.

I hung up with her as I pulled into the parking lot in front of the hotel. I walked around to the back to help Tyra out of her car seat and was dumbfounded to see her clad in only her shorts. Her shirt and sandals were nowhere to be found.

"Where are the rest of your clothes?"

"I was hot."

I searched around the floor of the car and didn't see anything. Tyra giggled. I looked at the open window, which I had forgotten to roll up.

"Did you throw your clothes out the window?"

She laughed. I looked at my watch; it was 11 on the nose. I didn't have enough time to run to the store and buy her something. I scooped her out of the seat and carried her into the building, hoping no one would ask why she was half-naked.

The minute we stepped inside, Tyra wriggled down and was running around. Sherrie, the event coordinator, showed me the ballroom. We reviewed the party's specs, how many tables I needed, and other points in the contract. I pulled out my notebook to see the requirements for the band. I couldn't concentrate because Tyra was touching everything that shouldn't be touched, running between tables and twirling in circles. The Terrible Two's was a disease, and I was convinced children shouldn't be seen or heard during that time. Sherrie smiled a tight-lipped smile as we tried to finish going over the contract details, but finally, we had enough. I told her I'd come back another time. I tried to take Tyra's hand and walk out, but she went boneless on me, forcing me to carry her horizontally like a suitcase.

"Nooooo!" she howled. "I wanna stay!"

She miraculously found the use of her limbs as I pushed open the glass doors. Her little arms and legs were flailing as I stepped outside. The firestorm of flashbulbs shocked both of us. She stopped crying and looked around.

Five paparazzi were waiting for me.

"What do you think about Coogan's death?"

"Was it murder?"

"Have you heard from your boyfriend?"

"Where's the money?"

They circled like sharks as I tried to navigate my way to the car. Tyra felt heavier and heavier as she wriggled and cried.

"I have to potty!" she wailed as she clung to my neck for dear life. I tried to pat her on the back and comfort her.

I was so tired of being photographed and having questions hurtled at me.

"What is wrong with you people? Can't you see you're scaring the baby?"

They stood between me and the car making the parking lot a sea filled with predators that I was wary of crossing.

A screech of tires startled everyone as a car pulled in between the closing divide between the photographers and me.

"Get out of here before I call the police!"

I looked up, and Lucas was there. His car was running with the driver's side door wide open as he walked over to the passenger side and opened it.

"Come on, I'll give you a ride."

Tyra was crying uncontrollably as I scooted into the back seat with her. And more than a few tears had slipped down my cheeks. I wiped them away with the back of my hand.

"Thanks," I said in a wobbly voice. I closed my eyes. What just happened? Tyra's sobs had subsided, and she said in a tiny voice, "I tinkled."

twenty-two

MY LIFE WAS BORDERING on the absurd. By the time I got home, I wanted to just go upstairs and sleep. Even that was a challenge. My mother needed the car, which was still parked in Long Branch.

The fight was awful. I never understood the dance we often danced, the tango between mothers and daughters. The push/pull nature of our relationship gave us the ability to strike one another to the core with truths only we knew.

"I come home from work to a sink full of dishes from this morning. There's no maid service here."

"I'm sorry. I forgot. Gigi usually does that stuff."

"Eleanor Paige Nixon! You are not a child anymore, so get a grip and grow up!"

No, she did not just use my full name! "Why are you yelling at me? It's just a few dishes! I said I was sorry."

"I just don't understand what's going on! Reporters are coming to our practice asking questions about you. How could you let this happen?" She yanked open the dishwasher door and started unloading it.

"Let? So typical. Blame me. Fine. I wanted this to happen. I couldn't wait to become 35 and get pregnant by some guy who was a crook. That was my master plan all along. My sole purpose was to shame you."

"Stop being so melodramatic! I need the car, and it's not here. I have an appointment I'm already late for because of you and this crazy life of yours. When are you going to grow up and settle down?"

"That's your answer to everything, marriage."

I walked out of the kitchen, my mother's voice trailed after me.

"You can't keep running Elle, one of these days, you're going to realize that your problems are wearing sneakers too."

In my room, I slammed the door shut. All that was missing was a term paper due because I felt like I was right back in high school. Michael and Prince stared down at me from their yellowed posters. I had to get out of here, get my own place. Reclaim my life. I pulled out my suitcase and started throwing in clothes. The urge to just pick up and go was so strong that it hurt. Angry tears marched militantly down my cheeks. I had plenty of airline miles but couldn't afford to stay anywhere once I arrived.

Why couldn't she understand that I was never running away from something? I was always running to something. A better job. A better man. Happiness. Guess the flight plan doesn't matter if you leave unfinished business behind. I stared at the graduation wallet photos that lined my mirror. Our smiles held so much hope and promise. How do you get that back? I knew my parents didn't ask for this upheaval, just as I never did, but it was here, and we were all coping the best we could. I sighed. I was tired of not being in control.

I went downstairs. She was still in the kitchen. She was sitting at the table, thumbing through mail. I sat across from her.

"You're right. I'm sorry."

"I'm sorry for losing my temper. This is just a lot to handle." She exhaled and then pressed her lips together, stopping herself from saying more.

"I know."

She reached over and patted my hand before getting up. "It'll get better."

Obviously, she still mistakenly thought being strong was a hereditary trait. She never complained while juggling her career, the house, the husband, me, and Evie.

She couldn't possibly understand. I never courted motherhood, and suddenly I had to get used to the idea that my life was going to change, and no one seemed to think I needed to mourn my old life. *Be happy. You'll be fine. You will be a mom. It's the greatest job ever.* People kept tossing these little phrases at me. But what did they mean? Why couldn't anyone say, I know you're scared. No husband. No boyfriend. I messed up. I accepted that. I wanted this baby. But I was still afraid of the birth, what to do when he cried, if he got sick. Everything. No one seemed to think it was natural to feel sad over all I was leaving behind. They felt I should just be happy about all that was in front of me. Nothing would ever be the same.

Déjà came over later that evening to drive me back to Long Branch. She couldn't stop laughing when I told her about Tyra throwing her clothes out the window and peeing in Lucas's car.

"I know it's not funny. You dropped my baby off in a pair of smelly wet shorts, barefoot and topless. We are two broke-down bitches aren't we?"

"Yeah, I think it's safe to say we're both pretty pathetic right about now."

"Doing crazy shit, is that just a by-product of love?"

"No, D, that's just you, Miss Graffiti Artist. Are you going to start tagging bridges and underpasses in your spare time?"

She laughed, we both did. It had been that type of day.

Her smile faded. "I'm going to be paying for that the rest of my life. Even when the kids are grown, he's going to throw that back in my face."

"Are you sorry you did it or sorry you got caught?"

"It's like sex with the wrong guy. Feels really euphoric while you're doing it, but afterward, when that rash pops up... It was the dumbest thing I ever did."

She hadn't fared much better in court. She had been ordered to attend ten anger management classes and ten parenting classes. Steve's request for every weekend had been temporarily granted. They had another court date in two months. At that time, the judge would make a decision regarding permanent 50/50 joint custody.

Lucas pulled up just as we stood in front of Déjà's car.

"I came by to give you a lift to pick up your car."

"Oh, thanks, but Déjà was-"

She jabbed me in the ribs, "Just leaving," she said. She gave me a wink and got in her car without me.

"And she's not subtle either." I walked over to the passenger's side of Lucas's car. Déjà beeped twice and waved as she drove off.

"I didn't think I'd see you anytime soon after the whole, you know, Tyra peeing in your car thing."

"Well, I thought you might need that," he said as he pointed at my purse sitting in the backseat.

"I didn't even notice! Thank you! I've been forgetting everything these days."

"No big deal."

"You are a glutton for punishment, aren't you? Are you sure you want to be seen with me? You might get your picture splashed across the gossip sites."

"I don't think you'll have to worry about those guys bothering you around here. I have a few friends on the force who owed me a few favors."

"Are you a cop? You seem to have some flexible hours..."

He laughed. "Go on and ask. You want to know if I have a job."

"It had crossed my mind because you always seem to just be around. Do you?"

"I did until me and 25 percent of the company got the option of a buy-out six months ago. I took the buy-out. Still looking for work."

He drove to the boardwalk in Long Branch. Found a little

hamburger shack. We ate on a bench overlooking the ocean. Seagulls spiraled lazily over the water. I loved the smell of the salty sea air. It wasn't quite the same in LA. You could practically taste the salt here. The crash of the waves added a nice backdrop to our conversation.

"How are you holding up?"

"Ha! You saw me in action. What can I say? I'm grace under pressure."

"Sorry to hear about that Coogan guy. Did you know him well?"

"Not really. I met him once or twice, but it wasn't like he and Diego were friends outside the office. It was just a business relationship."

"Do you think he and Diego maintained any contact since this whole thing went down?"

"I don't know. I don't even want to talk about this anymore."

"Sorry. You're right."

He was quiet for a moment, and then he smiled. "You know, I still remember the first time I saw you."

"Oh boy, here we go with the ancient history. If it's embarrassing, I will go ahead and claim no memory whatsoever of that meeting because of pregnancy hormones."

"No, it's all good. You were trying to help Victor Davis with his starting position, and he just ragged on you for being a girl. You were so mad, man. I could see steam puffs coming out of your ears," he laughed. "You were like, 'since y'all know so much, I'll race all of you,' and you challenged the whole boys' track team to a 200-meter race, and you served their asses on a platter." He was quiet for a moment; the hint of a smile still teased his lips.

"I had forgotten all about that! That Victor was easy on the eyes, but the premises were vacant upstairs. I don't remember you running, what happened? Chicken?"

"I knew there was no way I was going to win. You had this look of utter determination that scared the hell out of me. I was just 14," he laughed. "But whenever I think of you, I just remember you being this girl that got whatever she went after."

"Doesn't feel that way nowadays." In fact, it felt like what I wanted was coming back to bite me in the ass.

"Remember what your dad used to say all the time?"

"What? I can't wait until you get a job. Or get off the damn phone."

"'The success of your race isn't determined by how you start, but how you finish. It's the second half that counts.'"

I smiled in spite of myself. "I'd forgotten all about that too."

"You're going to be alright; just pace yourself."

After I picked up my mom's car, he followed me home to make sure I made it safely.

Lucas made me want to find that fearless girl. I pulled a box from underneath my bed filled with spiral-bound notebooks, pages from *Right On!* Magazines and loose papers. It was a time capsule of my childhood. As I rifled through it, I found an old, weathered list written in my big, curvy 10-year-old handwriting. It was a list of things I wanted to do before I turned 30. I lowered myself on the bed as memories of those faded dreams swooshed in.

1. own a mansion on the beach

2. become a lawyer/supermodel/animal activist

3. touch a glacier

I smiled. Where was that girl that believed she could do anything? I remember writing that list during the summer before Evie died. She had an equally audacious one of her own. *Veterinarian. Grammy-Award-winning singer. Founder of a Sickle Cell non-profit.*

She had her ups and downs with her disease. Sometimes she would go months without having to be rushed to the hospital, and other times it felt like she was in crisis every day. It seemed unreal when a neighbor came banging on our door one morning. A car had hit Evie, and she died instantly.

A cold, prickly tightness spread across my chest like an asthma attack. I didn't believe in ghosts or spirits or even the afterlife. Dead was dead. Despite my beliefs, I could feel Evie in the room with me. How could I not think of her when I thought of my younger self? We were inseparable. She was my babysitter, nemesis, and life coach. I hated being compared to her but secretly wanted to be just like her. And then one day, she was just... gone. We hurtled our last spoken words to one another like angry grenades over something silly. Words I wished, so wished I could take back. The bobbleheads, *her* bobbleheads, seemed to nod in agreement.

I knew about running away. Hiding from yourself to escape. I got ahead by not looking back. Now, for the first time, I realized I had never left the past.

I stared at my reflection in the dresser mirror. Survivor's guilt had made me co-opt Evie's dreams. I became my best version of what I thought she would be like if she were still here. You could run as fast and as far as you could, but you could never outrun what was in your heart. Maybe Diego and I were two halves of the same lesson.

twenty-three

THE NEXT MORNING, I removed the posters from the walls in my room. I needed a clean slate because I wanted all my energy focused on the future. Our future. Between working at the dental practice and Déjà's store, planning Cameron's album release party, and my parents' anniversary gala, I had little time to navel gaze. I was working on the slideshow for the anniversary party, and my mother wanted a big Hollywood production on a Netflix budget. *Six more days, and it would all be over.* During the slow times at the store, when I wasn't online hunting around on Craigslist for apartments, I created mini-displays for the products. Maybe it was early nesting, but I found myself designing nurseries with all the supplies on hand. I'd take a painting from one corner, pair it up with a rug, and bring over a glider and a Boppy.

"It's all about presentation," I told Déjà. People couldn't buy her goods if it was crammed in with a bunch of other things. In a multi-task, multi-purpose-driven world, folks wanted deals, but they expected them to be at their fingertips. I helped her email a newsletter with deal blasts that could also be texted to her customers.

On my off days, I went to look at apartments. For what I could afford, they were too small, too far, not in a great neighborhood, and unfurnished. It was always something. I tried not to let it discourage me. I wanted a place we could call our own before his due date. I needed to get the nursery ready for Johnny, short for John Doe. I didn't think I could come up with a name until I saw him. Was he a Beauregard or a Blaize?

Lucas was becoming a regular fixture. He would often pick me up from work if I needed a ride, quench my craving for chocolate-covered strawberries, and escort me to the movies, even the chick flicks. Déjà teased me about him. "He's working overtime to get in your good graces. You might want to keep him around."

"He's just a good friend. I don't need any extra drama in my life."

"Sure he is," she teased.

He was a good friend. Maybe I leaned on him too much. He filled the void left by Diego. Not in my heart, but just having a strong male shoulder to lean on and to assemble the crib was a big help. I knew it wasn't fair; I had nothing to offer in return, and sometimes I wondered why he kept coming back.

Lucas helped me coordinate the gift bags the night before the anniversary party. We'd developed a pretty good system. He filled the engraved toasting flutes with red confetti, and I put them in the ruby-colored gift bags along with chocolates wrapped in foil. Ruby was the symbol for the 40th anniversary.

"You know, you don't have to come tomorrow," I said.

"It's all good. I can't let you step into the fire pit of family without an escort."

I laughed. "They are going to be all over you with questions, you sure you can handle it?"

"Remember, I'm the youngest of five sisters? They make those Kardashians look Amish." He smiled ruefully, probably remembering all too well how hard it was to have to protect the honor of those Chavers' girls.

His sisters were beautiful and *wild*. His dad was a truck driver, often out of the house for weeks at a time, leaving Lucas in charge of the chaos in a crazy house full of women.

"Thanks, I know I probably should say it more, but I'm wrapped up in my own little world. You know, I appreciate you being here. It means a lot to me."

Lucas cleared his throat, wearing the uncomfortable look of a man not ready to discuss his feelings.

"Just say 'you're welcome,'" I laughed.

"You're welcome."

The day of the anniversary party arrived, and we decorated the hall in ruby and white crepe paper with plenty of balloons. A large banner read, "Happy 40th!" I hugged and kissed many cousins, aunts, and uncles I hadn't seen in years. I was decked out in a black maternity cocktail dress, compliments of Déjà. I was on my feet most of the time, making sure everything ran smoothly, the slideshow was up and running, the band playing, passing trays of hors d'oeuvres were plentiful, and ensuring everyone had a great time.

Whispers and side-glances seemed to follow me. Although the media had grown tired of chasing a ghost, apparently, my family had not. They were not shy in asking about Diego's whereabouts, if I knew what happened to the money and why didn't I go on the run with him? Fortunately, Lucas stayed by my side and tried to deflect much of the attention away. He cleaned up well in a dark blue suit and tie.

One of my favorite aunts, Grace, had flown out from Arizona for the festivities. She cornered me in the restroom and said, "I hope you're not naming the baby something crazy like Blue Jeans or Tree Stump. You people in Hollywood have forgotten good names like Jimmy, Theodore, or hell, what about Eugene?"

"No, I was thinking of naming him Aeiou," off her blank stare, I added, "and his middle name would be sometimes Y."

She pinched me on the arm once she realized I was only kidding.

Everyone seemed to be having a good time. The band played a mix of oldies and a few new songs. My parents stayed on the dance floor, swaying to the music. Lucas and I made our way to the table when the servers started bringing out the salads.

"Your parents make it look so easy," Lucas said.

I glanced at the head of the table, where they were smiling and holding hands.

"I know. I guess I assumed it would be that easy..."

"You just have to meet the right guy."

"And therein lies the challenge."

After the wait staff delivered the first course, I stood up to make a toast.

"I'd like to make this toast to two wonderful parents. You have weathered a lifetime together, raising a family, working together, and building a thriving business while maintaining your marriage and respect for one another. May we all be so lucky as to recognize and nurture true love. And to everyone else, yes, I'm pregnant by 'the guy that stole all the money from those celebrities.' I don't know where he is; even if I did, I would not split the reward money with you. So please stop asking me, and I'm looking at you, Charles."

There was a shocked pause and then thunderous applause. My mother looked like she wanted to strangle me, but she managed to laugh.

Lucas and I stopped at the beach before we went home. We walked along the boardwalk in the moonlight. A few other couples were out for a stroll. Everyone was locked in their own world. We stopped and leaned against the railing, watching the dark waves rolling in and crashing against the sand. The salt air stung my nose.

I leaned my head against his shoulder. "I'm so glad that's over!"

"So, do you think you'll ever get married?"

"Yeah, right. I'll get married when Whitney and Bobby get back together."

"Why do you always do that? You did it even back in high school."

"What?'

"Make jokes about everything."

"Oh. It's just me being me; I don't mean anything by them. Don't be such a wuss."

"See. What are you hiding? It's like you don't want anyone to get close. We never move beyond the small talk."

"I've never had to before. I don't operate in a world where people expect you to get all deep. Hello, I work in entertainment."

We walked down the steps and onto the beach and sat down. The water looked black in the moonlight. I dug a little tunnel with my toes in the damp sand. We could have been castaways on an island. Loneliness pulled at my heart.

"Well, I know you're deeper than that. I've seen it."

"What if you're wrong? And this is it? I've got a laundry list of fears bigger than the national debt. And even though I have friends and family, it's just me at the end of the day. I'm the baby's mother, I have to make it work, and some days I don't know if I can. Sorry if I try to inject a little humor in things to get me through the day."

"You don't have to do this alone."

He closed his eyes and leaned in. Reflexively, my hand shot up, so my open palm received the intended kiss.

"I'm not. I can't. I'm just not ready for this."

He leaned back from me.

"I understand, I do... but you know, it's like when you fall off a bike, you have to get back on at some point."

"I didn't just skin my knee, and a Big Bird Band-Aid will make my owie go away. An 18-wheeler hit me head on, ran over me, backed up, and ran over me again. You just don't pop up and hop on a bike after that."

"No. You don't. You heal first. And when the time is right, you swing one leg over the seat and put your feet on the pedals. It's fine to be afraid, that's normal, but it's not okay to let that fear stop you from even trying."

"Should we add armchair psychologist to your list of fabulous traits?"

"Yeah, right along with riding a horse backward. Look, I've been there, and I just don't want to see you holding onto something that's hurting you so much."

"That's sweet, and I appreciate it but don't rush me. I'm still in a full-body cast right now. Maybe you can help me find some training wheels when it comes off."

He leaned over and brushed his lips against my cheek.

"No matter what happens, I'll be there for you if you want me to."

We walked back to my place in silence. The funny thing about betrayal is that it doesn't go away. It casts a long shadow over your heart, and even when you believe you've parceled out the prerequisite forgiveness to move on... it's still there. Waiting. Sometimes it's camouflaged in anger. Uncontrollable. It rages out of nowhere at someone innocent over something insignificant. Surprising you. It's not about moving on. Life keeps going. You pick up broken pieces. Glue them back together. Tape them back together. Slap them together with spit. Whatever it is you have to do to pull yourself out of that hole. But you never forget those dark days and who put you there.

As much as I longed to hold Diego, sometimes I hated him with such a bitter vengeance; my thoughts traipsed along the borders of Tarantino territory of over-the-top movie violence. I struggled with forgiveness. The one person I thought would never hurt me did so with exquisite precision, leaving no scars but causing enough internal damage that I didn't know if I would ever heal. How do you forgive when every fiber in your being wants to strike back and inflict equal amounts of pain, not for revenge, but for empathy? No one wants to suffer alone.

He deposited me on my doorstep, making sure I had unlocked the front door before saying, "See ya later," and disappeared into the night like one of those shooting stars. I couldn't help but feel like I missed my opportunity to make a wish.

My walks to the beach were becoming slower and shorter. The last days of summer were winding down, and the beaches were packed, even in the mornings. Bodies were spread out on the sand like wall-to-wall carpet. I was becoming more and more anxious. I talked to my son a lot. Read him bedtime stories at night, put earphones on either side of my belly, and played classical music and jazz. He squirmed and kicked mostly at night and slept during the day. As much as I couldn't wait to see him, I knew I would miss this closeness. I didn't have to share him with anyone, and he was safe. Experiencing a life growing inside me was the single most beautiful thing I had ever done. I poured all the things I never knew I wanted, hopes and dreams into this little boy.

Work continued to be the salve that staved off any OCD compulsions I might have developed over Diego. I found I enjoyed being able to control my schedule with the various projects I was working on. Business was picking up at Déjà's store, and she was implementing a publicity plan I created for her. I was still filing in the evenings at my parents' practice so I could get health insurance, and I had picked up the business next door to Déjà's as a client. It was a flower shop; they wanted help with their marketing and publicity. I was exhausted. But I was surviving, something I wasn't so sure about a few months ago.

I almost forgot about Dillon Martin, Diego/Eugene's former roommate, until he replied to my Facebook message in September. We exchanged a few more emails and then decided to Skype. He was in Texas, and there was no way I was going to be able to fly out there. Cameron's album release party was coming up. Plenty of last-minute fires to douse. Guest list drama. Catering issues. The usual.

At 7 pm, I was staring at the delayed, stop motion image of Dillon, quippygirl12 needed to have her Internet connection checked. It was sluggish. His edges had become softer, fuller over the years. His cinnamon brown face was heavier, and his hairline was beating a hasty retreat to his neck, but otherwise, he hadn't changed much from his photo. In the background, muffled whoops and yells sounded like he had a troop of kids, and they were going to take over the house.

"Thanks for agreeing to chat with me."

"No problem, although I'm not sure how I can be of help. You were pretty vague in your email."

"I'm trying to find out information on Eugene Daly, your roommate from college. Do you know where's he from or any of his family members I can talk to?"

He exhaled and said, "just a sec." He got up and closed the door to what looked like a home office. Quiet descended upon the room immediately. Pictures were displayed in back of him on the wall. Progressive images of little boys aging from toothless wonders to T-ball champs. Hard to believe only two kids had been making all that noise.

Dillon sat back down.

"Listen, I don't know what's going on with Gene and you, but I don't want to get involved. Let the police and FBI sort it out, know what I mean?"

"I can't wait for the FBI and police to 'sort it out.' I need answers. This is my life too. Six months ago, we were happy, and now... I don't know what to believe. I just want to understand how this happened."

"I've seen the news. Doesn't look like he's coming back."

"Maybe. Maybe not."

"What if you don't like the answers?"

"In a few months, I'm going to have his son, and there's this... this hole. I'm just trying to fill it in. I don't know what else I'm supposed to do."

I turned my head so he couldn't see the tears slipping down my face. Pregnancy hormones had me crying at every commercial, red light, and cute puppy. Pregnant or not, I needed something from him. I just didn't know what exactly.

"If you're looking for *The Talented Mr. Ripley* or something, you're not going to find it. Gene was a good dude, full of hubris, but we all were at that age. Sometimes nothing has to 'happen.' It's just free will, and people make poor choices. Although, he took Diego's death really hard. It changed him. Gene came from a good family, and they wanted to help him, but he just turned his back on everyone."

"You know his family? Do you still keep in touch? Do you have a name or number?"

Now it was his turn to pause as he studied me. "I'm married to his sister, but I have to talk to her first. I'm not sure if she's going to want to talk to you. We don't need any reporters sniffing around, and we've been lucky so far that they haven't released his true identity. You show up, and people might wonder why..."

"I don't like the press dogging my footsteps either. It hasn't exactly been a thrill ride for me. This is personal. I swear, I won't jeopardize your privacy."

He ended the conversation by saying he would talk to his wife, although he wouldn't tell me her name. *Maybe* she would be in touch. I checked his Facebook profile again. She wasn't listed under relationships. So, I waited.

* * *

After another long day working in the store, I came home and had to push away the baby tub my mother had placed on my bed alongside the book, *What to Expect the First Year*, a few onesies and sleepers. Grandma was going to break the bank on her first grandchild.

When my parents arrived, I was sitting at the kitchen table polishing off my leftover spinach salad from lunch.

My mother had that look, wild-eyed and determined, and I knew whatever it was, it had to do with me, and I wouldn't like it. My father must have known that, too, because he didn't bother coming into the kitchen. He headed upstairs.

"Elle-"

"No."

"But-"

"Whatever it is, no."

"Well, it's too late."

In the living room, she stood anxiously in front of the large bay window peeking from behind the curtain to view our front yard.

I followed her to the living room with hands on hips, "Too late for what?"

Startling her, she pulled the curtains together. "Now, don't get mad. I'm only trying to help."

I pulled back the curtains, "Don't get mad at-" the words shriveled off the tip of my tongue. I couldn't finish my sentence as I saw some nut on a unicycle wobbling along the sidewalk carrying a dozen roses.

I looked at her, getting ready to make a joke about the loser who must be waiting for him, when I saw the sheer hopefulness radiating from her eyes.

"No!"

"Honey, Dr. Tower is a stable and dependable guy!"

"You've got to be kidding me!"

"Told you so," my dad's voice rang out from upstairs.

"You need to get out. It's not right; you holed up in the house all the time. This 'friend' stuff with Lucas, you need to think about your future."

"I'm pregnant! I have just a few issues to work out with the father. So, excuse me for not being ready to get my rose on the *Bachelor*."

"Well, it wouldn't hurt for you to just go out and have a nice time."

A loud clatter sounded on the porch... like someone falling off a unicycle, and then the doorbell rang.

"Please?"

"He's riding a unicycle... are you kidding me? Where did you find this freak?"

"He's an orthodontist, and he's interested in partnering with us."

"No."

"Elle, how many times have I asked you to do something for me?"

"Every day!"

The doorbell rang again.

"Just go out with the man. What can it hurt?"

Two hesitant knocks sounded on the door, followed by a tentative "Hello? Anyone home?"

"You owe me. Big time. If I want to name the baby Oompa-Loompa, you will have no opinion about it."

The doorbell rang again.

"You wouldn't!"

I folded my arms. A standoff.

"Fine, I'll stop with the names. Just go get yourself together and promise me you'll try to enjoy yourself."

She waved me upstairs. I don't know why she thought I would come back down looking any better. After a long day on my feet, this was as good as it got.

* * *

"So, what do you like to do for fun?" Ben asked.

"Oh, you know, Lamaze classes, shopping for baby stuff, counting my stretch marks. What about you?"

He looked so horrified; I felt guilty for being myself. Maybe Lucas was right about my snarkiness.

"I'm just kidding. Weird sense of humor. Shopping, going to the movies, traveling. The usual."

"Sounds interesting." He said it with as much conviction as though he were volunteering to be circumcised.

We picked at our food. Conversation had run out long before they brought water to the table. We were coasting on fumes at this point. I couldn't help but think how much easier it was to talk to Lucas.

I liked dinner and theatre just as much as the next girl, but I wasn't all that crazy about dinner theatre. Especially when horses were kicking up dust as knights were jousting while I was trying to carve off a piece of leather tough steak.

We were seated next to one another on benches, and it was hard to hear. Surrounded by a motley crew of rowdy diners dressed up in their Medieval finest, it was a sporting event. The bloodthirsty crowd roared every time it looked like the knight was going to fall off the horse or get impaled.

After tonight, I was revoking my mother's matchmaking license. Dr. Benjamin Tower was an orthodontist looking to combine his practice with a pediatric dental practice. My mother was looking for a suitable suitor for her unwed and very pregnant daughter. Somehow, she thought that was enough to make this match work. No matter that we had nothing in common, he loved football, tailgate parties, and paintball wars while I was a room service only type of girl... and I was almost seven months pregnant by a man I loved and loathed.

"You know, if you want to get that overbite corrected, I can make a retainer for you," he said as we waited for our dessert.

"*Excuse me?*"

"I mean, it's not noticeable really, but it's my job to notice. I thought if... you know..."

His voice trailed off when he saw my look. I ran my tongue over my teeth. I'd never felt self-conscious about my smile... until now. The evening couldn't end fast enough.

I had to drop him off at his place. I kept the car idling as I popped the trunk so he could retrieve his unicycle. The minute he slammed it shut, I was pulling off and calling "good night" out the window. We both knew the next time he saw me would be if I passed through my parents' office. By the time I made it home, my eyes were puffy and itchy. Wrong time to discover I was allergic to horses.

The night was so full of wrongs; it made what was right so much clearer. Maybe I needed to let Diego go. It had been almost five months, and he had yet to comment on my pregnancy. Didn't know if he knew about his impending fatherhood. Sometimes it felt like what we had was some fading dream, and every day it became harder and harder to remember the details. It was like trying to catch clouds. Watching the memories evaporate by the handfuls. What did he smell like? How did his laugh sound? What did his kisses taste like? How was I supposed to let go when I wasn't ready?

I felt I was trying to accept his death with no body to claim. All this time, I'd been waiting in suspended disbelief. Hoping. Needing a reason that made sense. There are no neat loose ends in love or life, just as there's no magic cure for a broken heart. Just living. Maybe it was time for me to start.

* * *

Having Cameron's release party in Manhattan was definitely a slap in the face to the record label, my former employers. If they wanted to represent, they would need to get on a plane and fly 3,000 miles as opposed to driving to one of many hotspots in LA. But I had a grudge to nurture. Cameron didn't care where we had the party as long as it was the biggest and the best. I found a sponsor, a new vodka company, to underwrite it; I didn't have to deal with the label at all.

So, in between ringing up customers at the store, I had planned and executed a flawless campaign, helped Cameron find new management, and the party would be my pièce de résistance. Everyone who thought they were someone was calling me, trying to get on the list. I felt like Eminem in *8 Mile*. I had one shot at getting my career back, and this was it. Tonight had to be perfect.

I had chosen a new club down on W. 23rd to hold the festivities. A converted warehouse, this would be the tipping point that would cause it to crash into the "hot" stratosphere. Even though Cameron talked about the track discrepancy in interviews on the radio, on the web, and in magazines to officially squash the beef, I invited Strykker to perform the disputed track, and Cameron would drop a little freestyle rhyme. Get a couple of photos of them on stage and circulate them. Beef over.

I invited Justine and Theo because she bugged the crap out of me to get them in. Apparently, a die-hard hip-hop head raged under Theo's smooth jazz, balding exterior. Déjà would have chewed off her left arm to go but had to stay home because it was her Thursday with the kids. With the looming court battle, she couldn't afford a misstep.

Theo drove us into the city. They dropped me off at the club early and went to dinner while I did a run-through to make sure everything was set up. I was pleased to see huge posters of Cameron's album cover dominating the walls. I found Sara, the event manager for the club, and did a walkthrough of the venue. We found Nell, the keeper of the velvet rope, the guest list holder. She had worked the doors at many prominent clubs and knew how to keep out the B and C Listers. The caterer was already set up, and the appetizers smelled delicious. I stood on the balcony and looked down at the darkened dance floor. John Doe gave a couple of lazy kicks, probably just rolling over. He wouldn't be awake until the middle of the night and would start his breakdancing routine in my uterus. "This is it," I whispered to him. This party would put me back on the radar and end my exile. I hoped.

Around 8 pm, people started trickling in, and by 9, the place was packed. Music was bumping, and there was an excited buzz in the air. People wore phoniness like mink coats. All night I heard, "Elle, you look fabulous," or "I felt so bad when I heard what had happened." Sure. That's why no one called to offer me a job. I drifted in and out of circles, feeling of that world but not in it. No longer caring about the hype of the next big act or needing to be on the guest list for the "hottest event of the year." I hadn't been to a party in months, and the universe hadn't imploded. I was still alive.

When Justine tapped my shoulder, I knew something was wrong. She was the type that could stay composed during a hold-up in a tornado, but now her mask was slipping, and panic tinged her voice, raising it up an octave.

"It's Theo."

I followed her as she wove through the maze of bodies surrounding the dance floor. Some of them were doing ancillary dance moves, not ready to commit to the sweat and action, while others stood and watched. Cameron was going to perform in 10 minutes; whatever was going on with Theo would have to wrap up soon.

She led me down the hallway to the men's bathroom. An incoherent Theo, shirt untucked, eyes glazed, and shouts of indignation reduced to a slur, was hemmed up between two bouncers. I looked at Justine.

"He gets like this whenever he drinks."

"Well, damn, how often does he drink?"

I walked over to the bouncer. "What happened?"

"He was trying to enter the women's restroom, and he got belligerent when we stopped him. We were going to call the police and have him taken away for public intoxication."

"Let me handle this. Please."

The other bouncer nodded, and they let Theo go, which had been his only means of support. He slid to the ground, still mumbling to himself.

Justine grabbed his arm and helped him up. I led her to the exit door on the side.

"Get a cab and go home. You going to be alright?"

She nodded. I watched them stumble away, him leaning heavily against her as she tried to balance on her heels. She got to the corner and hailed a taxi. A certain stoicism rested in her profile. I checked my watch; it was time for Cameron to go on.

The bass engulfed me as soon as I walked back in. It pounded in my chest like a second heartbeat. Cameron and Strykker performed on a stage built from risers in the center of the dance floor. Cameron also performed the title track from the new album, and the crowd went wild.

"I want to thank all y'all for coming out tonight and supporting me!" He told the crowd when he finished. "And I especially want to thank Elle Nixon, my publicist, for putting all this together and continuing to work with me even though she thinks I'm an asshole most of the time. Alright DJ, turn the music up, yo!" Laughter and clapping rippled through the crowd. That was as close to a public apology as I was going to get, and it touched me.

I found Cameron surrounded by a clusterfuck of groupies, wannabes, and his crew. He saw me and reached out to grab me in a bear hug, which was awkward with a belly the size of a soccer ball. He gave me a semi-shoulder thump and one-armed hug.

"I don't want to squeeze you too hard, and something pops out."

An impatient crowd rolled in like the tide and separated us. It was almost like the old times as I fielded business cards and tossed out the "I'll call you" phrase. Felt like I was being called off the bench and back into the game, but now it didn't seem as much fun.

* * *

I slept in the next afternoon; I had a slew of voicemails. Everyone from Macy to the publicity head at Triad had something to say. Justine was the only person I called back. We met for coffee after she got off work.

"I'm sorry about last night. Theo has a hard time with liquor."

I gave her the side-eye and a look that said, "Tell me something I don't know."

"He's not an alcoholic; even if he were, it's a disease. I wouldn't leave him because of that. That's like leaving someone because they're diabetic," she said while gripping her coffee, blowing away the curling steam.

"I guess when you put it that way..." I never thought I'd hear the day that Justine got off the bus in CrazyTown, but she sounded like she owned a timeshare there.

"Don't judge me, Elle."

"I'm not judging. You love him, of course. He's the father of your kids."

She gave me a quick nod because she knew where I was going.

"Is he getting help?" I pressed.

"He's sorry, Elle. He wanted to come with me to apologize, but... look, he's not perfect, no one is, but he's my husband."

"I understand. I just find it... hmm, what's the word I'm looking for... oh, I know... *hypocritical* in the way that you came at me so hard for wanting to believe in Diego when you're married to Mr. Sloppy-Drunk."

"How can you even compare our situations?"

"Seriously? I can't believe you just went there."

"First, Theo is not wanted by the FBI, and second, it's not that easy for me to just pick up and walk away. We have a family, a house, a life together."

"I never said you should walk away. I haven't said anything, unlike all the unsolicited advice I've received. We all make mistakes, Justine. Don't diminish my feelings because I fell for a man who didn't come pre-packaged with a goody-two-shoes badge and is a card-carrying Suburban Dad. I didn't need your judgment. I just needed a friend."

She was quiet as she twisted her wedding band back and forth. She spoke more to her lap than to me. "You're right. I'm sorry."

"I accept your apology, but there is one more thing I have to get off my chest. I've known you since forever, when we were little, and you wanted to collect dues every time we played at your house. So, we can be real with one another."

I took a deep breath. "I really think you used that dues money to buy yourself ring pops from the ice cream man."

Her left eye twitched, almost like a tic, and then she laughed.

The thing about love was that to outsiders, it was a foreign language understood only by the couple. Translations never quite captured the true meaning because it was a language meant for two, just like friendships.

twenty-four

A SLIGHT CHILL was in the air, which the orange and red leaves took as their cue to jump from the trees to their deaths. The days were shorter. People traded their windbreakers and light sweaters for heavier fare. Halloween decorations mean-mugged on doors and windows. I was in my third trimester, and all I could think about was *how much longer?* I was tired of being pregnant. I wanted to hold my baby, see his little face. Sleep was a rare delicacy to be savored. Most nights, I tossed and turned, trying to get comfortable while he kicked and danced in my belly like there was an iPod in there. My feet had officially increased a size, rendering my shoe collection useless unless I wanted to cut off my toes, not that I could see my toes.

My life had taken on a sense of routine. I worked the phones in the morning for my side hustle as a marketing consultant for small businesses. I had picked up another client; it was a mom-owned shop that designed diaper bags. I also had two offers on the table for publicity jobs. One was from a record label in L.A., and the other was a publicity firm in New York. Neither were dream offers, but a job was a job was a job. In the afternoons, I worked at Déjà's boutique, and in the evenings, I did the filing at the dental practice. If I kept busy and didn't dwell, I could get through the days and nights without acknowledging the fear that sat perched on my shoulder. I figured if I kept advancing in baby steps, I would eventually get to that place of—if not happiness, then at least semi-contentment.

One morning, my mother knocked on my door softly before opening and poking her head in. "Want to go for a ride?"

Even though I didn't want to, I agreed. We drove to the cemetery in silence. She had picked up a bouquet on the way there. Tulips were Evie's favorite.

Row after precise row of headstones dotted the ground as far as the eye could see. I hadn't been to her grave since the day of the funeral 25 years ago. I followed behind my mother as she walked. She seemed oblivious to the stinging wind that shook the trees and rustled the grass. We came to Evie's headstone, and she knelt down to place the flowers in front of it. *Evelyn Ruth Nixon, 1972—1986.* She patted the ground next to her for me to kneel.

"I usually sit awhile and visit."

"If I bend down, I'm not getting back up. I'll wait for you over there." I found a plain cement bench not too far away and sat down.

I hated this place. We stood in the cold rain that day as they lowered her box into the unforgiving ground. She was buried with a living visage that time would rob and turn unrecognizable. What was in the coffin now? Bones and dust, tattered remnants of her favorite dress? It was her but not her, and if she wasn't there in the ground, where was she? We had to swallow the bitterness of how unfair life could be and somehow find comfort in the deluge of platitudes. *She's in a better place. It was her time. She'll be waiting for you.* I would scratch through the hard earth until my fingers bled. I would tear apart the coffin if I could talk to her one last time and tell her I was sorry. I didn't mean it.

A hard lump was inside me, or maybe it had been around me, protecting me. It was starting to crumble and dissolve. I found myself in my mother's arms, crying, shedding the tears I could not do all those years ago. She locked her arms around me on that cold bench and held me. The words were clenched in my throat, the fight, the anger, the guilt. I should have been with her that morning. Things would have been different. I'd always thought, always known, things *could* have been different. Even though I couldn't say what needed to be said, it was as though my mother knew, and for once, I didn't need a witty comeback, a warrior's face paint, or expensive armor. I could just be. And it was ok.

* * *

On Halloween night, I got dressed up to go to Justine's costume party. We were instructed to come as a television character. I wasn't sure if I would be able to make it through the party; I was always tired. Falling asleep on the couch with the remote in hand was normal. I was ready for this baby to come out of me by any means necessary. Lamaze classes started next week, and I was already working on my birthing plan.

"Who are you supposed to be?" I asked when Lucas came to pick me up.

He did a stiff-legged walk around the living room. Off my blank stare, he said, "Fred Sanford. Suspenders? Plaid shirt, grey wig? Who are you, a hippie?"

"No, I'm Cher. 'I got you, babe.'"

I figured the floor-length, flowing dresses of the 70s would go well with my belly. I got a long jet-black wig, made a headband, and called it a day.

The party was a blast. Déjà showed up as Eartha Kitt in *Catwoman*, reigniting her love affair with spandex, much to the delight of every male with a pulse. She flashed way more cleavage than I remembered being allowed on network television at that time. Justine and Theo explored their dark side as Gomez and Morticia from the *Addams Family*.

I found a spot on the couch and worked the party from that space all night. Fred Flintstone, George Jefferson, and Homer Simpson were all in attendance. Lucas floated around and finally relocated to wherever the men were hanging out. Déjà plopped down on one side of me, and Justine filled the spot on the other.

"Justine, where is the beer? I want to get my swerve on tonight," Déjà laughed.

"There will be no swerving in here," Justine deadpanned. Turning serious, she lowered her voice, "Theo is going into the program."

"What program? Weight Watchers?" Déjà asked. I elbowed her. "What? I'm just asking."

"No, AA. He has a problem, and we're trying to get help. As a family."

"Oh girl, I didn't know. I'm sorry. I hope it works out."

"That's a good first step," I told Justine. I rubbed her shoulder in encouragement.

"You know, my mom went through the program once, twice, five times. If it's going to work, he has to want it. You can't do it for him. Trust me. I'm here for you if you need me," Déjà said and squeezed Justine's hand. "In the meantime, I'm going to wake this party up cause nobody's dancing." She popped off the couch in search of the iPod playing the music.

"You know I'll help you guys any way I can."

Before Justine could answer, "Planet Rock" by Soul Sonic Force was blasting through the speakers. I threw my hands up in the air. "She's taking it way back!" I laughed.

Déjà knew how to get the party started. She had plugged up her iPod and kept the old-school hits going all night. She made people get up and do the Wop, the Cabbage Patch, the Running Man, and all the other dances from our childhood. I even got up and did the Bump. She organized a *So You Think You Can Dance* contest; I was one of the judges and don't remember having laughed as hard as I did in a very long time.

For once, I was able to forget about everything and totally live in the moment. I was with friends; I was happy, and my baby and I were healthy.

twenty-five

THE WEEKS WERE SLIPPING AWAY as the temperature dropped lower and lower. I missed Los Angeles and our California winters. It was a week away from Thanksgiving, and already we had snow on the ground. It had been a long day, and I seemed to move slower and slower. My birth plan was complete. I wanted a natural birth, no epidural. I had already picked out the CD I wanted to play in the background as I did my breathing exercises to control the pain. Even though Lucas was going to Lamaze classes with me, it was understood that Justine and Déjà would be in the birthing room with me. Feeding me ice chips. My bag for the hospital was packed and sitting by the door. In a few more weeks, John Doe would be here.

It had been a long day. I finally found an apartment and signed the lease. I could move in on the first of the month. It was 15 minutes from my parents, in a quiet neighborhood, with a nice backyard. As I got ready for bed that night, my phone chimed. My heart paused after I read the text from a number I didn't recognize.

I need to see you. Where are you?

It was as though he were sitting on the bed next to me and whispered those words in my ear. All the emotions and memories charged in full throttle and trampled my resolve. I now had heart palpations to go along with the heartburn. It hammered an erratic beat in my chest as I tried to catch my breath. *He* had texted me. I wasn't sure what to call him. It was like Diego was just a figment of my imagination, and I felt very territorial about it. This fugitive, Eugene, I didn't know him. I didn't have any memories with him. How dare he come back and make me confront the truth, even though I've never stopped wanting to see him.

He was in the country, but he wouldn't tell me where. He said it would take him a few days, but he would text me when he was nearby. He had a passport for me and wanted us to start a new life together.

Three months ago, I would have probably jumped at the chance, even if it was to give Estella the finger by leaving with him, triumphant that he chose me. Not that life on the run was anything to brag about. Now, I was rebuilding my life, and I wasn't ready to drop everything for him, even if it meant I'd never see him again or that our son would never know him.

Diego and I had this thing. No matter how much he hurt me, I wouldn't be able to let go until I saw him again. Touched him. Our time together was nothing but worn memories, trotted out night after night. I needed to hear his voice, hear it from him, why he did what he did. A part of me still clung to a shred of belief that maybe it was a mistake or, for some greater reason... like he was raising a ransom for his kidnapped mother/sister/daughter. Dying of cancer. Something.

I waited on his text messages and would get a bolt of excitement after reading them. It was my only link to him. He wouldn't call, only text. I sent him my address, and he replied he would come. Every time my phone even sounded like it was going to ring or chime, I jumped. I wasn't expecting a fairy tale reunion. Until I saw him, I didn't feel as though I had permission to move on. Sounded silly, even to me, but he was in my heart. I loved him. I loved the thought of us. Even though it was impossible to regain all that we had lost, to return to who we were, I needed to compare notes on who we had become. Could we raise a child together? Although that largely depended on whether he was out of prison before the baby went to college.

At night, I mulled over the different ways he could react when he saw I was pregnant. A picture was worth a thousand words. Walking in eight months pregnant would save me the trouble of having to bring him up to speed.

"Are you feeling well? You seem distracted lately," Lucas asked as he drove me home from Yee's Chinese restaurant. We had grabbed something to eat. I had barely touched my plate. Clearly, a sign the apocalypse was coming. Usually, I'd threaten him with stabbing a fork in the back of his hand if he even looked at my shrimp egg rolls, but tonight they sat untouched.

"Nothing. Just feeling a little run down, I guess."

"Want to talk about it?"

"No, I'm fine."

As usual, he got out and walked me to the steps when he dropped me off. I could tell he wanted to say something as he watched me unlock the front door. I couldn't put him in the middle of this, so I stifled my urge to blurt out everything.

"See you tomorrow," I said as I closed the door on his unasked questions.

The girls were throwing me a baby shower tomorrow. Lucas was going to drive me over to Justine's. He said he was man enough to brave the shower games and girl talk. They were all convinced he was in love with me. I liked Lucas, but not in that way. He was dependable and fun, but there was no chemistry.

Diego texted me that night. He wanted to meet at a little diner off Highway 35 the following afternoon. We would appear to be an inconspicuous couple having a lunchtime tryst as we planned for our upcoming blessing. He didn't ask if I would be ready to run off with him. *Would I?* Isn't there a contradiction in all of us? The sane part of me knew there was no way in hell I was going on the run while pregnant, but the unpredictable, still-in-love with him part of me, I didn't know what she would do if she heard what she wanted to hear.

The next morning, I called Lucas to tell him I didn't need a ride to the baby shower. I couldn't decide what to wear. Everything made me look fat because I was. The ring Diego had given me no longer fit. My hair had grown evenly into a low 'fro. I looked nothing like the woman he left in Paris. I decided on my only pair of maternity jeans and a t-shirt that read *Warning: About to Pop*, with a black button-down cardigan.

I sat down on the bed. There was no coming back from this, whatever happened. Was I really ready to see him? Excitement, fear, sadness, and longing all raged inside me, fighting to be the dominant emotion.

"Today's the big day," my mother announced as I walked into the kitchen.

"What? What do you mean?"

"Your baby shower. I'm heading over there after my 3 o'clock patient."

Relief rushed through me, and I sighed.

"You seem so jumpy. Relax. Enjoy these last few weeks of pregnancy. Once that baby comes, there's no turning back."

"Tell me about it!"

The drive to the diner was a long one. I took the surface streets and seemed to catch every light. I replayed our last night together in my mind, searching for clues. Wondered what he looked like. Had he changed? What was I going to feel when I first saw him?

He was sitting at a booth in the back when I walked in. Even though it had been months since we had been together and he looked nothing like the last time we saw one another, I knew it was him. At first, his eyes glided over me when he glanced my way, and then shock registered on his face as he saw my expanding belly.

Slowly, I lowered myself into the booth. We were only a few feet apart, but a great chasm yawned between us, and somewhere a part of me felt as though I would jump off whatever ledge I had to in order to cross that distance.

He had a beard, and locks of hair peeked from underneath his beanie cap. I'd never seen him with hair except in that old college photo. I was expecting to see the upscale professional that left me in Paris on his way to Frankfurt. This man was a stranger wearing clothes I had never seen. We sat in silence. I rested my hands on my stomach, feeling the baby squirm, anxiously awaiting the outcome. *Single parent home? Two-parent home? Life on the run? What's up?* He seemed to ask.

"I'm sorry," he said.

For months I thought about what it would be like to see him, to touch him. I put one hand on the table, and he reached over and held it. It was a warm and familiar touch, but it brought me little comfort.

"You look good," he said. "I missed you."

"Why?" It slipped from my mouth and dropped into the space between us as though weighted with an anvil. I was supposed to play it cool. I wanted to act like I didn't care, but the pain was gnawing at my heart, and the fearless me, the girl who knew she could do anything, didn't want to pretend.

"You are the worst type of liar... you're too good at it."

"You don't understand-"

"No. I don't," I took a deep breath and pulled my hand away from his. I'd been having this conversation non-stop in my head for so long that it seemed weird saying the words aloud. "You made promises to me you knew you couldn't keep. Whether you told me outright lies or just forgot to mention a few things like a wife, you played me. You didn't trust me. You watched me fall in love knowing the man I was falling in love with didn't exist."

"I came back for you."

"What do you want? A ticker-tape parade? You're a fugitive."

"I haven't been served with an arrest warrant, so technically I'm not a fugitive."

I shook my head. "This isn't a game."

"What do you want me to say? That I fucked up? You don't think I know this? But I'm trying to—to make things right."

"How? By asking me to run off with you? Who will raise our child when we wind up in jail? It's too late for us."

"Don't say that. I can't do this without you."

"You've been gone for *months*, and you seemed to have made out just fine. I don't know who you love, but it isn't me. As far as I can tell, you only love yourself because this is all about you." I put his class ring and the key on the table between us.

"You have it," he exhaled. "This is good. We can make this work."

"I also met Estella."

"I know, but let me-"

He knew. "What? Explain?" A dry chuckle scraped along the edge of my parched lips. All these months, I had been clinging to the hope that there would be an explanation for the "why" of it all. My anger deflated like the last balloon at a forgotten party, and sadness crept in. He would never be the man I needed him to be. No amount of screaming, loving, begging, pleading, or crying would change that.

"Just forget it. Our son is due in a few weeks, just make sure you have a working phone, so I can send you pictures."

"A son? It's a boy?"

The excitement in his eyes was bittersweet; it needled the ache in my heart his absence had caused.

"Yeah, and he's awake."

Diego got up and slid in next to me. Every fiber of me was aware of him. The soft touch of his jeans brushed against my leg and sent waves of shivers through me. I hesitated before I took his hand and placed it on my stomach. I guess the baby wanted to investigate the new heat source because I felt a little karate chop in my tummy. The force of the kick startled Diego.

"Those leg muscles... My boy's going to be a football player," he smiled.

His reaction was just like I had hoped it would be, but instead of feeling ecstatic, all I could feel was a sense of loss. I had longed for him at doctor's visits and felt pangs of envy whenever I saw other pregnant couples. The way the husband or boyfriend would be so protective and proud of his partner, of the life they were creating. I wasn't supposed to be in this alone. Seeing him smile gave me a taste of what it could have been like. That alternative life where Agent Walsh didn't exist, and I still had my job. At night, I would mold my body into his, his arms wrapped around us as our pillow talk evolved into whispered hopes and dreams for our son. Instead, this meeting, this moment, was the end of our life together and a prelude to our life apart.

"How could you hurt me like this?" I clasped and unclasped my hands in front of me. Knowing there was no answer.

"I'm sorry." The two words rolled off his tongue and flip-flopped on the table between us.

"Sorry won't do me any good right now. I don't even know what to call you. Diego? Eugene? Why did you come back? Are you trying to get yourself killed? You're a fugitive, and you're Black. You might as well just give the police the bullets they're going to shoot you with if the people you stole from don't get to you first."

He shifted in his seat and looked around. I wanted to touch him one last time, feel his skin underneath my fingertips, and breathe in his scent that was my oxygen. Needed to see that he wanted me the way I used to want him.

"What do you want me to say?" he asked.

There were a million things I wished he would say, but I wasn't going to coach him.

I rubbed my stomach. This was the father of my child... I prayed my son wouldn't get any of his dumb ass traits.

I sighed. "Nothing, Diego. Have a good life."

In his eyes, I saw fear, anger, betrayal, and finally, resignation collide with one another. Not even in my worst dream could I have imagined this happening. Law enforcement surrounded us. They seemed to appear from everywhere like they were all actors on a set; they had a script while Diego and I were doing improv. The waitress who served us and the couple in the booth were all yelling and flashing badges. Was there anybody in the restaurant who wasn't a cop? Even the cook in the back seemed like he had a gun drawn.

Words tripped out of my mouth, their thunder stolen from the surprise attack. Everything was running in fast forward.

"Put your hands where we can see them!"

"It will all work out, Elle. Just go to Penn Station," Diego said to me. Our eyes locked, and although nothing else made sense, I knew what he meant.

Before I could fully register what was going on, hands were everywhere, and they separated us. Diego was being read his rights. He was patted down and pulled up. They were leading him out of the restaurant. I grabbed the ring and the key from the table and tried to push through the crowd to go after him. Arms were holding me back. Words were buzzing around me like angry bees while a sharp pain shocked me into silence. I took a deep breath and tried to breathe through it. I had to get to the car before they left. I put my hand on my stomach as though to quiet the baby and took another step toward the door. Lucas appeared before me.

"I'm sorry, Elle."

"What are you doing here? Oh my gosh, the police, they just took... wait, what *are* you doing here?" My initial surprise and relief faded as I noticed the badge strung around his neck. Agent Walsh's shock of red hair was bobbing through the crowd, making his way toward us.

It took me two seconds longer than it should have to realize what was happening. Anger fueled me. Otherwise, I would have been curled up in the fetal position on the floor.

I pushed by him. A loud roar of noise rumbled in my head as I struggled to comprehend the impossible. Bile rushed to the back of my throat. A vise was tightening around my lungs, snatching my breath away in increments. I stopped to breathe.

"You don't look so good. Let me take you to wherever it is you're going."

"Stay the fuck away from me," I said as hysteria etched my voice up a few octaves.

I saw Diego a hundred feet ahead of me in handcuffs, being led to an unmarked car. Being pregnant had its advantages. The sea of people parted when they saw me and my big stomach waddling through.

I tried to reach him before they left. Out of breath, it was like a slow-speed chase. Lucas easily caught up to me.

"I'm sorry Elle. I didn't mean for things to go down like this."

"How was it supposed to go down?"

"You don't understand-"

"No, obviously I'm too stupid to grasp that you used me. You men are all the same, you purposefully hurt people for your own gain, and you don't care what happens in the end." I shoved him out of my way.

"Wait!" I shouted. Another wave of pain wrapped around my belly like a vise squeezing it. I thought I was going to pass out. I gritted my teeth. "Wait!" I shouted again. Please, not now. It was too early!

Diego turned around. Someone had their hand on his head and was in the middle of pushing him down to get into the backseat of an unmarked car. I doubled over with intense pain; the dirty pavement swam before my eyes. A moan escaped from me as I tried to catch my breath.

Lucas grabbed my arm.

"Elle, you ok? Someone call an ambulance!" He sounded like he was underwater.

Diego lurched toward me. Pandemonium broke out.

"Don't touch me!" I pushed Lucas away when I felt my knees go limp like spaghetti noodles, and I had to grab his coat to keep from sinking into a sticky pool of darkness. It was going to swallow me up. I had to hold on. Words floated above and around me; they ceased to make sense, and then there was nothing...

twenty-six

IF ONLY... isn't that what people always said when confronted with the sudden realization they're not immortal? If only I would have done *ABC*, and then *XYZ* would have happened. Grasping at that elusive formula of *maybes, should haves* and *wish I dids* in the belief that things could have been different... *if only*. Maybe everything I did was leading me up to this point.

My life wasn't bad. I thought it was pretty good. Actually, I thought it was pretty damn good—not to think too highly of myself, but I was on top of my game. I had everything I thought I wanted. And then, in a nanosecond, the landscape changed, and I didn't have a map. What I had, who I was, who I thought I was on my way to becoming, were all gone. In the new world order, I thought I had nothing; I was nobody. Over the last few weeks, I discovered I had plenty. I wanted and needed more time. For us.

twenty-seven

THE FLIGHT MECHANISM was such a strong instinct. Survival. Sometimes it was just as important to throw caution to the winds and fight our battles from where we stood.

Something was different. I couldn't wrap my mind around anything; it kept slipping away like water through my fingers. I just had a feeling that something had changed. I tried to focus on a clock on the wall when it came into a hazy view, and then it slipped away. Wherever I was, I wasn't alone. Darkness enveloped me again.

* * *

"Ellie?"

My eyes fluttered open. I was in the hospital. Justine's face swam in front of me.

"She's awake!"

I looked at my stomach. My baby.

"Am I still pregnant?" My words rolled out of my mouth like lopsided marbles. I looked at my stomach again; I wasn't as big.

"Where is my baby? I want to see him."

Things started coming back to me in bits and pieces. A puzzle. I was too tired to put it together.

Justine squeezed my hand. "He's gorgeous, honey. You'll see him soon, although you're going to have to pry him away from your mom."

The lull of the waves was too appealing, and I was being pulled back under. It was dark, calm, and quiet.

* * *

When I woke up again, the first thing I noticed was my stomach was not flat. At all. I was no longer pregnant, but it looked like someone had shoved a pouch of lumpy dough under my skin. Between the stretch marks and a puffy middle that was bandaged, bikinis were definitely out of the picture for a while. I would have to go old school in a one-piece that looked like a girdle. I tried to sit up but could barely push myself up on my elbows. There was an IV and a catheter. I pressed the on-call button for the nurse. I watched the minute hand swing by as I waited.

It was 11 o'clock. Night, day? I couldn't tell.

Finally, she came in. "How are we feeling this morning?" she chirped.

"I don't know about you, but I feel like crap."

She took my blood pressure. Later on, they wheeled me to the Neonatal Intensive Care Unit. The first time I set eyes on Chance, he was bathed in blue phototherapy lights in a clear breadbasket with little eye covers. He was healthy except for jaundice. He was five pounds, big for a preemie. His arms and legs would give a sporadic jerk, and he would flail away imaginary flies. I wanted to cry. I put my palm against the glass. The nurse took him out, removed the eye covers, and handed him to me.

"Nice to meet you, little guy," I whispered.

His little face was scrunched up, lips puckered up in a howl waiting to happen, and the little feet that had been relentless in the middle of the night as he tried to break dance in my womb were still kicking. I fell in love with him. I wanted to protect him from everything and everyone. As I held him, I felt like home was wherever this little guy happened to be.

I left the hospital seven days later. Chance Nixon, who had burst onto the scene three weeks early, was also discharged. So much for my birthing plan. I had no memory of his entry into the world whatsoever. Not that I was surprised. Nothing had gone according to schedule this year.

Lucas walked into my room on the day I was checking out. I was packing our clothes in the suitcase when he arrived, holding a bouquet like a shield.

"Unbelievable." I flung my clothes in with more force than necessary.

"I'm sorry."

"That's supposed to make everything better? You acted so high and mighty, like you were morally superior to Diego. But you're worse."

"Elle, how can you say that? *Eugene Daly* is nothing but a liar and a common thief."

"At least he knows what he is."

"What's that supposed to mean?"

"Tell me one thing. Was all of this just a job to you?"

"Elle-"

"Was it?"

He paused. "Only at first, but then-"

"Were you following me? All those times you just happened to bump into me?"

"You don't-"

"How did you know we were going to be at the diner? Because that was pretty elaborate. Was that your big sting operation?"

I had stopped flinging my clothes and stood there looking at him. He clung to the bouquet and seemed to rethink his decision about coming to see me.

"You owe me at least that much. How. Did. You. Know?"

He sighed and looked as though he wished he were anywhere but here as he said, "I cloned your cell that time when you left your purse in my car after I gave you a ride home from Long Branch, and uh, I was able to hack into your computer after you logged on using quippygirl12's network."

"What? You're quippygirl12? That was months ago. All this time," I shook my head, unable to complete my sentence and my thoughts. I just knew he had to go. "Get out."

"You know, you're not so innocent in all this either, Elle. You conveniently ignored the fact that the FBI wanted him; he hurt a lot of people. You could have ended this and turned him in, but you didn't. What does that say about you? You're lucky you're not brought up on charges for aiding and abetting."

I grabbed the closest thing to me, a can of powdered formula, and threw it at him. The airborne missile would have hit its target if he hadn't ducked. It bounced off the door with a thud and dropped to the floor.

"Get out!"

Justine entered the room and gave him the serious stink eye before rearranging her face. "Oh. Is he bothering you? Do I need to call security?" she asked.

"Yes, this man is harassing me."

"I'm going, but you know I'm right," Lucas said as he placed the bouquet on the hospital bed and backed out. I grabbed the assortment of white and yellow roses and followed him.

"Take your stupid flowers with you!" I said as I hurled them at his retreating back. He flinched as they hit.

The nurses, doctors, and patients all stopped in the hallway and stared at us. Security was already blazing a path to my room. I pointed to Lucas and then ducked back inside.

Was he right? During those nights in the hospital, I had more than enough time to reflect on things and knowing what I know now. Was it worth it? I still didn't have an answer. Diego had been extradited to

Los Angeles, where he was held without bail. He had already proven he was a flight risk.

Even now, it all felt like a dream. Chance was my only souvenir from that world. Proof that it all happened. Somewhere in an alternate universe, my life was lurching along with the normal hiccups and happiness. I was at work, writing a press release or putting together a publicity plan. Life as usual.

In my new reality, I felt like a failure because my breast milk wouldn't come down, and Chance was throwing fits because he was hungry. It was also up to me to decide where we went from here. Did I really want to go back to working in music with the long hours and overabundance of traveling? I had turned down two offers and had received a third one to consider from another label.

After Justine dropped me off at my parent's house, I put Chance on the bed and kneeled over him as I took off his snow jacket. We were both exhausted. He gave me this look as if to say, "Now what?"

twenty-eight

THE CLOUDLESS BLUE skies of April marred by the swaying of tall palm trees were exactly as I remembered. Los Angeles hadn't changed. Traffic? Check. Inattentive drivers? Double check. Potholes with the circumference of baby hippos? You betcha. Elle's old life? Up in smoke. Although it had only been a little over a year since... my life imploded? Began? It felt like a lifetime, a stranger's lifetime.

Eugene took a plea bargain. He was to be formally sentenced this month, but Walsh told me he would get close to 12 years. Almost six million had been recovered and distributed amongst his victims. The news cycle cranked on, and there were bigger fish to skewer and rake over the coals. The core staple of politicians/entertainers/very important men cheating and lying to their spouses while doing very important business, the occurrence of natural disasters, and the passage of time, had given me my life back. Allowed me to slip into anonymity as the paparazzi hunted other prey.

I wrote to Eugene a few times and sent him pictures of Chance. Asked him to fill in the holes of where he had gone and why he had done it, but he refused to write back. Refused to tie up the loose ends of our story. His new home until his sentencing was the

Men's Central Jail in Los Angeles. The largest jail in the world. It took up a huge city block and housed about 5000 inmates. It looked like an impenetrable fortress, and Eugene was in there, somewhere.

Cameron's voice pulled me out of my thoughts.

"You sure you don't want to stop? I mean, we're right here."

"No, keep going."

He had long ago abandoned his tie, his shirt was unbuttoned, and his suit jacket was in the back seat.

"To the airport?"

"Yeah, I got someone waiting for me back home." The damp-ening circles on my blouse were a reminder I had a nursing someone waiting for me.

"You a'ight?"

"I'm good," I sighed. "It is what it is."

"You got through it, came out on the other side."

"You did too."

This morning we sat in court, not too far from the jail, and faced the man who shot up Cameron's Hummer. Anton Franks, a low-level banger trying to make a name for himself. Barely 19 and already on his third strike. Mandatory sentencing was life in prison if they found him guilty. Sorrow outweighed the happiness of getting him off the street. Pregnancy had unleashed empathy hormones that wreaked havoc on my conscience. Couldn't help but wonder about his mother. He was somebody's baby. Wanted to know what put him on the path to give up his life at such a young age. It was a path that never only claimed just one victim; it caused a ripple effect whose reach was incalculable.

* * *

The terminal in Atlanta wasn't that busy. There were a few folks at my gate already seated. I had three hours to kill on my layover back to Jersey. I sat down and started reading a magazine.

"How did it go?" A woman asked as she sat down in the seat next to me. It was Eugene's sister.

"It will be a while before that kid gets out of jail," I answered.

"And Eugene?"

I just shook my head. She understood. He hadn't written to her either. Not in a very long time.

She had the same chocolate brown complexion and midnight black eyes. Her features were softer, more feminine, but the height was there. She crossed her long legs at the ankle.

"You look so much like him."

"Creepy, I know. We're ten months apart. People thought we were twins growing up. So how was your first trip away from your little one?"

"I miss him. But honestly, last night was the best sleep I've gotten in months! You know, aside from my aching, leaking boobs."

She laughed. "It gets better. I can't wait to meet him."

I knew better than to ask about her childhood. We had established the ground rules. It had been three months since Robin Daly Martin first called me. When we found out we would be traveling through LAX the same day, we took the opportunity to meet in person.

I showed her the latest photos I had taken of Chance on my phone. She handed me a little plastic bag with yellowed photos. I pulled them out. My breath caught in my throat as I gazed at pictures of a hopeful little boy smiling at the camera.

"In case Chance wanted to see what his dad looked like as a little boy."

She had to leave shortly after; her connection to Texas had arrived. We made plans to get our families together. We had a tenuous bond of shared grief over two different men who had lived in the same body. She had lost a brother named Eugene, and the Diego I knew was forever gone.

I had begrudgingly accepted that I had loved and lost. It was even harder to accept that sometimes people came into our lives to reveal truths about ourselves. Rather than a destination, they were just one of many landmarks on our journey.

I learned that somewhere between the heartache and the ecstasy, the planned and the unplanned, you found and lost friends and loved ones in places you least expected. I wasn't going to let it slow me down. Chance wouldn't let me. Life was messy and ongoing. There was no such thing as happy endings, not if you were living; the best I could hope for was to be a steady work-in-progress and to know that sometimes when we think we've gone off-course, we were in fact, just taking the scenic route.

It was an uneventful flight into JFK. I took a cab to Penn station in New York. Before leaving for Los Angeles, I found Diego's class ring and key stashed away in a purse I no longer used. So much had happened since then. I'd almost forgotten about them. Seeing them again reminded me of his last words.

When I arrived at Penn Station, I searched for the bus lockers. I vaguely remember seeing them a long time ago, but I was told they had been removed after 9/11. A ticket clerk told me the closest luggage storage place was around the corner.

I fingered the key in my pocket. *What was I going to find?* The nondescript storefront was sandwiched between a wholesale clothing store and a jewelry shop. I paused before crossing the threshold; there was no turning back. I followed the numbered lockers along the wall all the way to 207. I pulled out the key and slipped it into the lock of a door no bigger than a wall safe. The sound of the click surprised me. My hands shook a little. I didn't know what to expect. Crammed inside was a black duffle bag. I recognized it. It was a freebie that had been given to guests at an event we went to in another lifetime. It had a little weight to it. I didn't open it there. I walked back to Penn Station, half expecting to be accosted by law enforcement at any moment.

On the train ride back into Jersey, I found a nearly empty car to sit in. The few other passengers were sleeping, on their cell, or reading a newspaper. I sat down in the very last seat and placed the bag on my lap. I knew in my gut what was in it before I saw the stacks of worn one-hundred-dollar bills tightly bound by rubber bands. An envelope with six different passports, all with Diego's picture and different names and countries of origin, was tucked on the side. I couldn't even guess how much money was in the bag. How much was ten pounds of one-hundred-dollar bills worth?

All too soon, I was at my stop, getting off the train. Wondering if everyone could see the secret I was harboring. I could justify thousands of reasons for keeping the money, even though it was the wrong thing to do. Made me no better than *him*. Maybe that's why he told me to go to Penn Station? To show me how easy it could be to get caught up, *especially if you thought you wouldn't get caught.* Or maybe he wanted me to believe we weren't so different. *But why cut off all communication with me?*

I took a cab to the small apartment I was renting. I was wrestling with my thoughts and so entrenched in figuring out what to do as I unlocked the door. The chorus of "surprise" startled me. If I had been pregnant, I probably would have peed on myself.

My mother, who was holding Chance, my father, Justine and Amara, Déjà, and her brood all stood in front of a small cake with a candle on it. I had totally forgotten it was my birthday. And so did everyone else because it had passed more than a week ago, but they were here now, and that's what mattered.

They broke out into a disjointed version of "Happy Birthday." I grabbed Chance and inhaled his sweet, baby smell of talcum powder and newness before I leaned down and blew out the candle. For once, thoughts of Evie didn't cast a pall over the occasion.

My call to Agent Walsh could wait a day; I wanted to enjoy the moment because, finally, I was home.

a note from sibylla

If you enjoyed *Bumped*, I'd love it if you'd tell your friends about it so they can experience Elle's hectic journey to motherhood. *Bumped* can be found on most retailers' platforms, so it's easy to share with friends.

For those inclined to leave a review on a retailer's site, Goodreads or even your blog, I'd love to read it! And thank you in advance, I appreciate it! You can send me the link at sibylla@sibyllanash.com.

I'd love to stay in touch with you and share upcoming releases with you. You can sign up for my newsletter to get the scoop.

about the author

Sibylla Nash lives in Los Angeles. Her work has appeared in various outlets including *The Gumbo, Lit Hub, Essence* magazine, *Vibe,* and others. She received her MFA in Creative Writing from Otis College of Art and Design and her BA in Journalism from the University of Southern California.

She is a proud mom (to a human and cats). To learn more, please visit: SibyllaNash.com.